D1414124

The
Disappearing Girl

A Novel by
Heather Topham Wood

THE DISAPPEARING GIRL
Copyright: Heather Topham Wood
Published: May 7, 2013

DEDICATION

To the girls who've never felt beautiful

CHAPTER ONE

I began to lose pieces of myself over the winter break.

I had returned home from college to spend time with my mother and younger sister until the spring semester began in January. Christmas was a trying affair; only the second one our family had endured since my father died a year and a half earlier. His stocking still hung from the mantle, his armchair left empty while we opened gifts— and his ghost ever present.

My father's death left my mother with a permanent scowl etched into her flawless features. My mother was beautiful in a way that made strangers assume she was a famous actress or a world-class model. Her hair was naturally dark with auburn highlights, and her eyes were the color of emeralds. Jaws dropped when it was revealed she was a housewife. Pitiful expressions betrayed their thoughts: what a waste of beauty.

My younger sister, Lila, and I were a disappointment to my mother because of our ordinariness. We both had straight brown hair and the same murky brown eyes as our father. No one stopped to compliment us on our stunning looks. Since middle school, boys would ask to come over to our house to glimpse my mother sunning in the backyard, clad in a skimpy bikini and rolled onto her back with the strings left untied. The boys' eyes would volley between my mother, Lila, and me, their thoughts leaking into their expressions: a beautiful mother didn't always guarantee a beautiful daughter.

Dad had always been our biggest advocate, shushing my mother's criticisms and making outrageous claims about how Lila and I were the greatest beauties that ever graced the planet. I never realized how much of a buffer he was until he was gone.

I had my own personal countdown for when I'd be able to return to my college campus, because each day brought a new barrage of insults from my mom. I tried to sympathize; she was drowning in her own misery, but all I craved was an escape. My father was the one great love of her life and his death undermined her chance of ever being happy again. Although she ate up the attention other men gave her, my father was the only man that could melt her iciness. My father would tell us about how all the boys in their small hometown were too intimidated to ask my mom out on a date—the walls around her seemingly impenetrable. My dad may not have been the handsomest man to ever ask her out, but he was the most devoted and kind.

Like most nights before, dinner was a stilted affair. My father used to regal us with stories from work. He was a veterinarian, and his tales of the wild animals he saw from one day to the next would have Lila and I laughing so hard we would have difficulty swallowing our food. But after his death, suppertime turned into an opportunity for our mother to discuss our failures and how we'd have to rectify them in order to transform from the ugly ducklings we were into the beautiful swans she deserved.

"Did you receive your final grades for last semester?" she asked me as I took a bite of the salad she had prepared for us.

"Yes, I did fantastic. My GPA is three-point-seven." I allowed the pride I felt over my accomplishment to seep into my voice. My mother had inspired obsessive perfectionism when it came to my life, and her disappointment in my grades had promoted me from a B to an A student. I thought excelling in school would be enough for her.

But nothing was ever enough. Her reply was a dismissive nod. She used her napkin to daintily dab at the salad dressing at the corners of her lips. I could feel her evaluation move on to my outward appearance as her eyes swept over me. Her perfectly sculpted eyebrows shot up as I reached across the table for another piece of bread from the basket.

She said, "Kayla, you really need to start making more of an effort regarding your weight." She pressed her lips together and looked at me with unmasked distaste.

I looked to my sixteen-year-old sister for help, but she had her head down and was silently eating. I didn't blame her—it was tough to be the target of so much vitriol over the course of a single meal. The week before, Mom had Lila in tears, threatening to confine her forever if she didn't stop running around with a boy my mom deemed inappropriate.

I didn't reply to her remark, having learned there was no battle she couldn't win against me. I'd never be what she wanted. My only refuge was to attend school an hour away and return home only on the mandatory breaks. I was hoping to get my own apartment off-campus in the near future, which would allow Lila to visit me more often. I hated leaving her. Guilt would gnaw at me when I imagined what it was like when Lila was the only one around to suffer the brunt of my mother's reign of terror.

"Kayla Marlowe, I am speaking to you," my mom said with exasperation. "Have you been watching what you eat?"

I swallowed the snide remark on the tip of my tongue. My mother was obsessive when it came to our weights. She was a size two and I'd never seen her weight fluctuate. I was only five when Lila was born, but I couldn't even recall her being swollen with pregnancy. I imagined she popped Lila out of her womb and slid right back into her skinny jeans.

The answer was no, I hadn't been watching what I'd been eating. Going to college had been eye opening, and I hadn't been prepared for the freedom of campus dining after living under the strict regime enforced by my mother. My meal plan allowed me a certain amount of money each semester for food. But instead of getting small portions of salads, grilled meats, and steamed vegetables, I was permitted for the first time in my life to eat whatever I wanted without answering to my mother.

After overindulging in late-night snacks, impromptu pizza study sessions, and flat keg beer at fraternity parties, I'd gained at least twenty-five pounds. I didn't consider myself overweight, but my mom's constant criticisms ate away at my self-confidence. I was wearing mostly size ten clothing, but I felt obese by her standards.

I sighed. "I know you're permanently on a diet, Mom, but that's not me."

"It's your life, Kayla, but men don't typically want girls who let themselves go. Have you gone on any dates lately?"

Her words stung me, and she knew it. I hadn't dated anyone seriously since breaking up with my high school boyfriend before I left for college. My friends blamed my lack of a love life to my shyness; social situations left me uncomfortable, and I preferred observing from the sidelines. But once I got to know a person, I was able to open up.

I rose from my seat. "I didn't come home to hear your criticisms about my life. My weight has nothing to do with me being single."

Her eyes narrowed, her expression telling me she thought it was exactly the reason I was unattached. My mother's glare made me acutely aware of every bulge under my sweater and jeans. I threw my napkin down and stormed away from the table. I ignored Lila calling out my name as I grabbed my jacket and purse and rushed out of the house.

I hated deserting Lila, but I was angry at her for not jumping to my defense at dinner. We were supposed to be a team against my mom. Whenever my mom harassed my little sister, I attempted to put myself in the middle and stop the verbal abuse. Lila was more sensitive than me and prone to teary outbursts. It roused my protective instincts.

I had a tendency to process the pain privately. Even if I was falling apart inside, I pretended to be tough on the outside. But burying the anguish deep inside was getting more and more difficult each day. An explosion was on the horizon, and I wasn't sure I'd still be standing once it erupted.

When I peeled away from my house in my burgundy Jeep Wrangler, I was clueless about where to go. My friend Tami's house had always been a refuge after the many fiery arguments with my mom, but she was in Florida with her parents for the holidays. Although my school was in-state, my Trenton College friends were spread throughout the tri-state area. My roommate and best friend, Brittany, the only person besides Tami I confided in about my tumultuous relationship with my mom, was two hours north of my hometown of Red Bank.

Red Bank was a mid-sized New Jersey town minutes from the beach. Years ago, redevelopment efforts in the center of town revitalized the city by adding a large number of high-end shops and gourmet restaurants. I'd lived in the same split-level, four-bedroom house a couple of blocks from downtown since I was a baby.

The disruption at dinner made me realize I was hungry. In fact, all of a sudden, I felt ravenous. I parked my car in front of the twenty-four-hour convenience store and walked inside, zombielike. My objective was singular: *eat.*

Thoughtlessly, I roamed from aisle to aisle, grabbing whatever caught my eye. Boxes of doughnuts, candy bars, and bags of chips—the brightly colored wrappers looked inviting, and I reached for them like a lifeline. Soon, I was struggling to carry my loot and had to dump it on the front counter.

My face reddened as the dull-eyed cashier rang up my purchases. I was experiencing a kaleidoscope of emotions; I was giddy over defying my mother, but humiliated over my plans to eat my weight in junk food.

As I got into the Jeep and drove away, I felt my self-control slipping. Greedily, I reached for a chocolate bar from my spoils and clumsily tore at the package. I shoved a large piece into my mouth and barely had time to swallow before I was inhaling another piece. In seconds, the chocolate bar disappeared and I was licking the residue from my fingers.

But the chocolate bar didn't provide the fulfillment I was desperate for. Driving was getting in the way and I pulled to the side of the road to continue my binge unencumbered. My hunger felt animalistic, and I was devouring whatever I could get my hands on. Before long, I'd finished off three candy bars, a large soda, two bags of chips, three packages of TastyKakes and a half box of doughnuts. As if I had come out of a trance, I gazed around at the empty wrappers in horror. My stomach ached and the residual sugar from the snacks left an unpleasant taste in my mouth. While maneuvering the car away from the curb, I became panicked.

I sped home and ran into the house. Slamming the front door, I ignored my mother's calls from the kitchen. I took the steps two at a time to reach the bathroom in the upstairs hallway. I locked the door and turned on the faucet as far as it would go, hoping the sound would drown out the noise from inside the bathroom.

My fingers found their way into the recesses of my mouth. When my fingertips brushed the back of my throat, my gag reflex kicked in. The food slid easily back out the way it had come in and plopped into the waiting toilet. Throwing up once didn't purge everything inside of me and I repeated the process until I was dry heaving and there was nothing left to bring back up.

I flushed the toilet and sat on top of the lid. I didn't feel at all disturbed about what transpired. A part of me wondered why I wasn't hysterical and disgusted over what I had done. Instead, an eerie calm permeated through me. I hadn't only been purged of the food, but also of the awful feelings that plagued me since I fled my mother.

A knock at the door startled me. "Kayla, are you okay? I'm sorry about Mom."

My sister's lilting voice drew me out of my reverie. "I'm fine, Lila, I'll be out in a minute."

After washing my hands, I dared a look in the mirror. My eyes were red-rimmed and glassy. The bitter stench of my own vomit polluted the air and my heart began to race as I worried about my family figuring out what I'd just done. My pallor grew and I took shallow breaths to alleviate the crushing anxiety I suddenly felt. I asked myself, *Who is this troubled girl?*

CHAPTER TWO

At first, I convinced myself it was a one-time occurrence. Throwing up to get rid of my food was sick, and I wouldn't succumb to the pressure to take extreme measures to get thin. I knew binging and purging wasn't healthy, and there were better ways to control my weight.

For the rest of winter break, I ate like a bird during the day, relishing the salads and raw vegetables that were plentiful at home. Diet soda and water were the only beverages my mom kept in the house; she avoided sugary soft drinks like the plague. Her health-nut lifestyle turned out to work in my benefit as I tried to slim down.

Then night would come, and my stomach would become dissatisfied with the slim helpings during the day. It would twist and beg to be fed something more than carrot sticks. I tried to distract myself, but nothing worked. Once my mother and sister were in bed, I'd leave the house on a mission for sustenance.

My car had become a safe haven for reckless eating, and I ate whatever I craved the most. Sometimes that meant ordering the entire dollar menu at McDonald's or grabbing a bucket of chicken from KFC. When I went into a feeding frenzy, I didn't have a chance to enjoy the taste of the food—it was more about getting the most food into my body as quickly as possible.

The purging became second nature. As I binged, I could feel the growing nausea threatening and the food begging to be released from my body. Although the aftereffects were unsettling—my eyes were bloodshot, and my throat ached—the emotional release I felt brought an overpowering sense of relief.

I was no longer comfortable in my own skin. When I undressed, I would stare at the flab on my body and feel compelled to shut my eyes to block out the source of my revulsion. Somehow, my mother's condemnations had snuck into my subconscious and altered my perception of myself.

My mom helped me load up my car on the day I was set to return to campus. Her piercing gaze softened as she gave me a quick once-over. "I've noticed how much effort you've put into your diet," she said. "It's really starting to show."

Two weeks of extreme dieting and a nightly ritual of vomiting had been what I needed to do in order to win my mom's approval. I couldn't even begin to psychoanalyze what it meant.

I shifted uncomfortably and took notice of how my clothes were hanging a little more loosely from my frame. I had weighed myself in the morning and found I'd lost five pounds. The few pieces of size eight clothing I owned fit perfectly, and I hadn't bothered to pack the outfits I kept for my chunkier days.

Mom embraced me in an awkward hug, but I stood there stiffly, not sure what to make of the sudden impromptu show of affection. I hated that something inside of me preened from her sudden attention. I wanted to be stronger, not just happy that I'd finally done something she deemed worthwhile.

I was self-aware enough to know our relationship wasn't healthy. She wasn't the worst mother in the world, but her own personal demons prevented her from giving Lila and me the unselfish love we craved the most. Our father spoiled us. He teased us with that type of love before disappearing from our lives way too soon.

When my mother released me, I snatched Lila up in my arms and hugged her as if our lives depended on it. I whispered promises into her ear and begged her to call me if she needed anything. I had the strongest impulse to steal her away and concoct an elaborate plan to smuggle her into my dorm.

Tears pricked my eyes as I drove away from home. Lila and my mother stood side by side on the sidewalk, watching me leave. My heart ached for Lila, but a selfish part of me finally felt like I could breathe once again. I no longer had to go day to day and worry about whether I'd be the cause of my mother's everlasting discontent. I was going to be twenty-one the next month, but I was still controlled by my mother's whims.

Brittany had arrived first, and she met me outside. I double-parked so I could unload everything into our dorm. As juniors, we had preferred housing, and we lived in one of the three-story townhouses on campus. The townhouses were clustered in a large complex and housed juniors and seniors exclusively. Trenton College was small, with all the dorms and academic buildings within walking distance of one another.

Brittany had been my roommate since our freshman year, and we'd been inseparable since we met. I envied her fearlessness and her ability to feel comfortable being the center of attention. She was different from my bookish high school friends, but I liked the idea of living vicariously through Brittany.

Our floor had four single rooms, with Brittany and me sharing the space with a set of twins named Danielle and Jessica. We'd grown close to the other girls since the last semester, and I'd kept in touch with them over break through email and texting.

Brittany said, "I'm so glad to be back! I swear, if my parents made me work at the restaurant one more time, I was going to lose it." Her parents owned a small Italian restaurant in North Jersey. According to Brittany, the tips were crap and the customers were rude.

"I'm happy to be back, too. My mother was driving me nuts," I admitted.

"And how was Charlotte Marlowe? Did she go into a tizzy because she spotted a split end?" Brittany joked. Brittany had grown accustomed to the outrageous tales about my mother.

Brittany was naturally pretty, with short, curly black hair and dark eyes. Her Italian heritage rewarded her with a year-round tan and a metabolism that allowed her to seemingly eat whatever she wanted and not gain an ounce.

"No, but she hinted I was grossly overweight and would remain single forever because of it," I said.

"Your mother has issues." Brittany shook her head emphatically as she propped open the heavy aluminum door of the townhouse. I coasted by her carrying one of my suitcases and headed up the two flights of steps with Brittany following me. "Besides, you look amazing," she said. "You've definitely lost weight; I can see it in your face. Great job, Kayla."

I bristled at the compliment. I'd always found it exceedingly strange how easily girls judged and shared their assessments of one another's weight. But I couldn't claim to be one of the innocents; I'd stood by with my friends, listening while they dissected who had lost and gained weight over summer vacations.

Brittany's comment made me question how I'd looked before. Had I needed to lose weight? Is that why Brittany felt inclined to congratulate me on the weight loss? My paranoia set in and I wondered whether I had blinders on before and hadn't seen how heavy I'd become.

"Thanks," I mumbled as I unlocked my room and rolled the suitcase inside. My single was tiny, just enough room for my twin bed, desk, dresser, and nightstand. There was also a small closet where I was able to fit most of my clothing. A bathroom and kitchen in the common area was shared with the three other girls on the floor.

Brittany stood in the doorway. "How's your schedule? Did you get all the classes you wanted?"

I nodded. Most of the classes in my junior year were focused on the core courses I needed for graduation. I was majoring in journalism and looking to land a position on the campus newspaper, but nothing had opened up. In the meantime, I'd been publishing web articles to build a portfolio I could use after graduation. The pay wasn't bad and the topics were easy to research. My mother didn't think I was cutthroat enough to be a journalist, and I sometimes wondered if she had a point. My passion lied in sharing human-interest stories.

I asked, "What about you?"

Brittany was an elementary education major and would spend most of the semester student teaching. She wasn't exactly thrilled over the development since it would cut into her late-night partying. Besides frequenting fraternity parties, Brittany's twenty-first birthday in November allowed her access to the bars on and around campus. She had joked that she had a countdown clock for my upcoming birthday.

"Yes, I've received my student teaching assignment. I'll be working with third-graders; kids are still pretty cute at that age, so I'm happy. Once they hit fourth and fifth grade, they begin to get whiny and annoying."

It was good to be home, I thought, as we caught up on what was going on in our lives. Maybe I could forget about winter vacation and get in shape the old-fashioned way. I had free access to a fitness center on campus, and I was certain I could find plenty of low-calorie foods to choose from at the school eateries. I knew I couldn't eat with abandon like before.

Although the compliments about my weight loss were off-putting, it was nice to be told I looked good. I'd never needed the validation before, but experiencing a taste of it made me crave it. I would use my perfectionist tendencies to turn my body into something beautiful.

CHAPTER THREE

My head was pounding the next day as I picked up my textbooks from the campus store. Brittany and I stayed up until after two in the morning, participating in a gossip fest. The twins had arrived a few hours after I had settled in, and we got caught up with them. Danielle and Jessica were charming girls from Maryland, both amazing field hockey players. I found it very surprising the way they turned into savage beasts on the field, considering their normally laid-back personalities.

Brittany had picked up subs and bags of chips around midnight from the Wawa five minutes away from the campus. Although I'd made a pledge to eat healthier, it was hard to resist the temptation once the food was in front of me. It took all my resolve to not eat it, and I went to bed hungry. I decided to skip breakfast as well and instead set off for the bookstore to get everything I needed for my classes, which would be starting the next day.

My messenger bag was laden with newly purchased textbooks as I cut through the Student Center. The Student Center had a large atrium in the middle, with couches and tables where people could study between classes. The Student Center was the central building on campus and housed the bookstore, information desk, computer lab, and a sandwich shop. Student groups and vendors usually had tables set up along the walkways. Since it was the first week of classes, the building was overcrowded.

As I walked toward the exit, a figure carrying a clipboard stepped into my pathway. I let out an annoyed breath and I knew I was in for a lengthy spiel. Getting accosted by overzealous vendors in the Student Center was commonplace.

"Hi there." The soft voice was male, with a deep timbre. I lifted my gaze to meet his and found a pair of electric blue eyes twinkling in my direction. His hair was medium brown, with lighter blond streaks that looked to come naturally from the sun. He had a mussed hairstyle going on that may have been unintentional, or could have meant he spent twenty minutes in front of the mirror to perfect the look. Since he stood a full head above my five-foot-three, his chin was tilted down to look at me.

"Good morning, would you be interested in signing up for a student MasterCard?"

I rolled my eyes. It wasn't surprising he was chosen for that particular job. A man as gorgeous as he was would have the girls lining up around the block to sign up for a new credit card. "No thanks."

I went to sidestep him and he shot me a disarming smile. His smile was sexy, without any traces of smarminess. I found myself staring at his lips as he spoke.

"You get a free t-shirt and a coffee mug for just filling out the application."

"And in exchange I get a card with an outrageous twenty-five percent APR? I think I'll pass," I said dryly.

His smile grew bigger. "You can cut up the card if you get approved. You don't have to use it."

"I don't think I could withstand the temptation."

He looked amused by my response. "I'm Cameron."

My pulse picked up and I was startled by my instantaneous attraction to him. A guy hadn't excited me in a long time. I'd had a few casual dates since I went away to college, but nothing that gave me the butterflies I was suddenly experiencing.

At my silence, he remarked, "Not telling me your name?"

"It's nothing personal, I just don't like credit card sales reps." I smiled shyly at him to reduce the sting of my words. I was awkward when it came to flirtatious banter. I always envied how easily it came to Brittany and Tami.

He laughed heartily. "A blanket judgment, but interesting to know."

I reached for the clipboard he was holding and he handed me a pen. I could feel his eyes on me as I scribbled my answers in the different fields. If I didn't know better, I would guess he was scoping me out. I talked myself out of that notion, figuring he was using some sort of sales tactic to get me to sign up. His commission was most likely dependent on how many naïve girls he charmed into filling out applications.

Once I finished, I held out the clipboard to him. He set it aside and I took the offered bag containing my free t-shirt and mug. "Thanks," I said, and I turned to go.

"I'll be here all week if you feel like stopping back," he called as I took a few steps away from him.

I dared a look back. His gray, button-down shirt was tailored exactly to his body and I could make out the ridges of his lean, muscular frame. His hands were stuck inside the pockets of his black pants and he had tilted back on his heels. I wanted to express an interest, but I wasn't in the right state of mind. My head was a mess and it wasn't a good time to get romantically involved with anyone.

I waved to him before hurrying away. Cameron had thrown me off balance. I was the girl who faded in the background, not the one who attracted sexy strangers. My past dates had the same personality I perceived in myself: They were quiet homebodies, more interested in their academic futures than in being social and going to parties. I assumed Cameron was the type of guy that demanded attention, his looks and personality easily overshadowing anyone else in his vicinity.

My self-confidence was at an all-time low. I'd cast myself in the role of a chubby plain Jane, and the categorization stuck, despite my friends telling me over and over again how pretty they thought I was. I needed to discover a way to feel better about myself.

As I passed the sandwich shop, I stopped in and bought only an apple and an orange, despite not having anything substantial to eat since the previous afternoon. I reasoned if I lost more weight, maybe I'd feel comfortable again in my own skin. My rationalizations, born out of insecurity, had taken over, and they would guide my every decision going forward.

CHAPTER FOUR

Thoughts of food consumed me, but every bite I took was torture. Guilt gnawed at me and took away any enjoyment I had over the taste of food. I designed convoluted food challenges to help me stave off hunger and offered up the chance to give myself a congratulatory pat on the back once I completed them. For one day, I vowed to eat only raw vegetables. Another day, I committed to skipping breakfast and lunch and only eating dinner. I had fast days, where I didn't eat anything solid, surviving on water and Diet Coke.

Each meal was carefully planned out in my head. I took my meals alone, blowing off invitations to join Brittany, Danielle, or Jessica for lunch or dinner. Instead, I ate alone in my room, taking small bites, trying to make the tiny amounts of food last as long as possible. I could make a slice of bread last as long as a three-course meal.

My first week of classes was hazy. The low amount of calories I was consuming affected my concentration, and I found myself rereading portions of my texts several times until I was finally able to grasp things. My writing assignments lacked finesse, and I had to do heavy revisions to get my work up to par.

However, my reward for the strict diet was the number on the scale. I purchased a scale from a local pharmacy and weighed myself every morning without a stitch of clothing on. By Friday, I'd lost four more pounds. It was all the motivation I needed to keep up with my eating pattern.

"Bella!" a voice called as I searched the bookstore for a supplemental text I needed for a desktop publishing class I was taking. "Hey Bella!" The voice sounded closer and more insistent. I spun toward the source and found myself face to face with Cameron.

Cameron's expression was inscrutable. "Bella Swan, right?"

A blond girl standing next to me browsing the bookshelves looked at Cameron, then at me, and started chuckling. She shook her head in disbelief and disappeared down the next aisle.

"I'm guessing you read my credit card application," I said. I tucked a strand of hair behind my ear nervously. I had mixed feelings about seeing him again, as thrilled as I was apprehensive.

"Sorry, I was curious." He leaned closer to me. "I didn't lift your number off of it though; I'm not a total creeper."

My heart pounded as he moved into my personal space. He was wearing a blue shirt and it brought out the vibrant color of his eyes. His scent reached me, and I had the sudden urge to move closer to him and deeply breathe in his clean, masculine smell.

"That's not my name," I said and I turned back to face the wall of textbooks.

"Ah," he said, "You put a fake name on the application."

"I told you I didn't want another credit card," I reminded him. "Unless you've been living under a rock, I figured you would've recognized the name I used."

"Maybe I should ask you to return the t-shirt and mug then."

I turned to him and was again disarmed by the dazzling smile he was giving me. He was putting me at ease, and I liked the sensation. "Sure, you can take back your cheap, oversized t-shirt and dollar-store mug."

He laughed. "How about you keep them, as long as you give me your real name?"

"Deal," I replied. "It's Kayla."

"See? That wasn't so hard, was it?" Cameron chided. "So what year are you?"

"I'm a junior." I found the book I was looking for and removed it from the shelf. As I faced Cameron, I tapped my foot to release my nervous energy. "Today is your last day working here, right?"

It was something of a relief to know he would no longer be in the Student Center. I wasn't certain about how to process the unexpected attraction I felt toward him. My mind had a hard time believing Cameron would be flirting with me.

"Yes, then on to harass more students at other campuses into signing up for credit cards." He shrugged. "It's a crap job, but the best I could get since I graduated last year."

My curiosity was piqued. "Where did you graduate from?"

"I have a business degree from Rutgers. My goal is to have my own business one day, but this gig pays the bills in the meantime." He fell in step next to me as I walked toward the register. "What's your major?"

"Journalism. I'm not sure what type of company I want to work for yet, but I'm hoping to line up an internship for the summer."

Cameron waited next to me as I paid for my book. When I went toward the exit, I remarked, "Shouldn't you be manning your table?"

He looked nonplussed. "I'm taking a break." He took a sip from the water bottle he was holding, drawing attention to his lips. It had been months since I'd been kissed, and at that moment I wanted nothing more than to feel his mouth on mine. His lips appeared soft and inviting, and I imagined him to be an expert kisser.

He caught me watching him and I glanced away. I mumbled, "Well, it was nice to meet you."

"I only live five minutes from here. Would you want to get together sometime?"

Yes, a part of me screamed. Why wouldn't I want to go out with someone undeniably gorgeous, who also seemed interested in me? Yet my fears made me hesitate, and I stood in front of him silently. I didn't feel worthy of anyone's attention. I was fat and plain, and I suspected that instead of being truly attracted to me, Cameron had an ulterior motive. At times like that, it sucked being inside my head.

"That's probably not a good idea," I said, without meeting his eyes.

"Oh, okay." I thought I heard defeat in his tone. "Do you have a boyfriend?"

"No, it's just I'm not interested in dating anyone right now."

When I made eye contact with him again, I could see in his expression he wasn't sure how to reply to that statement. After a second's pause, he suggested, "We could get together casually, hang out as friends if it makes you more comfortable."

"Umm…" I awkwardly said. I didn't know how to respond to his persistence. Was he not used to being turned down? It wouldn't surprise me; girls didn't say no to guys like Cameron. I considered his ego might be bruised since I wasn't champing at the bit to go out with him.

He pulled a business card from his back pocket and held it out before I could finish replying. "This has my cell phone number on it. If you want, give me a call sometime. No pressure."

My fingers brushed his when I removed the card from his outstretched hand. I tucked it into my purse. I stared at his shoes and hoped for the growing awkwardness to pass.

"It was good to meet you, Kayla." His tone was soft and intimate. "I hope you'll give me a call."

"Bye Cameron," I said.

With hesitation, he walked back toward his stand. I studied him and saw several girls' heads turn as he maneuvered across the building's atrium. His strides were purposeful, and he didn't seem to notice the attention he garnered. I envied his confidence.

After only two brief meetings, Cameron left a lasting impression upon me. I liked him, but my emotions were too raw. It felt like all of my feelings were being amplified, and if I experienced heartache, it would cut me too deeply. It was safer not to take the risk.

CHAPTER FIVE

By the next week, I'd lost a total of eleven pounds. My clothing was getting looser and my features appeared leaner. My cheekbones were more pronounced and my chin more defined. I had hoped the weight loss would chase away the melancholy inside me. My expectations were if I was leaner, I'd suddenly feel comfortable in my own skin. I wondered if I would ever be happy inside my own body.

My dieting was extreme and left me with little energy most days. I found myself sleeping longer and was glad for the respite. The longer I was unconscious, the less time I had to focus on food. During my waking hours, it was all I could think about. I could feel my attention fading in class while I planned what I'd be permitted to eat for that particular day.

At night, I longed for the binge eating of Christmas break. But scarfing down a lot of food and vomiting proved difficult while living in close quarters with three other girls. The communal atmosphere of our dorm meant we had our doors open most of the time. It made it challenging to sneakily consume copious amounts of food and then vomit it back up. When my roommates were scarce, I was able to make an exception to my own rule.

Brittany grew impatient with me one night and coerced me into going to dinner with her. My excuses for bowing out of dinner were getting weaker, and she stood her ground until I finally relented. Under her watchful eyes, I couldn't have my typical meal of either plain vegetables or fruit. Since Brittany was twenty-one, her new favorite place to eat was The Court. It was the only restaurant on campus to serve beer. The menu was made up of mostly fried foods.

Once we settled in, Brittany ordered a Miller Lite, and I opted for a Diet Coke, Brittany started. "I can't wait until your birthday. Only ten days away!"

The plan was to go bar hopping with Brittany, Jessica, and Danielle. Brittany was good friends with several guys in one of the campus fraternities and had also invited them along. I would've been looking forward to a night out if I hadn't been obsessing over how many calories were in alcoholic drinks. I had come to the conclusion that a rum and Diet Coke would be my best bet for the night, since it only had a hundred calories per serving.

"I'm excited, too," I said, and I took a sip of my soda after the waiter put it down in front of me. After mentally debating the menu items, I decided on a grilled chicken sandwich. Jealousy flooded me as Brittany proceeded to order mozzarella sticks and a cheeseburger.

"So, what's been going on with you?" she asked me. "I feel like I barely see you anymore."

It was true. I hadn't realized how much my relationships revolved around food. Without attending meals together and with her hectic student teaching schedule, I only spent time with Brittany late at night in our dorms.

"I've been busy with classes and homework. I've also had a lot of online articles to hand in this week."

I wrote articles for several different websites to make extra money. The pay was decent and I could work in my pajamas in front of my laptop. My father's life insurance policy had allowed us to live comfortably after his death, but I preferred to have my own spending money handy without being forced to rely on my mother for handouts. My mother had quit college after two years, and I couldn't remember her working a day in her life. Turning Lila and me into her perfect little clones was too taxing for her to do anything else.

"Oh, okay," she said. "I was worried you were mad at me or something. I've felt like you're blowing me off lately."

"No! I'm sorry; I haven't meant to flake out on you."

"You're forgiven." She leaned forward conspiratorially. "So, have you called that guy yet?"

In a moment of weakness, I went to Brittany for advice. I hadn't been able to stop thinking about Cameron since he gave me his card. Several times, I'd even pulled it out and tried to talk myself into calling him. When I told her how much I'd been attracted to him during our two brief meetings, she insisted I make a move. I understood Brittany's insistence: Since my father's death, I hadn't expressed any interest in a guy.

"No, even if I could get up the nerve to call him, I'm not sure what I would say once I did talk to him," I admitted.

"Kayla, you have to snap out of this *woe is me* phase you're in. If he gave you his number, he obviously likes you and wants to talk to you." The waiter came to the table and set the mozzarella sticks down. "You've been a downer ever since you got back from break. Don't let your mom mess with your head." Brittany picked up a mozzarella stick and shook it at me to emphasize her point.

I thought being away from my mom would make me feel more at ease, but I couldn't shake the oppressive mood that had plagued me since after Christmas. The normal things that brought me happiness—late-night movies with Brittany, Skyping with Lila, even my writing—no longer had any effect on me. It was as if I had somehow died inside and was numb to the world. Cameron was the exception, and the idea of relying on a stranger to feel *something* was terrifying.

"I'll think about calling him," I conceded after Brittany glared at me.

She nodded, satisfied for the time being. "I wish I had a new hottie to drool over. I'm so bored with campus guys. It's like the same old, same old. And they have the attention span of gnats! They want you in and out of their beds within the hour and don't even want your number at the end of the night. I'm hoping to meet someone new when we go out for your birthday next weekend."

Brittany's endless chatter about the lack of eligible men on campus was soothing. It allowed me to momentarily forget about my own problems. When the waiter placed our entrees in front of us, I stared at the chicken sandwich and fries with dread.

"Kayla, you're looking at that chicken sandwich like it's still clucking." Brittany's eyes shrewdly scanned me from head to toe. "How much weight have you lost anyway? You look like a total babe, but I don't want you taking this dieting thing too far."

"I'm trying to eat better, that's all," I said lightly. I didn't mind the part of her calling me a total babe, but the rest of her remarks forced me to pretend I wasn't going overboard with my diet. The chicken sandwich felt like it weighed a thousand pounds as I compelled myself to lift it to my mouth. I was in agony as I forced down a bite. I gave Brittany a tight smile once I swallowed.

"I never see you eat and I know your mom loves to bitch about your weight. You don't need the Charlotte Marlowe seal of approval; she has to learn how to accept you as you are." Brittany pointed to my chest. "You're drowning in that sweater and I remember it fitting fine last semester. You have to be careful about losing too much weight that quickly."

"I'm fine. My New Year's resolution was to try and be healthier," I lied. To prove my point, I took another bite of the sandwich. It was tasteless, and the only thing I could think about was how I was going to get rid of those calories later. "Why don't we go work out after this?"

Brittany's look was disbelieving. "We never work out. We don't even run to class when we're late."

"It'll be good for us. We could bond again over exercise." Brittany still didn't look convinced. "Plus, there could be hot guys working out at the gym."

"All right, you sold me on the idea. But there'd better be a lot of cute asses for me to gawk at."

I amped up the resistance on the exercise bike and drove the pedals down. After dinner, Brittany and I had changed into our workout clothes and headed to the campus gym. The fitness center had treadmills, stationary bikes, elliptical machines, weight benches, and free weights. It wasn't a high-tech gym, but access was free with our tuition.

Brittany was daintily doing bicep curls with the lightest possible weights while not so subtly checking out the butt of the guy standing next to her. I doubted Brittany had even broken a sweat. Meanwhile, I was red-faced with perspiration, which was causing my hair to stick to my skin. Although I wasn't in shape, I was trying to sweat out as many calories as possible on the bike.

I groaned in frustration when I checked the calorie counter on the display. I had been pedaling like crazy for half an hour and had only burned two hundred calories. I hopped off and climbed on a treadmill. I never ran on a treadmill, so I pressed the quick start button. Without a warm-up, I increased the speed and incline until I was running at a pace that burned one hundred calories in a mere ten minutes.

As I surpassed the ten-minute mark, I began to feel lightheaded and had difficulty breathing. My palm slammed down on the emergency stop button and I stumbled off the belt. The room started spinning and stars erupted in my field of vision. Desperately, I tried to cling to consciousness as I realized how close I was to passing out.

A guy working out next to me jumped off his treadmill and put a firm hand on my elbow. "Hey, are you okay? You don't look so hot."

Brittany was suddenly at my side. "Kayla, come with me and sit." With the help of the stranger, Brittany led me to one of the exercise mats in the center of the room. I fell into a sitting position, put my head between my knees, and closed my eyes. A bottle of water was pressed against my lips.

"Here, drink this," Brittany commanded.

I greedily gulped down the water. A moment passed and the dizziness subsided. Lifting my head, I noticed I'd drawn the attention of several people working out. A staff member made his way in front of me.

"Everything okay here?"

"Yes, I'm fine. I was dizzy for a minute, but I'm feeling much better now." I was still wobbly as I climbed to my feet, and the muscular guy who had helped me over to the mat reached out to steady me. I shot him a grateful smile. "Thank you."

"Yes, thank you," Brittany said and I could hear the flirtatiousness in her tone. I forced myself not to roll my eyes. There was never an inopportune time for Brittany to flirt.

"I'm Kurt," he said. Although he was holding me up, he addressed Brittany.

"Brittany," she said and did a cutesy hair flip.

"Can we go?" I asked her as she locked eyes with Kurt for a long minute. I hated to break up the party, but I was getting uncomfortable with the scrutiny of the others in the gym.

"Sure," she agreed readily. She turned to Kurt. "Do you think you could help me get her back to our dorm?" Her long lashes lowered and she pressed her lips together in a pout.

"I think I'll be fine," I insisted. When Kurt looked away, Brittany's expression turned pleading. I relented. "But I guess it wouldn't be hurt to have someone around in case I feel lightheaded again."

We made an awkward trio as we left the gym. Kurt had been ecstatic over being enlisted to walk us to the dorm, and I could see the sparks flying between him and Brittany. I trailed behind while they chatted during the ten-minute hike back to the townhouse.

Kurt fit in with Brittany's type perfectly. He had dark hair, dark eyes, and an amazing body. He towered over her petite frame and she had hit his arm playfully more than once, squeezing his enormous biceps. I guessed she'd found her latest conquest. Brittany seemed ready for something more than a casual fling, and I hoped she'd find someone soon to get serious with.

Once we got back to the dorm, I excused myself while Brittany and Kurt continued to talk out front. Hurrying into my room, I collapsed on my bed. I was exhausted. My mind and body were tired, and I didn't know how much longer I would be able to stand it. I craved oblivion; the chance to disappear and not have to deal with the anxiety that food and my weight caused me each day. I wanted to fall asleep and wake up in a new body I could be content with.

CHAPTER SIX

"Happy twenty-first, Kayla!" Brittany's jubilant voice rang out as we downed our second round of shots for the night.

We were at the second stop in our planned bar crawl for the night. Brittany's plan involved us having a shot and a maximum of two drinks at each place before moving on. We'd taken a taxi to Main Street, a long stretch of road containing the most popular bars frequented by Trenton College students.

We had a pre-celebration in our dorm before heading out around ten o'clock. Brittany ordered pizza and purchased a delicious chocolate cake from a local bakery. As I indulged, it became a struggle to not rush off to the bathroom and purge the high-calorie meal. However, I vowed to not let my food issues ruin my night.

My mom hadn't been thrilled that I wasn't coming home for my birthday. She would only surrender after I promised to spend the next weekend at home. I was excited to see Lila, but dreading the time I'd be forced to spend with my mother. Birthday celebrations were especially hard, since most of the time I'd stare at my father's empty chair and wish he were there. If I closed my eyes, I could still hear him singing *Happy Birthday* off-key at the head of the table.

As we lined the glasses back up on the bar, I pulled on the hem of my dress. Brittany had insisted we go shopping for something new for me to wear out. She made it clear the oversized sweaters and jeans I'd been living in were unacceptable. After I saw her outlandish choices, we compromised, and I bought a simple black dress, with a rounded neckline that dipped startlingly close to my cleavage, and a hem resting on my thighs. I'd been thrilled that I fit into a size six—a size I hadn't been since high school. My good mood over the revelation allowed me to forget how out of character I felt in the dress.

Kurt leaned over and whispered something in Brittany's ear. She tossed back her head and let out a high-pitched giggle. Since my almost-collapse at the gym, Kurt and Brittany had been inseparable. Kurt was a senior finance major and seemed to be a nice guy. As long as he made Brittany happy, I approved of him.

Jessica and Danielle were seated at the bar and talking to Todd and Dan, a couple of fraternity guys Brittany was friendly with. Dan and Jessica had been flirty since we left for the night, and I had a feeling they'd be hooking up before the night was over. The twins were casual daters, and I didn't expect anything serious to develop.

When I scanned the bar, my jaw suddenly dropped. Panicked, I grabbed Brittany's arm and pulled her away from Kurt. I whispered harshly in her ear, "He's here."

Brittany drew her eyebrows together. "Who?"

"Cameron," I said nervously. "Don't look now, but he's wearing a green polo shirt and sitting with a group at the table to our left."

I groaned as Brittany snapped her head in Cameron's direction. Inconspicuously, I snuck a look past her to where Cameron was seated. He was with three other guys and two girls. A redhead was seated next to him, and I was

31

surprised by the surge of jealousy I felt when I saw her lean toward him and say something that made him laugh.

"Let's leave," I urged Brittany.

After Brittany was done eyeballing him, she spun back around to face me. "Are you crazy, Kayla? He's hot," Brittany asserted and mimed fanning her face for emphasis. "I'll let you call dibs since you met him first."

"He's probably on a date with that girl. I really don't want to run into him," I moaned.

"Kayla, get a grip. You look freaking gorgeous! Guys can't stop staring at you. I'm telling you, even if he *is* with that girl, he won't be once he sees you." I went to protest, but stopped when Brittany added, "You're too late anyway. He just saw you."

I locked eyes with him from across the bar. Recognition dawned on Cameron's features. He addressed the group at his table as he rose to his feet. They looked my way and I was relieved the dark lighting of the bar could hide my blush. Brittany's smile was charming as Cameron approached. He kept his eyes on me the entire time.

"Hey," he greeted me.

"Hi," I replied. I gestured toward Brittany. "This is my roommate, Brittany."

"Cameron," he said, with only a brief glance in her direction. "It's nice to meet you."

He held my gaze again and I swallowed visibly. Brittany's expression turned sly. She patted us both on our shoulders. "Well, I'll let you two catch up. I'm going to grab a drink with Kurt." She addressed Cameron. "It was great to meet you."

I leaned into the wall behind me once Brittany slithered away. I took a sip of my drink and tried to come up with something witty to say.

"You never called," Cameron stated. It wasn't an accusation, but his tone told me he had hoped I would be in touch with him.

"I wanted to," I said softly into my glass.

"I wasn't going to come out tonight." When he paused, I shifted my gaze to his face. "I'm really glad I did."

"Kayla! Dan bought you another shot!" Jessica stumbled in my direction and thrust a shot glass into my hands. The alcohol was already hitting her hard and I suspected she wouldn't be upright for much longer. When she saw Cameron, she tossed back her blond hair. "Whoa, are you Kayla's present?"

Cameron laughed. "It's your birthday?" he asked me.

"Yes, first time legally in a bar."

"Can I buy you a drink?" he asked, taking note of my near empty glass.

"That would be great, thanks. It's a rum and Diet Coke." After asking Jessica if she needed a drink, he elbowed his way to the bar.

Jessica's eyes were wide as she watched him walk away. "Who is *that*?"

"Just some guy I met in the Student Center a couple of weeks ago. He was doing credit card sign-ups." I was trying to play it cool. I was frightened by how much I liked him already. But there was a recklessness about the night working in my favor. It was my twenty-first birthday, and I wanted to shed my normal insecurities and have a fun night.

My skin was abuzz with anticipation when I saw him turn away from the bar and return to me. I loved seeing him out of a suit. His polo shirt highlighted his lean muscles, and the pair of jeans he was wearing accentuated the nice shape of his behind. His hair still had the mussed style I'd found sexy when I saw him at the college. My hands itched to run my fingers through it.

When Cameron handed Jessica her beer, she thanked him and darted back to our group of friends. Cameron opened up his mouth to talk, but a shout from behind interrupted his thought. "Cam!" I pivoted toward the source of the voice and saw the redhead calling to

Cameron from their table. She was motioning emphatically, and I didn't want to be labeled the interloper.

"I shouldn't keep you from your friends." I fiddled with the silver bracelet on my wrist. "Thank you for the drink."

"A table opened up next to them. Do you want to have a seat with me?"

The alcohol was diminishing my nervousness and I suddenly felt emboldened. "Yes. I'll just let my friends know."

Brittany sent me a wink after I let her know I'd be heading to a table with Cameron. He took me by the hand as I walked away from my friends. His hand was warm and I loved the feel of his skin again mine. I hadn't realized how much I'd been craving affection until his fingers intertwined with my own.

Cameron introduced me to his friends at the table. They were a group of his high school friends who still lived in the area. Besides the redhead, who introduced herself as Taylor, his friends were polite and asked about where I lived and what I was studying. Taylor was silent, and I felt derision come off her in waves. I was allergic to girl drama and felt relieved when we sat at the adjacent table.

He pulled out the chair for me and took the seat across from me. "I wish I would've known it was your birthday, I'd have brought a gift."

My smile was wry. "Really?"

"Well, since you didn't call to let me know, you'll have to settle for my company." He leaned back into his chair and took a long sip of his beer. "Was there a reason you decided not to call me?"

"It wasn't anything personal, I'm a shy person," I said.

"Oh," he breathed. "A rookie mistake, I should've asked for your number. You were giving off the vibe that you weren't interested, so I didn't want to come off as too pushy."

"You're a credit card rep, it's in your nature to be pushy," I teased.

He winced and put a hand to his heart. "You wound me with your low opinion of credit card reps."

I liked our rapport. I hadn't felt that relaxed with a guy in a long time. He was helping me loosen up. It felt natural to smile and laugh with him, reminders I could be a normal human being if I wanted to.

"So, was I right? Was I coming on too strong and you were being too nice to tell me to get lost?"

I dared a look into his brilliant blue eyes. "No," I said softly. "I'm interested, but I'm not going to step on any toes if you're seeing someone else." I sent a meaningful look toward his table.

His mouth turned down and he asked, "Do you mean Taylor? I'm not with her."

I used the tip of my ring finger to trace the rim of my glass. "I was getting a *hands-off* vibe from her when we were introduced."

"We dated back in high school, but it's been over for years. She tries to act possessive about me, says it's because she's looking out for me. But we're only friends."

His sincerity was disarming. The college boys I'd had brief flirtations with were disingenuous. They would ply me with compliments, but they turned their attention elsewhere when I didn't put out. But Cameron seemed honestly surprised I'd feel threatened by Taylor. I was making assumptions about what kind of person he was based on how attractive I found him. I had to stop expecting the worst in people.

I said, "You're single, then?"

He opened his mouth to reply. After a brief hesitation, he pinched his lips together.

"What?" I asked. "You do have a girlfriend then?" Settling back in my chair, I waited patiently for his answer. My stomach clenched as I waited for him to admit he was in a relationship.

35

"No," he laughed and a flash of embarrassment crossed his features. "I was going to say something like 'hopefully not for long,' but I'm thinking I should back off a little bit. I like you and I don't want to come off like a cocky jerk."

My eyes lit up. "You're not."

"Good, because you're a little hard to read. But I like that about you. It makes me want to try and figure out what you're thinking," he said, and he scooted forward in his chair.

His knee brushed against mine under the table. His touch made my skin come alive, and I wanted to thank Brittany for insisting I wear a dress. I took a breath. "So, what else should I know about you, Cameron?"

"Well, my friends call me Cam, but I find the way you say my full name very sexy, so keep calling me that."

He was something else. My ineptitude with men made me glad he was taking the lead. His self-assurance was appealing, and I found myself turned on. I liked the emotions he was invoking inside me, and I couldn't deny the appeal of being desired by someone like him.

"Anything else I should know? Besides the fact that you're an incurable flirt." I laughed.

"I live in an apartment a few blocks from here. Just me and my dog, Angus; he's an English bulldog and he's pure awesomeness."

I smiled at his description. I doubted he could get any cuter, and I was suddenly grateful I'd run into him.

"My parents live about twenty minutes away, and I have a younger sister who just started her sophomore year at Rutgers."

"I have a younger sister, too. Her name is Lila and she's still in high school." I conjured up Lila in my head and felt a pang as I realized how much I missed her. The last time we'd talked over Skype, she was irate over my mother trying to control her daughter's social life and deciding who was good enough for her to date. "I'm from Red Bank, it's about an hour away."

"I saw a concert there last year with my sister, Scarlett. We went for drinks afterward, seemed like a cool town. I'd like to go back some time."

"It is a fun place. The bars always have amazing bands playing. I couldn't wait to turn twenty-one to check some of them out."

Cameron laced his fingers behind his neck and grinned. "Sounds like we have a date then."

I laughed. "You're pretty sure of yourself."

"You did tell me you were interested," he pointed out. "Are you going to keep saying no each time I ask you out? Because it's okay to admit you want me."

Although he was teasing, heat crept into my cheeks. His grin turned wicked and I gulped down the rest of my drink nervously. He was making my need for control slip, but I was enjoying the sensation.

Brittany appeared before us. "I hate to break this up, but we still have three more bars to hit."

I shot Cameron an apologetic smile. "We're doing a bar crawl for my birthday. Meaning everyone will be completely smashed by the time we get home."

"Yes, and we're already behind schedule." Brittany placed her hands on her hips and sulked.

I stood up and squelched my annoyance over her interruption. I was compelled to remind her of whose birthday it was. "Fine," I answered shortly. "Just give me a minute."

Brittany took the hint and scampered back to Kurt. My annoyance disappeared when I saw the twins glance in my direction. They had all come out for my birthday, and I couldn't ditch them for a cute guy.

Cameron got to his feet and walked around to my side of the table. "I really don't want you to leave." His voice had taken on a seductive quality as he tilted his head close to mine. "I can't stand the thought of anyone else seeing you in that dress."

My breath caught. His hand slid down my bare arm and gooseflesh emerged once his fingers pulled away. "Come with us," I said, my voice thickened with desire. Within minutes of seeing him again, I was already entranced by his presence and I wasn't ready to let him go. I frowned when I remembered his friends seated next to us. "I guess it would be rude to leave your friends."

"I'll see if they want to come," Cameron suggested. "If not, I'll catch up with them later."

His eyes searched my face and I felt in tune with his thoughts. We needed more time together to see where this was going. There was chemistry between us, and I hoped he wasn't only feeling a sexual connection. My thoughts were lustful, but I was also attracted to the sweet guy I'd seen glimpses of during our brief encounters. He was a mystery I was excited to unravel, and I wanted the night to never end.

CHAPTER SEVEN

Fifteen minutes later, we exited the bar and were greeted by the frigid February air. My teeth were chattering as we walked to the next bar on Brittany's list. Cameron's friends had ordered pitchers of beer at the last bar and declined to join us. I was relieved; the last thing I wanted was to have Taylor clawing my eyes out for flirting with Cameron.

Cameron must have noticed my shivering because he quickly pulled me to his side. His body heat warmed me, and I grinned at him gratefully. I wasn't sure if it was Cameron's presence or the alcohol, but I'd become someone I didn't recognize. For the past couple of hours, my weight and what I was going to eat hadn't crossed my mind once. I missed the simplicity of not being obsessed with my appearance.

Cameron insisted on paying my cover charge when we arrived at the next bar. The pub was overcrowded, and we could only find a spot for our group in the back recesses of the bar. After Brittany forced us all to do the obligatory shot of Southern Comfort, she dragged Kurt into a corner to make out. Dan was holding Jessica up, and I doubted she would be able to stay much longer. Todd and Danielle had gone in search of the bathroom, and I guessed they'd be a while, based on the number of people in the bar. I was grateful for the chance to continue talking to Cameron alone.

"Are you enjoying your birthday?" Cameron asked in my ear.

"I am now."

Gently, he twirled me around to face him. Taking my drink out of my hands, he set it on the high-top table next to us. His left arm encircled my waist and he slipped his right hand behind my neck. I closed my eyes in anticipation.

His lips covered mine and our mouths moved in a gentle rhythm. His embrace tightened and I was crushed against the firm planes of his chiseled chest. I could feel every inch of hardened muscle, and it incited my desire. I gripped the back of his head and dragged my fingers through his hair. Shivers ran up and down my back as his hands caressed me in time with our kiss. I parted my lips and allowed his tongue to slip inside my mouth. Our tongues caressed, and he deepened the kiss.

His kiss floored me. It surpassed my expectations in every way and kept me wanting more of him. I felt swept away and I wanted to cry out when he pulled away. It wasn't until I regained my senses I realized I had been close to devouring him in the midst of a crowded bar.

"Wow," I muttered, surprised I was able to form a coherent sentence. "You must really want me to sign up for a credit card."

Chuckling, Cameron twirled me around to face the rest of the bar. "I think your friend has been trying to get your attention."

Danielle was calling out my name and waving her hands frantically. Jessica was slumped against the wall, without any shoes on and sandwiched between Todd and Dan. Groaning, I pushed my way toward the group. Danielle's expression was apologetic at my approach.

"I'm sorry to cut out early, but I have to get my sister back home before she passes out in a pile of her own puke in the middle of the bar."

"Will she be okay? Maybe we should all head out." I grimaced when I saw Jessica smile drunkenly at Dan and attempt to kiss him. I was poised to intervene, but I saw him holding her gently away from his lips. The effects of the alcohol were beginning to hit me hard, too, and I wanted to avoid making a fool out of myself in front of Cameron.

"I'll take care of Jess, she needs to rehydrate and sleep it off. But you absolutely can't leave early. It's your birthday." Danielle was insistent. Motioning to Brittany, who was dirty dancing with Kurt in the corner of the bar, she added, "Also, Brittany will kill me if you go home with us."

"Okay," I said reluctantly. I was the good girl who took care of everyone. It was strange to hang up my duties for the night.

"Besides, you'd be out of your mind to leave that delicious man," she chided. Cameron was standing where I'd left him and had his hands shoved into his jeans pockets. He grinned when he saw me watching him and lifted an eyebrow in my direction. My lips were swollen, and I could still taste his kiss. Danielle was right: I'd be crazy to leave him so soon.

Danielle was giggling when I faced her again. "Just keep in mind that my room is next to yours and the walls are very thin."

I playfully shoved her shoulder. "Call my cell if Jessica needs anything. Do you have cash for a cab?"

"Yes, and stop worrying. You only turn twenty-one once." She kissed my cheek and headed toward Jessica.

I returned to Cameron after I said goodbye to Jessica, Todd, and Dan. With Brittany and I already paired off, the guys no longer saw the point of staying at the bar. They bought me an Irish Car Bomb before they left, which I quickly handed over to Cameron.

"Please drink this," I insisted. "I will face plant soon if I don't stop drinking."

"But it's your twenty-first, it's like a twisted rite of passage to drink until the point of unconsciousness," he teased.

"Why? Is that what your twenty-first birthday was like?"

"Worse. I woke up with a tattoo."

I was pleasantly surprised by the revelation, figuring he was too preppy to have an edgy side. The more I was getting to know him, the more my crush was growing. My damaged psyche questioned why a good-looking, funny, and nice guy like Cameron would be attracted to me. His ex-girlfriend was beautiful; she was most likely a size zero and had a gorgeous face. I was fat and ordinary.

But I wouldn't allow myself to succumb to my hang-ups. Even if it was just for one night, I'd have fun and enjoy spending time with Cameron. The chemistry between us could be fleeting, and I didn't want to waste time thinking up all the reasons he shouldn't like me.

"So, are you going to show me the tattoo?"

He closed the space between us and brushed his cheek against mine. His breath was warm as he whispered into my ear. "That's my party trick for later."

The rest of the night felt ethereal. I felt like I was existing on an entirely different plane from everyone else, and the only other person I could see was Cameron. His eyes were captivating, and they held me prisoner for the entire time we stood together, talking. Each time we touched, I melted, dissolving into nothingness and becoming only sensation. Cameron didn't paw at me; instead, he was affectionate in a natural way, making every excuse to touch me. He held my hand for most of the night, tracing small circles over my knuckles. Each caress made me envision what else he could do to me using his fingers.

The night came to an end too swiftly. Brittany had her arm laced through mine when we were ushered out of the final bar on our pub crawl. Cameron and Kurt were behind us, bonding over their shared love of the New York Giants. Brittany and I were struggling to walk, both of us equally intoxicated.

Brittany stage whispered, "He's so freaking sexy, Kayla, you should totally go home with him."

I dared a look behind me and was met by a pair of glittering blue eyes. Cameron winked my way as he continued his conversation with Kurt. I hissed, "I'm not going home with him, I barely know him."

"That didn't stop you from letting him perform mouth-to-mouth on you in the bar."

"Like you should talk," I reminded her.

Brittany giggled in response and spun around to face Kurt. She ran behind him and hopped on his back. He carried her down the road to the intersection where we were going to wait for the cab to pick us up.

"Do you want a ride back to the dorm?" Cameron asked me while Kurt and Brittany charged in front of us. "I haven't been drinking for hours."

My feet throbbed and my head was beginning to pound, and the thought of being chauffeured home by him was tempting. However, through the alcohol induced haze, I understood it would probably be best to stay with Brittany and take the taxi home. I may have been ready to kiss him senseless, but I didn't want to wake up with regrets the next morning by allowing things to go farther than I felt comfortable with.

"Thanks for the offer, but I should probably head back with my friends," I said softly.

"I was going to drive you all back," he elaborated.

"We already called a cab. Anyway, if you drove us home, I'd feel obligated to invite you up. Call me old-fashioned, but that's pretty quick, considering we haven't gone on a date yet."

"This night turned out much better than I expected. I thought I'd be at the bar all night, whining to my friends about the girl who never called me," he said.

We stopped walking and I began to shift from foot to foot to stave off the bitter cold. I shoved my hands into the pockets of his wool coat and smiled up at him. "Thanks for a memorable birthday."

The wind picked up and my hair was blown into my face. He smoothed my hair back and cupped my chin. His lips grazed mine, and I sighed in contentment. He drew back and then planted a gentle kiss on my forehead.

"Will you call me this time?" The husky timbre of his voice was stirring up lustful images of the two of us in my head. I conceived of things he could do to my body to help me forget how much I loathed it.

"Do you want to take my number just in case I lose my nerve?"

He pulled out his cell phone and I relayed my number to him. Smirking, he quipped, "This is your actual number, right, Bella Swan?"

"Yes," I said, and I blushed. I hoped he would call but didn't want to say it. The night brought out a side of me that had been dormant for a long time. I'd begun referring to that period as the *before*. Before my dad died and broke my heart, before I transformed into the calorie-counting maniac who abused her body for skinniness.

When the taxi pulled up, I disentangled from his arms. I kissed his cheek, lingering for a second too long. I breathed in his scent, already addicted to the subtle masculine aroma. As I took a step backward, I hoped his smell lingered on my skin, reminding me of the incredible night I'd had. Cameron escorted me into the cab and leaned over for a quick peck once I was crammed into the backseat with Brittany and Kurt.

Brittany kissed her palm and blew it in his direction. "Bye lover boy!" she exclaimed. Her dark curls fell forward, concealing her face, and she began to laugh hysterically. I had a hunch I wasn't going to live the night down anytime soon.

When the door closed, I studied Cameron through the smudged windows of the cab. He stayed at the curb, watching us disappear from view. I was frightened by the intensity of my feelings, and I couldn't help but speculate about when the other shoe would drop. He was too perfect, our time together too incredible, for it to turn into something more than a casual flirtation.

CHAPTER EIGHT

When I was a little girl, I would play a game that involved me spinning around in circles for as long as possible. When I'd finally fall, I'd press my head against the ground and revel in the dizzying sensation. Waking up the next morning to a spinning room after a night of drunken debauchery was decidedly less appealing.

As I climbed out of bed, nausea snuck up on me and I made a beeline for the bathroom. The mixed drinks and shots stung my throat as the contents of my stomach emptied into the toilet. Once my stomach settled, I leaned my head against the chilly tiled walls. I hated that my first thought was I'd liberated myself from the exorbitant number of calories I'd ingested the night before.

I flushed the toilet and splashed ice-cold water on my face. My eyes darted up to the mirror and I inspected the damage. Mirrors had been my enemy for a long time now. I despised my reflection. My face was puffy, and my eyes glittered with moisture. Last night's mascara had blackened under my eyes and my lips were dry and cracked.

As I fled from my reflection, Danielle was emerging from her room. She rubbed at her weary eyes and gave me a wan smile. "You sound just like Jess last night. I was holding back her hair for an hour. After I finally got some water into her, she passed out."

We could make out Jessica's snores through her door. She sounded like a drunken sailor. Brittany's door was firmly shut, and I was glad I lived across the hall and not next door. Kurt had slept over and, according to Brittany, he was a shouter during sex. Since the couple had seemed to be reenacting a scene from *Taxicab Confessions* on the way home, I could only imagine what happened once they were removed from a public place.

Brittany got a kick out of telling me about her sexual exploits. She considered herself my teacher due to my inexperience. I'd slept with my high school boyfriend, Grant, once on prom night and one other time before we broke up and left for college. Losing my virginity was anticlimactic, and the two times I slept with Grant were forgettable. We weren't attuned to each other's bodies, and sex had been awkward. I decided to sleep with Grant because I felt like it was time to get rid of my virginity, not because I loved him. I suspected Grant was in the same mindset, and it made our breakup decidedly painless.

During my time at college, I hadn't felt a strong desire to sleep with anyone. There wasn't enough of a spark with anyone to consider taking things to such an intimate physical level. What happened with Cameron was a fluke. His confidence and sexiness didn't just ignite a spark—it had me ready to burst into flames.

Danielle bypassed me and opened our refrigerator. Downing a bottle of water in a couple of gulps, she heaved a huge sigh. Her long blond hair was mussed and she looked about as hung-over as I was feeling. Reaching into the fridge, she pulled out another water bottle and passed it to me. I pressed the bottle against my temples to ease my worsening headache.

"You should eat something; it'll make you feel better. Want me to make you some toast?"

I shook my head emphatically. "I don't think I can keep anything down."

Danielle shrugged. "Well, don't keep me in suspense. What happened with Cameron last night?"

I bit my lip as I thought about the night before. When I relived it, I kept returning to our first kiss. It had electrified my body and filled me with a deep longing. The connection couldn't have been completely one-sided; Cameron's desire had been unmistakable since the second he saw me at the bar.

"We hung out and went to a few more bars. He was a lot of fun and very sweet. I gave him my number, but who knows if he'll actually call." The crack in my voice betrayed me. Pretending I didn't like Cameron wasn't going to fool anyone. I yawned and stretched. "I think I'm going to veg out in front of the TV today and try to recover from last night."

I returned to my room and bundled up in my burgundy comforter. I was shivering, and I felt iciness circulating through my veins. My stomach growled, but I disregarded the noise. Instead, I turned on my small TV set and tried to divert my attention from my bodily needs.

I dozed for a couple of hours. Finally, I rallied enough to get out of bed and go in search of my cell phone. It had been left off the charger all night and had probably died hours before. I found it in my purse and attempted to turn it on without any success. But after a few minutes plugged into the wall charger, it came to life.

I held my breath when I saw a text from an unknown number: **I had a great time tonight and wanted to make sure you got home safely. Cameron**

The message was time stamped three in the morning. I swooned slightly as I imagined him going back home and still having me on his mind. I wrote several drafts of a reply text before I was satisfied. **I had fun too. Thanks**

for checking up on me. I've been spending the day recovering from last night.

Ten minutes later, my cell phone rang. I dove for it, but hesitated a second before answering. "Hello."

"Hi, it's Cameron." His voice was rich and smooth. Butterflies fluttered in a frenzy within my belly. "How are you feeling?"

"Like I got run over by a truck," I confessed. "I'm obviously a lightweight when it comes to drinking."

"I'm guessing you're not feeling up to meeting for a drink then," he teased. "Are you free for coffee?"

I had forgotten the rules of dating. Would it look bad if I agreed? Was I supposed to pretend I was busy and give him more of a chase? It was evident he wanted to see me again as much as I needed to see him, so I decided to avoid the games.

"Coffee sounds good. Where do you want to meet?"

We settled on getting together at the Starbucks in town. Since we were meeting in an hour, I had to rush to shower and decide on what to wear. As I hurried into the hallway, Brittany was coming out of the bathroom.

"Hey," she said sleepily. It was close to three in the afternoon and Brittany appeared ready to go back to bed already.

"Rough morning?"

"Ugh, I didn't get to sleep until six. I thought alcohol was supposed to kill a guy's sex drive, not turn him into an insatiable beast," Brittany complained. Once again, I was thankful for being a heavy sleeper. "Don't mind me if I'm walking a little funny today."

I shook my head in disbelief and smiled. "As charming as it is to hear about your sex life, I have to run. I'm meeting Cameron for coffee."

Brittany waggled her eyebrows suggestively. "He can't get enough of you, huh? Maybe he'll help you get rid of that pesky v-card."

"Too bad I'm not a virgin."

"It's been three years, Kayla. I think you're considered a virgin again after that long," Brittany said drily. "Was he a good kisser?"

"An amazing kisser. It makes me wonder if a boy has ever kissed me properly."

Playfully, Brittany pulled on a strand of my long hair. "You're so cute sometimes. I want all the details of your date later."

My indecision over what to wear made me ten minutes late to meet Cameron. My black dress the night before had left little to the imagination, but in the light of day, I didn't have the same confidence. The desire to cover up my body was too ingrained into my consciousness. The gray sweater I chose was pretty, but oversized. It would hide my flaws from him. The outfit was completed with a pair of jeans and boots.

Despite the cold, Cameron was standing outside the Starbucks when I arrived. His smile was warm when I hopped out of my car and approached him. He nodded toward my car. "I like your Jeep."

I appreciated the compliment. I loved my car. In the summer, I had the top off as much as the weather permitted. I'd speed down the highway with the wind flying through my hair, drowning out my mother's voice in my head telling me how much I'd never measure up. My father had gone with me to pick it out a few months before he died, and my Jeep made me feel like we were still connected somehow.

"You look like you're freezing," I told him. "You didn't have to wait out here for me."

"I'm just glad you're here," he said, and he kissed the top of my head. "I was beginning to worry you were going to stand me up."

The idea seemed laughable. Cameron wasn't the type of guy girls stood up. "Not a chance."

He took me by the hand and led me into the Starbucks. I liked how comfortable I felt holding hands with him. It gave me the sense we'd known each other for much longer than we had.

My thoughts of Cameron were momentarily halted when the aroma of pastries and coffee assaulted my nostrils. My eyes were drawn to the display cabinet, stocked full with cookies, muffins, and cupcakes. My mouth began to water and my stomach rumbled in protest. It was after four o'clock and the only thing I'd eaten for the day was a handful of saltine crackers.

Cameron was talking. "Do you want to grab us a table and I'll order?" My head bobbed up and down mechanically. "What would you like?"

I wanted to drown in food, eat until I couldn't stand another bite. However, if I wanted to keep losing weight, I would have to call on my willpower to help me avoid the fatty treats. "A green tea with one Splenda."

Green tea had no calories and was said to have fat-burning qualities. These were the types of things I discovered online as I became obsessed with losing weight. Sometimes at night, instead of doing my homework, I would scour the online forums for weight-loss tips and tricks. I'd started eating more low-calorie bread products since I found they kept me fuller, for longer, than fruits and veggies. I'd also taken to chewing gum, since I read mindless chewing could cut down on the cravings for food.

The worst part of starving myself was the side effects. Exercise was unimaginable because of my low energy level, and I'd begun carrying around a bottle of pain relievers to treat the headaches I was prone to.

After double-checking to make sure I didn't want anything else, Cameron went to stand in line. I watched him remove his jacket while he waited to order. His t-shirt gave me a glimpse of his well-developed biceps. He wasn't beefy like Kurt, but instead had just the right amount of definition. I dreamed up a visual of what he looked like shirtless, and it made me smile. My curiosity was also piqued over where he could be hiding a tattoo.

As if he could sense my eyes on him, he spun to face me. His eyes glittered when he caught me checking him out. Before he stepped forward to order, he winked in my direction.

Five minutes later, my hands were trembling as he handed me my tea. The shaking was from both my nerves and how chilly I felt. I was constantly battling the cold that had settled in my bones. My roommates had yelled at me for cranking up the heat, but no matter how high the temperature in the dorm, I could never get warm enough.

"How much do I owe you?" I asked and dug into my purse for my wallet.

"My treat. I bought us a chocolate chip cookie to share, too." He put the cookie on the table between us. My eyes widened involuntarily at the sight. Cameron noticed my expression and asked, "Are you not a fan of chocolate chip cookies?"

My laugh was unnaturally high and rang false. "Of course I love chocolate chip cookies. Who doesn't?" In fact, I had consumed an entire box of Entenmann's Chocolate Chip Cookies in a single sitting during a recent binge. To erase the questioning expression on his face, I broke off a piece of the cookie and shoved it into my mouth. Hurriedly, I changed the subject to stop talking about food. "I'm really glad you called."

"You sound surprised I did. What, did you expect me to do the guy thing and wait three days?"

"I wasn't sure what to think." I shrugged. "I'm pretty clueless when it comes to guys."

Cameron broke off a piece of cookie and chewed thoughtfully. "I find that very surprising."

"Why is that?"

"You're very sweet and a knockout. I couldn't actually believe my luck that you're single."

I contemplated his words. I tried to find the sarcasm in his tone, but it was non-existent. His cerulean blue eyes were deadly serious as he stared at me from across the table. I wasn't Brittany or the twins; they were the ones who guys flirted with and asked out. I was the fat, awkward friend who just came along for the ride.

I cleared my throat and tactfully avoided responding to his compliment. "What about you? Were you dating anyone recently?"

"No," he said. "I met this one girl at Trenton College, and I haven't been able to get her out of my head."

I smiled broadly. Cameron was charismatic, and I liked how he was flirty without coming off as creepy. "You're quite the charmer, aren't you?"

"Only when it matters," he remarked. "But to answer your question, I haven't dated anyone lately. I had a girlfriend for about a year, but we broke up more than six months ago."

"Was it serious?"

"Not really." He shrugged. "She was leaving for grad school in Massachusetts and neither of us really wanted to do the long distance thing. It wasn't a messy breakup or anything, we're still friends."

"Are you friends with all of your exes?"

Leaning back into his chair, his expression turned sheepish. "What can I say? I'm a nice guy." The cookie had provoked my hunger and I stared at the last piece longingly. Cameron followed my gaze and chuckled. "Please, finish the cookie. Should I get us another one?"

The idea was horrifying. I was already concocting ways in my head to get rid of the calories from the piece of cookie I'd already eaten. I shook my head vigorously. I could tell he was waiting for me to finish the cookie, prompting me to polish it off in a single bite.

"What about you?" he asked, as he took a long sip of his coffee. "Any sordid details I should know about your past relationships?"

There were sordid details about my life, but not about my relationship history. "No, I had a boyfriend my senior year of high school, but we broke up before we both left for college. I've dated a couple of boys from campus, but nothing serious."

"Your family lives in Red Bank?"

"Yes, my mother and sister. My father..." I trailed off and fiddled with the hem of my sweater before continuing. "My father died a couple of years ago."

"I'm so sorry," he said softly. His eyes held the question most people had when I brought up my father's death, but Cameron was being too polite to ask it.

"Thank you," I replied sincerely. "It was sudden. He had a massive heart attack while mowing the lawn. I found him in the backyard ..."

Tears flooded my eyes. I couldn't think about *that*, I scolded myself silently. Shutting my eyes, I saw my father slumped over, face down on the freshly cut grass. His brown hair was wet with perspiration and stuck to his cheeks, concealing his face. I screamed when I fell before him and wrenched him onto his back. My hands pounded his chest, doing CPR, frantically trying to bring my father back to life. A neighbor saw us and dialed 911. EMT workers pushed me aside while I continued in vain to get his heart beating again. My father was pronounced dead at the scene.

I never permitted myself the time to dwell on that day and what I had seen. My objective had been to focus on only the happy memories of my father. His death was too painful, the reason I couldn't bring myself to visit the cemetery since the funeral. He was in his early fifties when he died, and I'd mistakenly believed we would have decades together. He was supposed to give me away at my wedding and be a doting grandfather to my kids.

"Hey, it's okay," Cameron said and scooted over to me. He intertwined his fingers with mine. I studied our hands and waited for the tumultuous feelings inside me to pass.

"I'm sorry. It's hard to talk about my dad. We were close and his death still feels raw. He was so young." I sniffed as the tears continued to threaten to spill over.

Since his death, my father had grown to mythic proportions in my mind. Everything was better before he died. My mother's narcissistic tendencies and obsession with beauty were kept in check. My father treated her like the queen she imagined herself to be and limited the criticism from her Lila and I were forced to endure. She'd never been the affectionate type with us, but my father more than made up for it.

"I can't imagine what that must've been like," he said kindly. I shyly peered up at him and found myself mesmerized by his eyes. They held me in place, and I wanted to disappear inside of them.

"I'm guessing you didn't picture comforting a crying girl when you invited me out for coffee," I mumbled. "Are you close to your parents?"

His expression suddenly turned distant. Then I blinked, and the hardness was gone. I wondered if it was ever there in the first place. "Yes, they're great. I try to visit once a week. They pull out all the stops for me when I'm there. I get a huge home-cooked meal, my laundry done, and enough leftovers to last a week."

"A mama's boy?" I joked.

His eyes were humorless. "I guess so," he responded, but something sounded off about his tone. I couldn't tell whether the mood change was from talking about his parents or my teary outburst.

As I took the final sip of my green tea, I said, "I have a presentation tomorrow for class, so I should probably get going to prepare."

He nodded with understanding, most likely realizing how embarrassed I was about crying in front of him. Cameron was too unnerving. He was making me open up and talk about things I had buried deep inside myself.

Being with him was effortless, and I was afraid to develop that kind of connection with someone I barely knew.

Clearing off our table, he held out my jacket while I slipped into it and then put on his own coat. I was silent when he walked me to my Jeep.

He broke the silence. "I would really like to see you again."

"I haven't scared you off yet?" I said half-jokingly.

"No way," he asserted. "Your father died, of course you're going to get upset talking about him."

I broke away from his intense stare and surveyed the parking lot. "Are you parked close by?"

Cameron pointed to a car in the rear of the parking lot. My jaw dropped as I turned back to face him. "Are you serious?"

"Is it a deal breaker? Not everyone likes it," he said with a chuckle. I was relieved to see his mood lighten. Something about our conversation had made him uncomfortable and I couldn't pinpoint what had bothered him so much. Since we'd only met, I figured spending time together would allow him to open up in the same way I did.

"Are you kidding me? What's not to like?" I demanded incredulously. "Can I check it out?"

"Of course."

We crossed the parking lot and I stared in awe at his metallic blue Mustang. It looked like a model from the mid-1960s, but it had been restored to its former glory. The paint looked fresh, and it sparkled in the sunlight. "What year is it?"

"A 1967," he replied. Giving me a sidelong glance, he remarked, "I bought it last year after talking to the owner at a classic car show."

He opened the passenger door for me, and I slid in and got comfortable in the black leather bucket seat. It was a two-door model, and the interior was as pristine as the bodywork. Cameron climbed into the driver's seat and turned the key. The engine revved to life, and I found the loud rumble of the motor satisfying.

"Wow, you have the best car ever," I sighed. I grazed my fingers lovingly over the dashboard.

"I think it's really cute how excited you're getting about my car," he joked.

Leaning toward me, he caressed my cheek with his thumb. I tilted toward him and pressed my lips against his. I set the rhythm of the kiss, starting out slow, leisurely exploring every bit of his mouth. As the fire built between us, my kisses turned fast and passionate.

I pulled away with a whimper. "I've wanted to kiss you since the coffee shop." I motioned to the inside of the car. "This is surprising. I figured you'd drive something more businesslike, a sedan or something."

"Nope," he said, shaking his head. "I have a shitty job; I have to find ways to have fun outside of work."

"And what other ways do you like to have fun?" I asked flirtatiously.

Without any warning, his mouth crushed against mine and I parted my lips for him. As we pulled apart, the tip of his ring finger traced a line across my swollen bottom lip. "I also have a motorcycle. You'll have to take a ride with me once the weather warms up."

I blanched. "I think I'm too much of a wimp to ride on a motorcycle."

His eyes danced with amusement. "You'll love it, I promise."

I rested against the seat and took a minute to study him. "You're a credit card rep who has a muscle car and rides a motorcycle. You're certainly unique."

"I like you a lot, Kayla." Cameron's tone softened. "Will you have dinner with me?"

I almost groaned out loud. Why did so much of our lives have to focus on food? "That sounds nice," I said noncommittally.

"Are you free Friday night?"

"No, I'm going home for the weekend. My mother wants to spend time with me for my birthday." That was the nice way of putting it. In actuality, my mom wanted to continue her reign of emotional damage until I was close to imploding.

"How about Thursday then?"

Since I was free on Thursday, we made plans for him to pick me up from the dorm at seven. My anticipation level would be at an all-time high waiting for our date all week. Maybe Cameron would be able to help me rediscover what happiness looked like.

CHAPTER NINE

The stomach cramps began at eight in the morning. They woke me from a deep slumber and I clutched my midsection in agony. I made it to the bathroom with only seconds to spare.

After leaving Starbucks, the cookie began to haunt me. Along with the cake and pizza from the night before, I suspected the weight I'd worked so hard to lose would creep back on. All the nights I went to bed crying because I was ravenous would be for naught.

By the time I returned to the dorm, it would've been too late to throw up the cookie. With this in mind, I ended up pulling into the closest pharmacy. I combed the store until I found the aisle with the digestive aids. I had no idea how effective the laxatives were and chose the box labeled maximum strength.

As I swallowed two pills, chasing the medicine down with a sip of the bottled water I purchased, I skimmed the directions on the back. The laxatives would produce a bowel movement within twenty-four hours and should be taken with plenty of water. The recommended dosage was two capsules, but I swallowed another two to be sure the pills would empty out whatever was left behind from my two days of snacking.

I cried out as I sat miserably on the toilet the next morning. The cramps stabbed at my gut and wouldn't let up. Once I finished going to the bathroom, I thought the worst was over. But instead, the ache continued and I was unable to get off of the toilet. There would be no possible way I'd make my presentation at nine-thirty; it was ten percent of my grade in Press History, and I was already struggling in the course.

I was in the bathroom for over an hour. My roommates would be getting up soon and I felt humiliated about the stench emanating from the bathroom. Despite spraying half a can of air freshener, the area still remained toxic. Slinking out of the bathroom, I rushed into my room and gently shut the door. If I pretended to be invisible, I wouldn't have to face my roommates.

As I collapsed on the bed, I came to the conclusion I didn't care that much about my Press History grade. Nothing else mattered in my quest to be skinny.

"Christ, Kayla, you look so small! How much weight have you lost?"

Brittany stood in my doorway while I dressed for my date with Cameron. I had on a camisole and black pants and was browsing through my closet trying to choose a shirt. Brittany scrutinized my body, her eyes narrowed, and I could see her trying to calculate how much weight I'd dropped over the past few weeks.

"I don't know," I said nonchalantly, "maybe ten pounds."

The accurate number was nineteen pounds. I weighed myself religiously at the same time each morning and again before bed at night. During winter break, I'd been one hundred forty-five pounds. That morning the scale had displayed one hundred twenty-six. In only six weeks, I'd dropped three dress sizes.

"What kind of diet are you doing? I barely see you eat anything at all."

I was flustered. I had tried to hide the shameful things I was doing to become skinny. I always ate alone in my room, and I only binged and purged when my roommates weren't around. I had tried to simply eat five hundred calories a day to keep up with my weight loss. Yet, after a day or two, my stomach would twist in protest and I found myself craving the food I'd been denying myself. I couldn't stop eating until I greedily consumed enough junk food that my belly felt close to explosion. As I vomited the food into the toilet, I would finally feel a stillness inside me. I hated passing the mirror as I exited the bathroom, my cheeks flushed and my eyes red-rimmed, the evidence of how I was powerless against food plain on my face.

"I told you about my resolution," I said. "I'm really trying to watch what I eat. I'm not following a set diet." I continued the exploration of my closet, praying Brittany would stop her line of questioning.

As I dug a red sweater out of the closet, Brittany snorted with distaste. "You're not seriously thinking about wearing that, are you? It's a date, not another day for you to bum around in your hideous sweaters."

Elbowing me out of the way, she reached in for a white top with the tags still attached. "Wear one of the shirts I bought you for your birthday."

"It's see-through," I pointed out. It was a sheer white lace top with a floral design stitched into the fabric.

Brittany rolled her eyes. "You don't wear it without anything underneath, you'd be arrested. Keep on the black camisole you're wearing. I'd change into a skirt, too, but since you dress like a nun, I'm guessing you'll stick with the black pants."

Assuming she'd harass me until I submitted, I put on the top. I shifted uneasily, hating how much my body was on display. Gazing into the full-length mirror on the wall, I criticized every bulge visible. The only thing I saw in my reflection was how horribly fat I appeared. This was what my life had become inside of my mind. The mantra of *fat, fat, fat* on constant replay.

"I look awful," I protested.

"Are you on drugs, Kayla? Cameron's tongue is going to fall out of his mouth when he sees you." Chewing on her thumb thoughtfully, she added, "You better wear your sexiest pair of underwear, too."

"I'm not sleeping with him tonight. It's our first date." I picked up a hairclip from my desk, gathered my hair into a loose bun, and clipped it to the nape of my neck. My makeup bag was on my desk and I began to apply my mascara.

"I beg to differ. It's your third date, and by most standards that's when you're supposed to have sex for the first time." Brittany perched on my desk, observing me.

"How do you figure? We've never been on a real date yet."

Brittany counted with her fingers. "The night at the bar for your birthday, the day after when you went to coffee together and now tonight."

Smiling wryly, I asked, "Is that how long you waited to sleep with Kurt?"

Brittany stuck out her ample chest and huffed, "Yes. Our first date was when he walked us home from the gym, our second date was when we went to dinner at The Court and the third was when he took me to ice cream after dinner."

I giggled. "I think calling that three dates is a stretch."

Brittany rolled her eyes and changed the subject. "Where's Cameron taking you to dinner?"

"La Villa Rosa. I told him to pick a place and he said they have good Italian food there. I'll be too anxious to eat much anyway so it doesn't matter where we go."

I browsed the menu online to prepare for the date. I wanted to have a game plan ready so I could order something that wouldn't ruin my diet. Cheesy pastas, steaks in heavy sauces, and fried fish dishes contained enough calories to surpass my calorie goals for the week. I'd have to order the grilled chicken with vegetables or a salad with fat-free dressing to avoid overindulging.

"Don't be nervous, it's only a date," Brittany told me. "Try not to be uptight, and have fun."

If only it was that simple.

"They have a wine list. Do you want to order a bottle?"

I drummed my fingers on the table and tried to remember how many calories were in a glass of wine. If I was correct, I believed white wine had fewer calories than red wine. At my lengthy pause, Cameron had begun staring at me. This had become my life, disappearing into my head in an obsessive quest to be thin.

"Any type of white wine would be good. I don't know much about wine, so you can pick a type," I said.

"I'm typically a beer drinker, so I'm clueless about wine. We'll ask the waiter to recommend something," he said, setting down the wine list.

"You should never do that; he'll swindle you into ordering the most expensive bottle."

"You're probably right," he acknowledged and his lips upturned into a seductive smile.

I took the opportunity to study him. For the date, he had dressed in a light green dress shirt, tailored perfectly to accentuate his broad shoulders and chest. His gray dress pants were neatly pressed and belted around his narrow waist.

The restaurant was upscale, the atmosphere romantic. The lighting was low, and soft piano music played in the background. Cameron was going to great lengths to impress me, which was unnecessary, since I was already infatuated.

When it was time to order, I chose a salad with hearts of palm and artichokes, seasoned with lemon juice. Before

Cameron ordered, he frowned my way. "Are you going to order anything else? I think that's a starter salad."

As the waiter and Cameron stared at me, my palms began to sweat. I felt smothered by the questions and opinions everyone seemed to have lately about my eating habits. "Umm, I'll also have the vodka rigatoni with chicken."

It was a horrible choice. The prosciutto and the heavy whipping cream gave the dish an astronomical amount of calories. However, throwing up my food for two months had taught me what type of meals would come up easier than others. Creamy foods and desserts weren't as likely to become lodged in my throat and produce a coughing fit.

"What are you thinking about?" Cameron asked me when the waiter left.

"Hmmm?"

"You sometimes get this faraway look on your face. It makes it difficult to read you." He paused. "I wouldn't mind having a peek inside your head to figure out what you're thinking."

What an appalling thought. I couldn't stand to be inside my own head, no less wish my thoughts on anyone else. "I'm thinking about how much I don't want to go home for the weekend."

"Why?"

"I miss my sister," I insisted, "but my mother is a lot to handle. She's a critical person and has only gotten worse since my father passed away. Usually when I'm home, she spends our time together lecturing me about how I'm disappointing her."

"She sounds intense."

"She'll scare you away when you meet her." I gasped and covered my mouth with my hand. "I'm sorry, that was presumptuous. I mean, we've only hung out a couple of times, I wasn't trying to suggest we're serious enough to meet each other's parents—"

He interrupted my rambling. "Kayla, it's okay." He sucked on his lower lip, momentarily allowing me to forget my embarrassment, instead fantasizing about his kiss. "I like you, Kayla—a lot. If anything, I'm worried I've been coming on too strong. You seem a little skittish when you're around me, and I wonder if it's because I'm making you nervous."

I wasn't uncomfortable around him; I was terrified of being with him. Cameron created a yearning inside of me, a need to be in his arms and forget about the outside world. My heart was too fragile to hand over to someone who could easily crush it.

"You're not coming on too strong," I said softly. "I like you too."

"Good, because I've wanted to ask you out since I first saw you walking toward me in the Student Center."

I could hear the smile in his voice as he talked about our first meeting.

He laughed. "I was in the middle of talking to another student when I saw you. I think he was pissed when I cut him off mid-sentence to stop you."

I tilted my head to the side. "Why?"

"What do you mean?"

"What was it about me that you liked?"

It wasn't the most polite question, and it gave him a peek into my insecurities, but I was desperate to know. Cameron could have any girl he wanted—what was it about me he found appealing?

He laughed uncomfortably. "Kayla, are you messing with me? Or are you seriously that modest?"

My eyebrows lifted quizzically.

He continued, "As soon as I saw you walk out of the bookstore, I couldn't tear my eyes away from you. You're gorgeous, but in such an unassuming way, like you have no idea of the effect you have on men."

"Now, are you the one messing with me?"

He shook his head insistently. "Maybe it's because you're shy and you don't notice it, but I swore I was going to get into a fistfight at the bar when I saw all those guys ogling you."

I wanted to believe him, I did, but my self-image was warped to the point where I pondered whether I should avoid my reflection altogether. The best tactic was to change the subject. "Thanks for wanting to defend my honor."

"Anytime." He grinned. "I want to be the only guy allowed to ogle you."

My spine straightened and my pulse picked up. It was too late to protect myself from Cameron—he was unraveling my defenses and forcing his way into my guarded heart.

CHAPTER TEN

"Miss, are you alright? Should I get someone for you?" The female voice sounded elderly and called through the bathroom stall.

"I'm fine," I croaked.

I had waited for the bathroom to clear before I stuck my finger down my throat, but someone had walked in while I was throwing up. As quiet as I tried to be while getting rid of my dinner, the noise had been loud enough to alert the other person using the bathroom.

It took five minutes before the woman finished going about her business and exited the bathroom. Emerging from the stall, I cringed at my sight in the mirror. I was flushed and my eyes were tearing up. Dampening a paper towel with cold water, I used it to pat down my neck and face. I concealed the redness with the powder from a compact I brought and reapplied my red lipstick. After popping a mint in my mouth, I ventured back into the restaurant.

"I was starting to worry about you," Cameron remarked when I returned to the table. Leaving your date for fifteen minutes while you vomited up dinner wasn't the best way to make a good impression, I thought as he knitted his eyebrows together.

"Sorry, just freshening my makeup," I said.

"I ordered a chocolate cake for us to share." He motioned to the dessert plate in front of him.

"No thanks, I'm stuffed from dinner." I noticed a piece of chocolate on the corner of his lips. Reaching across the table, I used my thumb to brush off the crumb. Before I could pull away, he gripped my wrist softly. His fingers moved in gentle circles around my bare skin.

"Do you want to hang out after dinner? I could show you my apartment."

"Umm …" I trailed off awkwardly. The lust in my belly was screaming out in protest, demanding I go with him to his apartment. My practical side was telling me I wasn't ready to jump into bed with him. An emotional attachment to him had already started, and sleeping with him would leave me completely undone.

"No pressure, I only wanted to spend more time with you," he said.

"Maybe we could go to my dorm instead?" At least with my roommates there, I'd be assured we wouldn't get carried away. I wasn't Brittany; I'd be mortified if my roommates overheard us having sex.

He agreed and requested the check. Despite my forceful attempts at giving him money, he paid the bill, leaving a generous tip. I wished I could accept his kindness without questioning what his true motives could be.

My heart was hammering when we arrived back at the dorm and found the floor deserted. I'd forgotten the twins and Brittany were headed to a fraternity party with Kurt and a few of his friends. My voice caught as I unlocked the door to my room and announced, "So, this is my room …"

As he walked to the center of my room, his presence was overpowering. I did a quick inventory of my surroundings and was relieved I had cleaned up before heading out for the night. Cameron turned toward my desk and began inspecting the photos I had lined up. He held up one of the last family pictures I had that included my dad. We were dressed for my cousin's wedding and standing in front of the church where the ceremony was held.

"You and your little sister look so much alike," he said, casting a glance at me before looking back at the picture. I silently begged for him not to make a comparison of me against my mother, where I would fall irrevocably short.

"You have the same eyes as your dad. I've never seen such a dark shade of brown before—they're remarkable." He put the picture back down without another word. I stayed still although I had the strongest urge to kiss him.

"Do you want to put a movie on?" I asked and turned on the TV.

After ten minutes of postulating on the merits of the *Twilight* films, I was able to get him to finally relent. As I switched on the DVD, I said disbelievingly, "I can't believe you've never seen this movie." Since I only had a single desk chair, I sat on the edge of the bed. I patted the space next to me. Sinking into the mattress, he pressed his back against the wall next to my bed and stretched out his long legs in front of him. He held open his arms and I climbed comfortably into his embrace and sighed contentedly.

Twenty minutes into the movie, Cameron's soft snores drew me out of the film. Moving slowly, careful not to wake him, I took my time to study his sleeping form. His hair had become more unruly than usual, with one of the lighter locks falling across his forehead. His eyelashes were dark and thick, set against his perfect complexion. A small amount of stubble had erupted on his chin, and I wanted to feel the roughness of his skin.

His eyes popped open when I shifted closer to him. "What did I miss?"

"Just the beginning of an epic love story," I chided. "Tired?"

"Long and shitty day at another campus. Remind me to update my resume so I can find a new job."

"You know you love it," I teased. "Your job requires you to score the names and numbers of dozens of pretty college coeds."

"I get it now, that's what you think I do all day," he said sarcastically. "Meanwhile, I'm thinking about you at work and counting the minutes until I can do this again." His hand cupped my chin and guided my mouth to his.

The privacy of my room gave us the opportunity to not hold back. He kissed me expertly while running his hands down my back. His touch caused my nerve endings to sizzle, and I ached with need each time his mouth moved away from mine. My neck flushed as his lips began to trace a line from my jaw line to my ear. I tilted my head back and let out a low moan.

Sweeping his hand behind my head, he pulled out my hair clip and tossed it aside. My hair tumbled down past my shoulders and he combed his fingers through it. His lips trailed down the nape of my neck until stopping at my collarbone. Seizing the back of his head, I tugged him toward my mouth and sucked gently on his lower lip.

He grunted and I snuck my tongue inside his mouth when his lips parted. As our kisses became impassioned, Cameron settled me on my back. His hands swept under my shirt, and his fingers splayed across my ribcage over my camisole. Cameron's mouth teased me, moving leisurely from my collarbone to the swell of my breasts.

I momentarily disappeared into a chasm where only Cameron and I existed. I was falling, falling hard for this man with cerulean blue eyes and a tempting smile. If I stayed there with him forever, things could be different for me. I would no longer have to wake up each morning feeling leaden, as if the weight of the world was crushing me.

We were panting when we broke apart. His eyes glittered with desire as he ran his gaze down the length of my body. He was propped up on his elbow next to me, the both of us squeezed together on my small twin bed. While the seconds passed, I became anxious, unsure of how to tell him I wasn't ready to go too far with him.

Cameron appeared to take note of my worried expression. "Maybe we should slow down."

Adjusting my shirt, I said, "I'm glad you came over."

"Me too," he replied. "I wish you were going to be around this weekend."

He had no idea how badly I wished to stay in town. I would've loved to pick up Lila and take her back to the dorm for the weekend, giving us both a reprieve from my overbearing mother.

I planned to keep the moment close when I went to visit my mother. Each time my mother would toss an insult my way, I would remind myself there was someone out there who genuinely liked me and didn't only see my faults.

CHAPTER ELEVEN

"Kayla!" Lila squealed, launching her body into my arms.

I pressed my chin on top of her head. Lila was the shortest in the family; at five foot three, I was at least four inches taller than her.

"I've missed you, kiddo," I said softly. My arms tightened around her for a long minute, before releasing her.

"Kayla, you lost so much weight!" she exclaimed as she took a step back. "Did Mom brainwash you or something?"

"No," I replied shortly. I fiddled with my hands as I said, "I've just been trying to get fit and lost some weight in the process."

The longer I struggled with my weight, the more easily the lies were slipping from my tongue. I barely had the energy to crawl out of bed each morning, much less spend any time exercising.

"Once she sees you, Mom is going to be on my case now to lose weight," Lila complained.

Lila and I inherited the same body shape from my father's side of the family. We carried our extra weight in our hips, thighs, and butts; we were mirror images of my paternal grandmother. My father wasn't exceptionally tall, and he always joked about the extra thirty pounds he carried around despite my mother's healthy cooking. He'd compliment her on the delicious meals she prepared, but he would frequent fast food restaurants while driving to and from work. Besides that propensity for fatty meals, my mom also despised how much he smoked. He'd been a heavy smoker since high school, and that, coupled with his diet, likely contributed to his heart attack.

My mother anguished over how we didn't have the same genes as her side of the family. Her mother was tall and willowy; a preview of what my mom would look like in twenty-five years. Although Lila and I had always been close in weight, any excess pounds she gained became more apparent due to her shorter frame.

"Don't let her bother you. I wish I was half as beautiful as you are," I said. I fluffed her hair. "Don't let it give you a big head though. You're still a little brat."

I was being sincere with my compliment. I wouldn't change a single thing about my sister. With a laugh, Lila stuck out her tongue.

I followed Lila upstairs to deposit my suitcase on the floor of my bedroom. "Where's Mom?" I asked as I sat with her on my bed.

"She went shopping for dinner tonight. Just to warn you, she's making angel food cake topped with fat-free whipped cream. In her head, that counts as a birthday cake," Lila said, and she snorted.

My sister was repressed when she was around my mother. Lila seemed to be truly herself only when my mom wasn't near. After my father died, we had turned to each other for solace since our mother offered none. This bonded us in a way where a glance in the other's direction could reveal what we were thinking. I'd been terrified to return home, horrified over the possibility Lila would take one look at me and know I was starving.

"How was your real birthday? Did you go out to a bar and get trashed?" Lila leaned forward.

"Brittany had us bar hopping for most of the night," I acknowledged. "How have you been? I hope you haven't been going out and getting trashed."

"Like that would ever happen under Mom's rule," she said and leaned onto her back on my bed, propped up on her elbows. "She hates all my friends and won't let me date the guy I like."

"You're a junior, Lila. College will be here before you know it," I assured her.

"It seems like forever now." Lila added wistfully, "I wish I could live with you."

"Me, too, but even if I got my own apartment, Mom would never let you stay with me while you finished high school." Flopping on my back, I shot her a forlorn look. "I wish Dad was still here. Maybe she'd still be happy then and let us be."

"Do you think they were happy together?"

"I always thought, why him? What was it about an average-looking guy who was a vet that made her fall in love with him? But she needs someone to revere her, to make her feel like she's the most beautiful woman in the world. Dad did that. Remember their anniversaries? He would start planning months in advance and give her the most outlandish gifts: trips to the Caribbean, diamond necklaces, a new car. We aren't super-rich, so I'm guessing he had to save every penny to afford those presents."

"The wrong parent died that day," Lila whispered vehemently. Her hands were clenched into fists and I hadn't seen her that angry in a long time.

"Lila, don't say that."

Flipping onto her side, her brown eyes grew wide. "Don't lie and say you don't feel the exact same way. Our mother is a bitch that basically tells us every day how we're fat, ugly losers nobody will ever love. Dad was the only one who gave a crap about us."

What had my mother done to us? My sister was full of a black rage that made her wish death upon her own parent, while I was retreating farther and farther into myself.

"Do you want to guess what she offered to buy me for my next birthday?" Lila demanded. "A nose job. I didn't realize I needed one until she suggested it."

I shook my head in disbelief. "You don't need a nose job. Our mother is certifiable."

Her eyes softened. "I'm glad you're home. It's so embarrassing to talk about her with any of my friends. When we Skype or talk on the phone, she's usually hovering so I try and watch what I say."

"You can call me whenever, Lila. And I'm sure Brittany and the twins would be fine if you came up to visit for a weekend. I could pick you up or you can take the train up."

Her face lit up with excitement. "Are you serious? Can you take me to a frat party?"

"Yes, I'm serious; but no, I won't take you to a frat party." At Lila's crestfallen expression, I said, "But we'll find something fun to do."

I had an hour with Lila, an hour with my real sister, who wasn't eclipsed and diminished by the presence of my mother. But when we heard the front door open, we reverted to our shadowy existence, hoping to avoid the wrath of Charlotte Marlowe.

Lila shrank behind me while my mother made a spectacle of greeting me. "Kayla, my word! You look fantastic! I see you've been keeping up with your diet."

I wouldn't call what I was doing a diet, but I didn't interrupt. The way I was keeping the weight off was my secret, my shame. "Thanks Mom," I said meekly. I had to be suffering from some sort of mental disorder because I was briefly pleased by her compliments.

"I'm so glad you finally took my advice to heart. I hadn't wanted to say anything, but you were getting rather plump. It wasn't very attractive." Her crimson-stained lips were pressed in a thin line as she appeared to conjure up a picture of my former self. My pleasure over her compliments vanished. I hated her—she was a monster. How could my kind and tenderhearted father ever have fallen in love with her?

Her bony hip bumped into mine. "Who knows? Maybe we'll be the same size one day?" Her tone hinted it would be cause for celebration. If I could finally be a size two, she'd love me unconditionally.

She swayed on her heels as she walked into the kitchen. Studying her, I realized I did envy her grace and beauty. Her dark hair was luminous, and her emerald eyes effervescent. I understood the hours she spent on her appearance, but to outsiders, she was praised as a natural stunner.

While my mother stowed away the groceries, she called out, "Without all that extra weight, I'm sure you won't be single for long."

"I'm actually seeing someone," I responded distractedly.

Did my mother have a point? Was Cameron only attracted to me because I lost weight? If I'd still been a size ten when we met would he have asked me out? Doubts were swarming like bees, stinging me with the harsh truth that I'd been single for years before I lost the weight. If I dared to gain any weight back, would Cameron's eyes wander to someone new?

Lila, who had remained silent, perked up at the news I was dating someone. "Tell us about him."

"I met him at the college, and he works for a credit card company. We've only gone on a few dates, but I really like him," I confessed.

"What does he look like? Is he cute?" Lila asked eagerly.

"Very cute," I insisted. "He has brown hair with streaks of blond and gorgeous blue eyes. He's also so nice, he's very considerate and he seems genuinely interested in what I have to say. He took me out to the nicest restaurant."

Lila heaved out a lengthy sigh. "I can't wait to go to college."

"You sound a little too serious about him, Kayla. Men don't want to be chased. Remember to stay aloof with him and let him do the chasing," my mother advised.

Lila rolled her eyes behind my mom's back and I suppressed a smile. My mom was the queen of unsolicited advice. Determined to ignore her negative energy, I instead resolved to make the most of my time with Lila.

Lila crawled into bed with me later that night. After she snuggled into my side, I began to run my fingers lovingly through her hair. Her voice was laced with unshed tears when she said, "Maybe I should lose weight. Mom was actually nice to you at dinner."

"No, Lila, you don't have to lose weight," I hissed fervently.

I didn't want this life for my little sister. I was a prisoner to food and there was no reprieve in sight. Despite my weight loss, I was still unhappy with how I looked. Earlier, it had been a struggle to eat my birthday dinner and cake. After Lila caught me cutting the chicken into small pieces and moving it around my plate listlessly, I felt compelled to eat everything on my plate. Under my sister's watchful eyes, I couldn't head to the bathroom to vomit up my dinner.

A battle was raging inside me. I wanted so badly to allow the food to stay in me. My mother had made chicken with steamed vegetables and angel food cake, and the calories were low enough that it wouldn't undermine my diet. But I couldn't. In a panic, I got up and snuck off to my room to take two of the laxative pills I had stashed in my purse.

When I got back into bed, I said, "Lila, I don't think it matters how much we weigh. Mom is unhappy, and unfortunately we're the only targets around for her aggression." I believed it with my whole heart, but the damaged part of my brain still hoped she would love me again if I turned into the perfect daughter.

"Kayla, you seem sad. Shouldn't you be okay now that you're mostly free of her?"

The unspoken question was in her eyes. Would she be allowed to finally be happy once she escaped our house? "I'm not always sad," I answered truthfully. "I like hanging out with Cameron and my roommates. It's just sometimes I feel a little lost; like I'm in this dark place desperately trying to search for the way to the light."

"Kayla, be happy," she ordered. "Cameron sounds great, and you deserve someone who sees how amazing you are."

"You deserve it too, Lila," I whispered. "I love you."

"I love you, too."

CHAPTER TWELVE

"You look beautiful," Cameron murmured in my ear. "Are you certain we shouldn't just call it an early night and head back to your dorm?"

It had been two weeks since my visit home, and I'd been spending a few nights a week with Cameron. He'd taken me on several dates, with most of them ending at my dorm room for a hot make-out session. I still didn't feel ready to sleep with him, in spite of Brittany's insistence I could lose him if I didn't start putting out. Cameron was sweet, he hadn't pressured me, and it didn't faze him when I declined his invitations to go back to his apartment after a date.

Cameron and his friends had joined Brittany, Kurt, and me at a local bar called Rosie's. Like he'd been with the redhead, Taylor, Cameron had been friends with Alex and Chuck since high school. Alex and Chuck took an immediate shine to me and had me laughing while they shared the most embarrassing stories about Cameron possible. Taylor was distant, speaking only directly to the other boys, although I tried to make small talk with her. After it became clear I was an unwelcome presence, I left their group to stand with my friends on the other side of the bar.

I played the part of the laid-back girl. I wanted to be the cool girl, not the needy girlfriend who insists her boyfriend stay glued to her side. I forced myself to tell him, "Go hang out with your friends. We'll always have later to be alone."

After a quick kiss, Cameron was hauled away by Chuck to get another beer from the bar. Once he left, I tried to fight the fatigue that had plagued me all day. It was a battle to keep my eyes open.

After losing another six pounds, I was at my original goal weight of one hundred twenty pounds. This was around the weight I'd been when I started college and what I considered my ideal weight. My size-six clothing was loose, and I would certainly be able to fit in most size fours. But I didn't feel the relief I expected as I stared at the numbers on the scale. I hadn't lost enough—I still saw the fat bulging out of my hips and thighs. I couldn't stand to look in the mirror most mornings, my reflection feeling like a horror to behold.

"What are you doing?" Brittany slid up next to me; I jumped in surprise at her harsh voice.

"Zoning out, I guess." I took a hesitant sip of my drink.

"Well, while you were daydreaming, Taylor has been making a move on Cam."

Brittany tilted her beer bottle toward Cameron and his friends across the bar. Although there was ample room in the bar area, Taylor had her generous breasts pushed up against Cameron's left arm. While I spied on them for several minutes, she made every excuse to touch him and would tilt forward to show off her cleavage to the greatest advantage. But Cameron seemed unaware of her flirtation, and in his defense, he hadn't snuck a pe ek at Taylor's breasts.

"What am I supposed to do? They're friends," I said miserably. I didn't exactly have the authority to stake my claim on Cameron. We'd only been dating for a couple of weeks, and no one had mentioned exclusivity. He hadn't given me the impression he was seeing someone else, but I wouldn't have minded the verbal reassurance from him.

"That girl doesn't want to be friends," Brittany asserted. "She wants to bang your man." At my silence, Brittany nudged me hard. "Don't just stand there, Kayla. Do something about it."

I glared at Brittany. I didn't have her self-assurance, and she knew that about me. I didn't have the confidence to push Taylor out of the way and drape myself over Cameron. "Britt, leave it alone."

Taylor's giggle carried over to us and we returned to staring in her direction. She had wrapped her arm around Cameron and was leaning into him while her body shook with laughter. Brittany's eyes practically bulged out. "I'm warning you, Kayla, if you don't stand up for yourself, I will go over there and pour my drink down her shirt."

With a huff, I said, "Fine."

Moving across the bar, I stood awkwardly behind Cameron and Taylor while he told a story about one of his campus visits. Taylor said nothing about my arrival, although we locked eyes as I approached. Instead, she inched closer to Cameron and stared up at him with adoration clear on her features.

Annoyed, I gave her a dirty look before tapping Cameron on the shoulder. Spinning around, his arm snaked out and pulled me close. I felt smug when Taylor was forced to step aside. "Hi babe," he said and brushed his lips against mine.

I stayed planted to Cameron's side while he continued talking with his friends, his arm around me. I shivered as he traced small circles around the small of my back. It distracted me from the deadly looks Taylor lobbed at me each time Cameron showed me affection.

I wasn't comfortable with being hated openly. I was unassuming, preferring to stay on the sidelines and observe life rather than go after the spotlight. I'd never had fights with other girls, and I always thought it was silly to rip each other's hair out over a boy. My old boyfriend, Grant, was quiet and studious, the same as me, and I'd never had to deal with jealousy from other girls.

As much as I didn't want to fight over Cameron, I acknowledged that I would. I liked him too much to share him, and I couldn't be with him if he planned to see other girls.

An hour later, once his friends had disappeared to order a round of shots, Cameron turned to me and said softly, "Are you okay? You seem a little tense." He had passed on the shots and only had a couple of beers for the night since he planned to drive us home from the bar. My stomach had been in knots and I barely choked down half my drink.

"I have something I want to talk to you about," I replied, tilting my head back to stare up into his gorgeous face. I swallowed hard and marveled over how much he affected me. I was filled with anticipation each time we were together, looking forward to the delirium that took over when he kissed me.

"Why don't we leave now? The bar is only open for another hour anyway," he suggested. At my nod, he kissed my forehead. "I'll get our coats and start saying goodbye to everyone."

Minutes later, we were walking outside toward his car, my steps matching his. The street was quiet with the only sound being my heels hitting the pavement. Cameron cleared his throat. "What's going on, Kayla?"

When we reached his car, I stood before him and did an awkward shuffle. Instead of meeting his eyes, I addressed his shoes. "I don't want you to think I'm pressuring you or anything. I mean we've only been going out for a couple of weeks …" I trailed off. Squaring my shoulders, I continued. "I'm just curious about whether I'm the only girl you're seeing."

I cowered inside myself within those seconds of silence. I imagined all the ways he planned to let me down easily. I should've known my feelings were stronger and he wasn't ready to commit to being exclusive.

His hands found mine and he pressed something cold and metallic into my palm. Opening my hand, I saw his car keys. Finally, I forced myself to lock eyes with him and I gave him a questioning look.

I released the tension in my muscles when I saw his grin. Gripping the back of my neck, he pulled me forward for a searing kiss. As our lips parted, he said, "I want you to drive us back to the dorm."

The corners of my mouth lifted, and I demanded disbelievingly, "You're going to let me drive your car?" I cut a glance to the Mustang and my heart picked up. I desperately wanted to be behind the wheel. The thrill of speeding through town in his beloved car made me forget Cameron hadn't answered my question.

"Yes, but I don't let just anyone drive it. I'm only letting my girlfriend," he said. "So, what do you say? Would you be willing to date only me?"

The tension of his jaw betrayed his confident tone. He wanted to be with me as much as I wanted him. Lacing my fingers behind his back, I pressed my body against his chest. I could feel every hard ridge beneath the fabric of his shirt and my desire for him spiked. I hadn't seen him without his shirt on, and I looked forward to the opportunity.

"Cameron Bennett, I'd love to be your girl." My smile was in my voice and I felt lighter suddenly.

After a gentle kiss on the mouth, he opened the driver's side door for me. With a squeal, I catapulted into the driver's seat. When he got in, he adjusted the seat and mirrors for me. "You're fine to drive, right? I only saw you with that one drink, but I don't want you driving if you had any more."

"Yes, I'm sober," I said and sent him a mock indignant look. "You're not trying to renege on your promise to let me drive, are you?"

"Of course not," he asserted and squeezed my knee. "Besides, you look hot behind the wheel of my car." He pointed to the stick shift and asked, "Do you know how to drive a stick?"

"Yes, I was taught to drive on a car with a manual transmission."

I exaggerated my smile as I turned the ignition key. The rumble of the car's engine was satisfying as I revved the engine. Tires squealed when I popped the clutch and pressed down on the gas pedal. As the car shot away from the curb, Cameron laughed heartily. "We're not drag racing, babe, you can slow it down."

"No way, I've been dying to drive this car since I saw it and I'm going to make the most of it."

Cameron put his hands up in defeat. "Fine with me, but remember I warned you if we get pulled over."

I smiled to myself as I shifted into gear and raced through the deserted streets. My father had loved classic cars and had been the one to teach me how to drive a stick shift when I was sixteen. He would've loved to see me driving Cameron's car, and I was wistful when I thought about how much my father would've approved of the man sitting next to me.

I wanted to feel this way always: fearless, the doubts lifted from my conscience. Bliss was within my grasp, and I had only to learn how to hold onto it forever.

CHAPTER THIRTEEN

"Why don't you tell him no? I always blow off Kurt when he asks me to work out," Brittany said as I dressed for my jog with Cameron.

"Doesn't he remind you of how the two of you met when you refuse?"

"Yes, and I'm honest about it. I was only at the gym to meet guys."

Jessica poked her head in. "I hope you have layers on. You'll get overheated running in the sweatshirt. Here's my armband case to hold your iPod," she said and handed me the black holder.

"Thanks," I said, tightening my shoelaces. I stretched for a minute and jumped up and down in place. "I didn't realize Cameron ran daily until he invited me to come with him. I figured he was naturally that hot."

Brittany snorted. "Very unlikely. I think that only happens in the movies. If Cam looks that damn good, he's working for it. Kurt's at the gym every day and gulping down protein shakes between meals."

"He's not the only one," Jessica mumbled. "If you're still together, I swear Kurt's banned from the dorm during

85

finals. Every night he stays over, it sounds like an animal that needs to be put out of its misery."

"Sorry I'm the only one with an active sex life in this dorm." Brittany gave me a challenging stare.

"Really, Kayla? You haven't slept with Cameron yet?" Jessica asked. I shook my head, and she said, "I think that's cool. Why rush it? You only get one first time with a person, it should be special."

Brittany shook her head in disgust. "Romantic drivel. What if he's crap in bed? You have all these *feelings* now and you'll be stuck with him."

"Don't listen to her. The longer you're together, the more comfortable you'll be when you decide to take that step. The sex will be much better than if you jumped into bed with him the first night."

Jessica's words were encouraging. I'd been nervous about postponing sex, and she eased my worries. Brittany had been scandalized a twenty-three-year-old warm-blooded American male hadn't made more of an effort to get me into bed. But Cameron seemed genuine about letting me set the pace for how physical we got.

Fifteen minutes later, I met him at a park a couple of miles from campus. He was sitting on the ground, looking relaxed, staring at a flock of birds flying overhead. I took a minute to study him undetected. He always looked self-assured, no matter what situation he found himself in.

He stood up at my approach and greeted me with a peck on the lips.

"Is this what you wear running?" I asked teasingly.

He was wearing a pair of black shorts that displayed his toned legs and a white tank top that clung to his chest. His skin was already a golden hue, despite the weather only recently turning warmer. I was dressed to ward off the frequent chills I had and wore a Trenton College sweatshirt and sweatpants.

"Usually; why?"

"I'm surprised you get any running in when you probably have to stop to catch all the swooning women you pass."

He laughed. "What? The women I catch help me get my upper body workout."

I playfully slapped his arm and resisted the urge to squeeze his bicep. I coughed instead. "I might slow you down today. I'm not much of a runner."

"I'm not in a rush. We can take our time. There's a trail I follow that loops around the entire park."

We started off with a slow jog. I was able to keep pace for about a quarter of a mile. But when Cameron broke into a run, I was too winded to keep up with him. I wanted to push harder, but my body wasn't cooperating. I didn't consume enough calories to handle intense bouts of exercise.

He glanced back as I fell further behind, then he ran back to where I was walking briskly. I said, "You should go ahead. I'll catch up."

He stopped jogging and matched my strides. "I invited you to hang out, not to leave you alone."

"Okay, but I was enjoying the view of you from behind."

I liked this side of me. There were many facets to my personality, and I preferred the carefree and flirtatious Kayla to any of the others. I wanted this thing with us to work. His hands wrapped around my waist and he tickled me gently. He pulled me in closely and my giggles subsided.

His eyes searched mine and the last of my laughter caught in my throat. He cupped my face and closed the gap between us within seconds. An inch from my lips, he said quietly, "I like this ... I like us."

"I like this, too," I whispered. "I'm not good at talking about how I feel, but just because I don't say it, doesn't mean I'm not feeling the same things as you. I like how you're confident and say what you're thinking." I swallowed roughly and admitted, "I'm worried we won't last because I'm not like that."

"I think we're good together. I don't want a girl who is exactly like me. I may seem confident, but I'm talking out of my ass most of the time. I like how you sit back and observe; I love trying to guess what you're thinking."

My lips began to tingle when he brushed his mouth against mine.

"The fact that you're very pretty doesn't hurt either."

"You're not so bad yourself."

I was grinning when he picked me up off the ground. He hoisted me onto his back and I gripped his neck tightly. He took off in a sprint and I pressed my chest to his back. I bounced up and down as he gave me a piggyback ride through the park. My sides hurt from laughing so hard when he finally set me down on one of the benches lining the walkway.

"You're trouble, Cameron. And I think I like it."

CHAPTER FOURTEEN

"Angus approves of you, so I guess you can stay for dinner," Cameron joked as he watched me coddle his English bulldog. Angus rolled onto his back and let out a satisfying snort when I jiggled his fat belly with the palm of my hands.

"Who's the sweet puppy?" I cooed to him. "*You're* the sweet puppy."

Cameron held out his hand and pulled me back into a standing position. "Hey," he protested, "enough with the baby talk. He's a manly dog."

I rolled my eyes. "Sure he is."

Wrapping his arms around me, Cameron kissed me softly. "I'm glad you're here."

It was the middle of March and the first time I'd gone to Cameron's apartment. We'd been together for a month and a half, but I'd been leery about staying over at his place. He hadn't pressed the issue and didn't ask for the reasons behind my hesitation. For some reason, I got it into my head that coming over to his place translated into sex.

In some ways, I was completely ready to take the next step with Cameron. He was funny, kind, and his sexiness seemed effortless. I fantasized about spending hours exploring every inch of him, discovering what was hidden beneath his layers of clothing.

The problem was my terror over being naked, both emotionally and physically, in front of him. Over the last month, I'd only lost another five pounds. I wasn't sure why I wasn't losing weight as swiftly as before, but I suspected my metabolism had slowed because of the back and forth between starving myself and binge eating. The new clothes I bought for spring were a size four, but it wasn't good enough for me. I'd gotten it into my head I wanted to be a size zero. That size would best my mom and I'd never have to endure another one of her scathing remarks about my weight.

All I could think about was when Cameron took off my clothes, the fat girl I had tried to keep hidden from him would be revealed and he'd be repulsed.

"What made you change your mind about coming over?" Cameron asked as he led me into his kitchen.

The apartment was cozy and much cleaner than I suspected his bachelor pad would be. Cameron had a one-bedroom apartment with an open floor plan. The oversized living room led directly into a smaller eat-in kitchen, with his bedroom and bathroom in the back. I took a seat at the kitchen table and watched as he set two place settings.

"To see your dog, of course." I laughed when Angus waddled across the room and settled his paws on my legs. Although my mom never permitted us to have pets in the house, I'd taken after my father and adored all four-legged creatures. I grew nostalgic when I remembered all the days he allowed me to tag along to his office and help out with his furry patients.

Cameron's phone rang and he groaned as he picked it up. "Hi, Dad." Cameron paused and smiled tightly in my direction. His posture straightened and he ground his teeth together. "I'm not talking about this right now with you, I told you I have nothing to say to her. I wish you would stop making me feel guilty, I wasn't the one who did anything wrong." After a brief silence, Cameron sighed. "Dad, I have to go, Kayla just came by for dinner."

Cameron and his father seemed to get along fine, and their exchange confused me. Cameron's uneasiness remained after he hung up.

"Everything okay?" I questioned, watching him warily.

The discomfort slipped off his face and his eyes warmed as he stared in my direction. "Yes, just my father being a pain. He means well, but he seems to forget sometimes I'm an adult. Let's not get into it now; I'd rather have a fun night with my beautiful girlfriend."

I could tell the subject was closed with him and decided to let it go. "Are you cooking?" I asked him incredulously as he walked over to the stove.

"I did invite you over, you know. Of course I'm going to feed you while you're here." He turned off one of the burners and looked at me over his shoulder. "I'm not the best cook, but I'm getting better since I started living on my own."

It was a thoughtful gesture and it took a concentrated effort to not think about how fattening the meal would be. I didn't want to get sick at his house or offend him by refusing to eat. I could think about ways to get rid of the extra calories later.

Minutes later, he presented me with a plate piled high with spaghetti and chicken Parmesan. My stomach revolted at the sight. I couldn't eat it without having an exit strategy. Instead of food, I saw calories that would make my body expand to the point where I'd transform back into the unlovable blob I was before I started dieting.

"Kayla?" Cameron's concerned voice brought me out of my own personal hell. "Is something wrong?"

"No," I forced out. "I'm just shocked you went to so much trouble. The food looks delicious."

"I was hoping you'd say that. You seem a little intense when it comes to your diet," he remarked, twirling a piece of spaghetti on his fork.

I was taken aback by his perceptiveness. I mistakenly believed I was a convincing actress, never revealing how much food ruled my life. I couldn't let him see the freak I truly was or I'd lose him. Although it killed me a little inside, I lifted the fork and took a bite of the chicken. He smiled across the table at me. I could do this, I thought with determination. This was my existence, constant give and take in order to survive.

I awoke with my head on Cameron's lap. When I shifted, he tilted his chin down to face me. Brushing a strand of hair away from my eyes, he murmured, "I liked how you felt sleeping in my arms."

We had settled on his couch after dinner to watch a movie. I needed the distraction. As Cameron held me close, my anxiety over dinner faded and I relaxed into his arms. I must've fallen asleep at some point, exhausted from the constant disquiet I felt over my weight.

I sat up and glanced at the clock, it was after eleven. "I guess I should head back to the dorms."

"Or you can stay over."

"Or I can stay over," I parroted back, mimicking his tone.

Reaching across the couch, he took my hand in his. "I'm not pushing you into something you're not ready for. I was just sitting here thinking about how nice it would be to wake up next to you."

I shot him a wry grin. "Do you honestly think we could spend the night together in the same bed and nothing would end up happening?"

"Only if you wanted it to …" he trailed off. His fingers ran up my arm and I shivered involuntarily.

My yearning for him was too strong to resist. I scooted over until I was sitting on his lap. Instead of a tender kiss filled with longing, I crushed my mouth against his and began to kiss him passionately.

He kissed me back with just as much fervor and ran his hands down my back. He cupped my behind and tugged me close. I moved my right leg to the left side of him, allowing me to press my body flush against his.

I was gasping for air when I moved my mouth away from his. Kissing his neck, I said in a teasing voice, "You do realize I never got to see that tattoo you told me about."

His laughter was choked with desire. His eyes were feverish as he stared down at my body, watching how I straddled his waist. My hands inched under the edge of his t-shirt and he helped me remove it. This was the first time I had seen Cameron shirtless, and I was desperately trying not to drool.

Every part of him was cut and lean. My eyes were immediately drawn to the hard muscles of his abs. His arms and chest were toned as well, and I imagined how it would feel to have my lips on his exposed skin.

The tattoo was on his left side, placed inches above his hipbone. The tattoo was of a tombstone, and it held the epitaph, "Everything Was Beautiful, And Nothing Hurt." The words resonated with me and it brought upon feelings I'd tried to bury. I swallowed audibly as I searched my memory for the source of the quote.

"I didn't realize you were a Kurt Vonnegut fan. It doesn't fit with your cheerful persona," I said.

"It's my mom's favorite quote. I'll warn you again about how it's never a good idea to get a tattoo after you've been drinking."

I leaned down closer to get a better look, but snapped back up when I realized the suggestive position I'd put myself in. Cameron lightly gripped my hair behind my head and gazed at me intently. "You have no idea how badly I want you right now, but please tell me if we're moving too fast. I'm trying to show restraint and not rip off your clothes and haul you off to bed."

I was instantly aroused by the growl in his voice. I couldn't resist anymore and ran my hands slowly over every hard plane of his sculpted upper body. Stopping at his tattoo, I mindlessly began to trace the outline with my fingertips.

"I want to be with you," I said, but I couldn't meet his eyes. "But I'm a reserved person and I'm nervous about getting undressed in front of you."

His hand rested against my cheek. "You have nothing to be nervous about. I think you're absolutely beautiful, but I get the sense ..." he hesitated. Then he said, "That you don't realize how gorgeous you are."

I ducked my head shyly. "You don't have to say those things; you've already won me over."

Cameron didn't let me finish. "Kayla, stop. I'm serious. I've noticed how little you eat and how much weight you've lost since we first met. I have a younger sister, and I understand how extreme some girls can get about their weight. She's always trying some sort of crazy diet."

He was scratching at the truth, getting too close to the heart of the matter. I was suddenly ashamed, understanding I hadn't been able to hide my weaknesses from him after all. Cameron wanted to know all of me and he wasn't going to permit me shutting him completely out.

Standing up, I felt myself at a crossroads. I could leave, run away from the only happiness I'd known since my father died. Or I could try to work through my issues and trust Cameron not to break my heart.

"You never showed me the rest of your place," I whispered.

He rose from the sofa and held me tightly. I rested my head against his chest and listened to the frantic racing of his heart. I smiled to myself and found myself falling more and more for him.

I laid awake long into the night. My heart couldn't stop pounding as I became hyperaware of Cameron sleeping soundly next to me. I was clad only in a t-shirt he had lent me and desire churned in my belly each time my bare legs brushed against him.

My mouth was sore from the ferocity of our kisses. Although there'd been plenty of exploring with hands and lips, we hadn't slept together. As he pulled at my clothes, I lost my nerve. I didn't have the confidence for him to see every flaw of my body under the harsh overhead lights in his bedroom. After I confessed I wasn't ready for sex, he had reassured me we were in no rush. He cradled me against his chest until I pretended to sleep.

Under the cloak of darkness, I was brave. My body was invisible, every imperfection hidden from view. I could pretend I was someone else while being close to the man I cared deeply about.

Climbing on top of him, I wrapped my legs around his waist. My long hair brushed against his bare chest when I bent forward to kiss his neck. My mouth moved down the front of his body until reaching above his belly button.

"Kayla," he mumbled sleepily.

"Hmmm?"

"Am I dreaming?" he murmured.

I giggled. "Not a dream, just your girlfriend trying to take advantage of you while you're asleep."

"Okay, then I won't interrupt."

Pulling me closer, he kissed me deeply. His hands moved under my shirt, his fingertips grazing my breasts. I moaned into his mouth, letting him know how much I desired his touch. I pulled the t-shirt over my head and tossed it aside. I fell onto my back and he kneeled over me. His breath was warm as he rained soft kisses on my neck and the top of my breasts.

When his tongue flicked across the peaks of my breasts, I moaned, "Cameron …"

Stopping for a second, he said softly, "You have no idea how many times I've thought about you naked in bed with me, calling my name."

Lord, he was sexy, I thought. The feelings he was inspiring in me were incredible. I hated my body, but I loved the things he was doing to it. Hooking my thumbs around his boxer shorts, I pulled them down. With trembling fingers, I reached for him.

He caught my arm before I could reach him. "Kayla, you're shaking. Do you want me to stop?"

Absolutely not, I wanted to scream. "I'm nervous," I told him. "I don't have a lot of experience and I want things to feel good for you, too."

He coughed uncomfortably. "Kayla, believe me, I like *everything* you're doing to me. In fact, I'm trying to give you an out now because I'm not sure how much more I can take."

I wanted all of him. I tugged him to me and purred into his ear, "I can't take much more, either."

Hurriedly, Cameron retrieved a condom from his dresser and put it on. I was convinced my body was made for Cameron's when he entered me. I'd expected the same awkwardness and fumbling that happened with my high school boyfriend. With Cameron, everything was *right*. I was overwhelmed by the intensity of my feelings and moaned in ecstasy as he took his time, prolonging the pleasure of joining our bodies for the first time.

Afterward, Cameron ran his hands soothingly through my hair, as I lay curled up next to him. "That was the best way to be woken up, *ever*."

I smiled in the darkness. "I thought you might like that."

"I did," he said and kissed my forehead.

"Well, since you're in such a good mood, maybe it's a good time to spring something on you." I wondered if he could hear the strain in my voice.

"What would that be?"

"My mom has been bugging me about meeting you. Since I'll be home for spring break, I was wondering if you'd come to dinner at our house this week?"

"Of course, I'd like to meet your mom and sister."

He had no idea what he was getting into. A part of me hoped Cameron would refuse, but I realized my mother would harass me forever if I didn't introduce her soon. Selfishly, I wanted to keep Cameron to myself, not let him see how truly toxic my home life was.

CHAPTER FIFTEEN

"You're here," I breathed into Cameron's ear, greeting him at the door of my mother's house.

It was a relief to feel his arms wrap around me. After four days with my mother, I was craving the comfort of being with Cameron again. He bent down to kiss me and gave me a boyish smile. "Sorry I'm late; I got stuck on the phone with my mother. Once she heard I was coming here to meet your family, she insisted on having us over for dinner. How does Friday work for you?"

I nodded and took him by the hand into the living room. "Lila, this is Cameron."

Lila tossed the remote control she was holding aside and twirled around to peer at Cameron. Her lips twisted up into a cynical smile. "So, you're the credit card guy. You're not gonna try and sell us something while you're here, are you?"

Grabbing one of the pillows off of the couch, I launched it in her direction. "Be nice."

Cameron didn't look offended and he laughed heartily, his eyes crinkling with good humor. "No problem, I'll hold off until you're legally old enough to have a credit card, then I'll start actively harassing you."

When we first started dating, I worried Cameron's job was a touchy subject. Like most things, Cameron was optimistic and didn't dwell on how much he disliked his career. It was only a job to him and not what he wanted to do for the rest of his life.

Cameron dazzled me. He made me hopeful for my own life and for the possibility I could emulate his attitude one day. I visualized reaching inside him and stealing some of his light to chase away my darker nature.

My smile faded when my mother came out of the kitchen. As much as I stressed that the meeting was casual, she had overdressed. She wore a black-and-white, empire-waist cotton dress with a hem above her knees and a low-cut neckline. Her ebony hair was piled on top of her head to show off her long, graceful neck. My mother was in her mid-forties, but looked like she could be my older sister.

Upon my mother's insistence that I change, I came back wearing a maxi skirt and white blouse. I had warned Cameron about how difficult my mother could be, but I still wanted to make the introductions go well. If dressing up made her happy, I would surrender this battle in the Cold War we seemed to be in.

I gestured toward Cameron. "Mom, this is Cameron."

"Nice to meet you, Mrs. Marlowe."

My mom's hips swayed as she approached him. "It's a pleasure to meet you. Please, call me Charlotte."

Lila's eyebrows darted up and she locked gazes with me across the room. I hadn't imagined it: My mother's voice had turned sultry as she greeted my boyfriend.

I coughed into my hand. "Would you like something to drink?" I asked Cameron while my mother continued to stare unabashedly at him. Her eyelashes were thick with mascara and I noticed the way they fluttered, bringing attention to the perfection of her eyes.

"Sure, whatever you have is fine," he answered.

My mother took his jacket and instructed him to take a seat. When I returned with Cameron's soda, she had perched in the spot next to him on the couch, forcing me to sit on the loveseat with Lila. Instead of offering up her place upon my arrival, she continued to talk animatedly to Cameron.

My mom was telling him about how excited she'd been to meet him and how she was making sausage and peppers because I told her it was his favorite meal. I paled as I watched her pat Cameron's knee several times as they spoke.

"What the hell is she doing?" Lila hissed in my ear.

"I have no idea," I whispered back.

It wasn't true. I was fully aware of what she was doing. She was trying to prove she could have what was mine if she wanted it. In the past, I always retreated to the sidelines to allow her to shine. It was one of the reasons I never said anything when boys I liked would come over to simply gape at my mother in her revealing outfits. But this was Cameron. She couldn't have *him*.

Cameron's voice broke into my inner thoughts. "I'm really glad your daughter agreed to give me a shot. I haven't been able to stop thinking about her since we met." Although he was addressing my mother, his eyes didn't leave mine.

My mother smiled indulgently at us both. "I'm glad to see Kayla is finally dating someone, especially someone as handsome as you. I was worried she'd never find anyone since she has a tendency to be a wallflower."

Better than an attention whore, I silently seethed, but I kept my mouth shut. "Should I check on dinner?" I forced out.

"No, I'll get it," she said and breezed out of the room.

My shoulders relaxed once she was out of sight. Lila blew out a shaky breath. We were constantly in suspended animation under my mom's watchful eyes. She was our puppet master, her moods deciding how Lila and I would react. Cameron's expression was questioning.

"Is everything okay?"

Maybe I was the problem. Perhaps all mothers were like mine and I was only imagining her oppressiveness. Cameron didn't look like anything was amiss, so maybe it was all in my head.

"Yes, I'm fine," I answered quickly. I moved over to the couch and brushed my leg against his.

"I'm only asking because you seem tense. Were you nervous your mom wouldn't like me?" Cameron asked and massaged my shoulders.

I didn't answer at first. Instead, I focused on the feel of his hands on me. The truth was I hadn't mentioned my mother very often around Cameron, aside for telling him how difficult she was to be around. How could I explain the complexities of my love/hate relationship with her? Our relationship was at the center of most of my problems and I didn't want him to see that side of my life. A couple of complaints here and there probably didn't clue him in to how awful she could truly be.

Lila snorted. "You didn't warn him our mom is a raving bitch." Her voice was low enough that it didn't carry out of the room. Lila was as complacent as I was, and she wouldn't want to deal with my mother's fury.

"Lila," I admonished.

"What?" She held her hands up. "It's true. Tell me you didn't want to jump on top of her just now and strangle her for hitting on your boyfriend."

"She was hitting on me?" Cameron's face was an innocent mask. "I thought she was only being nice."

Lila shook her head ruefully. "Kayla really didn't tell you about how Charlotte Marlowe operates." Leaning forward, she said, "My mom will work her moves on you until you're drooling over her and offering to leave Kayla for a chance with her. She's like the Wicked Queen from Snow White and there's only room for one fairest of them all in this house."

"Lila, that's enough," I whispered. I gripped the edge of the couch cushions tightly before saying to Cameron, "She's joking."

Suddenly, I knew it was a mistake. I should've never brought Cameron here. Lila was bitter and angry, hating my mother, wishing she'd been the one to die instead of my father. I was a tragedy in the making, despondent unless I had my boyfriend by my side. My mother was conceited and selfish, not caring about either of us enough to realize how messed up her daughters both were.

And now Cameron was looking uncomfortable. Lila's eyes softened when she saw my distraught expression. "I'm exaggerating," she told him. "My mom isn't that bad. I'm sixteen, so I have the whole teen angst thing going on."

Cameron smiled politely as I mouthed "thank you" in Lila's direction behind his back. My mother called us for dinner and I hurried into the dining room. I couldn't wait for the disastrous night to come to an end.

My mother served us after we sat down. Cameron's plate was close to the point of overflowing with the sausage and peppers she placed on it. My portion was miniscule in comparison, but I wasn't surprised, since serving a fatty meal was an anomaly in itself for my mother.

With Cameron seated next to me, his hand resting on my knee, I relaxed. Cameron was a salve to all the wounds inside me. But as I thought it over, I had a sense of foreboding. This couldn't be good, the way I was becoming dependent upon him. I should be strong, self-reliant.

Cameron dug into his meal and complimented my mother on her fantastic cooking. She preened and faked false modesty. I sliced through the sausage and pushed the pieces around my plate. As the conversation surrounded me, I created patterns with the pieces. Cameron squeezed my knee softly to grab my attention. "You should try the sausage, you'll really like it."

"I'm not hungry," I muttered.

We caught my mother's interest from across the table. "Kayla has been doing wonderfully keeping up with her diet. I honestly didn't think she had the willpower." Pointing to my sister eating a piece of sausage, she remarked, "Lila, on the other hand ..."

"Mom," I interrupted softly.

"My girls take after my husband's family, they're all rather heavyset. I had thought about taking them to their doctor to rule out a thyroid problem, but I figured the problem was they were eating too much junk.

"But all it took was a little bit of effort, and Kayla now looks a hundred times better." My mother smiled serenely at me. I detested her at that moment. I hated my father, too, for deeming her worthy of his love.

"I don't know you and maybe I'm out of line for saying this, but I can't believe the things you're saying about your daughters."

I stole a glance at Cameron. A muscle ticked in his jaw and his back straightened up as he glared at my mother.

My mother's eyes narrowed. "You *are* out of line."

"Do you know Kayla barely eats? I take her out to dinner and she stares at the food like she's scared of it. I thought Kayla was being coy when she'd get embarrassed when I complimented her. Now I understand why she has such a low opinion of herself." Cameron rose to his feet.

"You have no idea what you're talking about. I'm only trying to help my daughters. You're kidding yourself if you think that you would've looked at Kayla twice before she lost the weight."

Cameron pulled me to my feet. Tears blurred my vision and I felt the room tilt. "Kayla, look at me," he commanded. When I didn't comply, he used his hand to turn me toward him. His tone was kind. "Why don't you get your and Lila's jackets? We'll take her out for ice cream."

"Lila is *not* going out for ice cream."

My mother sounded livid. I couldn't bear to look at her. I was humiliated Cameron had come to my home and felt forced to stick up for my sister and me. Lila and I were brainwashed into believing every word my mother said. Most days, it never even occurred to me I should disagree with her.

"Let's go, Lila," I said and held out a hand for her. Her fork clanged against her plate loudly when she dropped it abruptly. After shooting my mother an uncertain look, she nodded and grasped my hand. Hand-in-hand we walked away from my mother's outraged cries.

"I'm sorry," Cameron said when Lila went to refill her ice cream cup.

"For what?"

I swirled the vanilla frozen yogurt in my cup with the spoon before giving him a confused look. The car ride had been silent. Once we arrived at the ice cream shop, Lila had tried to snap us out of our funk by sharing a few funny stories about her fellow classmates. I laughed because it stopped me from sobbing.

"I didn't have any right to come to your house and talk to your mom like that." His expression was tortured. "I understand if you're pissed at me—"

I didn't let him finish. "I'm not mad, I'm embarrassed. I should've warned you more about how my mom was before I had you come over. It was foolish to hope we could be a normal family for the night."

"Kayla, the stuff your mom said …" He paused. "You have to realize none of it's true. You're amazing and the reason I'm with you has nothing to do with your weight."

"I know," I said automatically, understanding it was what he needed to hear. He needed to be reassured of his decency, his ability to see beyond how I looked on the outside. He wouldn't want to admit his own vanity and concede his unwillingness to date someone overweight.

"Kayla, I've noticed how much thinner you are since we first met and how little you eat." He pinched the bridge of his nose, hinting at his unease at broaching this topic. "It's not healthy. And now that I've met your mom, a lot of stuff I've been trying to figure out about you is starting to become clearer."

"Please don't psychoanalyze me after one meeting with my mother," I begged in a small voice.

"Kayla, I care about you and I'm only trying to look out for you. I really feel like you're starving yourself because of the warped things your mother says about you—"

I pressed my palm over his mouth to silence him. "I'm fine. I've probably taken the dieting thing too far, so I see where your concern is coming from. But things are good now. I have you and…" I trailed off and shifted uncomfortably under his scrutiny. "I'm happy. It felt amazing to see someone stand up to my mother." I pulled my hand away and gave him a hesitant smile. The torn expression remained fixed on his face and his lips turned down into a deep frown.

"Come back with me tonight. You can stay with me at the apartment until classes start up again next week." He looked over at Lila, who was requesting ice cream samples from the cute guy behind the counter. "Your sister can stay with us, too."

He was sweet, earnest, and deserved so much more than I could give him. "Lila has school and I promised to spend the week with her. Her spring break isn't until the end of the month. Why don't I stay at your place after dinner at your parents' house on Friday?"

Cameron gave a reluctant nod. "I hope I didn't make things worse for you with your mom. She seems too demanding about what she expects from you and your sister."

I laughed humorlessly. "It seems funny now when I think about how you asked if your car was a deal breaker. You had no idea what you were getting into by asking me out."

He didn't join in with my laughter. "Kayla, I'm not perfect. I've gone through rough patches and allowed the wrong kind of people to control my life."

"Why? What have you been through?"

"Not now. We'll save those depressing stories for a rainy day," he answered.

I was desperate to pull back the curtain and reveal what was beneath Cameron's cheerful façade. Yet it didn't feel like the right time. He was like me in that way: We loathed burdening others with our problems, and I could tell turning the conversation toward him was unnerving him.

He pleaded, "Please don't let your mom make you feel bad about yourself while you're home."

I smiled tightly at him when Lila returned to the table at the ice cream shop. He changed the subject and began discussing his favorite Xbox games with Lila. Lila was a guy's girl and loved any kind of game involving blood and guts. I assumed it was her outlet for stress relief.

I wished I could give Cameron what he wanted and block every ugly word out of my mom's mouth. But twenty-one years of being told I was fat and ugly was hard to erase.

CHAPTER SIXTEEN

As we walked up the path to his parents' home, Cameron shot me a reassuring smile. "You look really nervous. I told you, my parents are cool, they'll love you."

"I've never met the parents of someone I'm dating before. My high school boyfriend's parents went to the same church as my parents, so they already knew each other."

"I guessed this might be new to you. You went a little overboard on the fruit and wine basket," he said eyeing the oversized basket I clutched in my arms. It contained a bottle of red wine with an assortment of fruits and chocolates. It cost me a hundred dollars, a major purchase for a college student on a budget.

"Should I leave it in the car? I'm probably trying too hard, but I really want them to like me," I said. It was my way of making up for the disastrous meeting with my mom. I doubted his father would hit on me or there would be a screaming match at the dinner table. His family would be normal and my family's dysfunction would scare him off.

"It's a nice gesture. My point was you only had to show up for dinner. My family knows I like you, so they'll like you, too."

Cameron had the uncanny ability to say exactly what I needed to hear. I relaxed and took a minute to study his childhood home. The neighborhood was similar to my own: blocks of suburban mid-sized homes. The Bennett house was a bi-level with a two-car garage and brick siding. When he led me inside, we walked into a large living room with a set of matching brown leather couches. The TV was on and someone I guessed to be Cameron's sister was flipping channels mindlessly. She swung her head toward the door when we entered and grinned at us.

"Loser!" she yelled cheerfully.

The girl looked to be a couple of years younger than me. Her corn silk hair was cut to her chin and she shared the same eyes as her older brother. She was tall, with an athletic build. Cameron addressed me. "This is my pain-in-the-ass sister, Scarlett."

"Language!" a new voice admonished. A middle-aged woman with a strawberry-blond bob and green eyes strode toward us. She hugged Cameron tightly and kissed his cheek. A pink lipstick stain was left behind on his skin. I resisted the urge to wipe it away. She turned her attention to me. "Hi, I'm Maggie Bennett."

"Kayla," I responded and saw who I presumed to be Cameron's dad entering the living room.

He stuck out his hand to me. "I'm Cameron's father, Jack." I smiled as I took in Jack's appearance. I didn't detect any resemblance between Cameron and his mom, but he was the spitting image of his father. His blue eyes twinkled with the same good humor and mischief I often found in Cameron's, and he was tall, just like his children. The trio studied me openly and my cheeks began to burn from fixing a wide smile on my face.

Cameron seemed to detect my awkwardness over being appraised that way. He said smoothly, "Mom, can you take the basket from Kayla? She looks ready to drop it."

I smiled gratefully at him before passing the basket to his mom. "I wanted to bring a little something. Thanks for having me over for dinner."

"Kayla, this is such a nice gesture. Thank you so much!" Maggie trilled.

Scarlett's eyebrows shot up as she watched her mom gush over my offering. "I hope you used Cameron's money to pay for that. I'm guessing he's paying you to pretend to be his girlfriend. You seem way too nice to be dating my brother."

"Ha-ha," Cameron said sarcastically. "Ignore her. She's just jealous because she had to break up with her last boyfriend when he got caught running an illegal gambling ring on campus."

Cameron's mother returned from placing the basket in the kitchen and raised her eyes heavenward. "Children, please be nice to each other." She smiled indulgently and told me, "Sorry for our lack of manners. I think everyone has been just so excited to meet you since Cameron started talking about you."

I gave Cameron a questioning look and he responded with a wink. "What do you want to drink?" After I requested water, he said, "Have a seat with my sister and I'll be back in a sec."

I sat on the couch next to Scarlett while Cameron and his parents went into the adjoining kitchen. Scarlett sat crisscrossed on the couch with a curious expression on her face. "My mom's right. My brother doesn't normally talk about girls with us, so I couldn't wait to meet the girl he can't shut up about."

"Really? I heard about a few of his past girlfriends and the relationships sounded serious."

"Who; the grad-school girl whose name I can barely remember? Stacey, I think. Or Taylor, the leech who is constantly calling my brother for some sort of ridiculous favor? Do you know a few months back she asked him to go change her flat tire in the pouring rain? I told him to tell her to get lost and call Triple A, but Cameron is the nicer one out of the two of us," Scarlett said.

Checking behind me to make sure Cameron hadn't returned, I leaned forward conspiratorially. "I thought I was the only one who noticed it. She's always calling him when we're out on a date and he has to stay on the phone to calm her down because she's crying over the latest drama in her life."

"My brother tries to be the hero too often. He suffers from an acute case of white knight syndrome." Scarlett opened her mouth to say more, but stayed silent when Cameron returned to the room.

His sister's words were intended to soothe me, but they had the reverse effect. Did Cameron see me as a girl in trouble that needed rescuing? Was this the source of his attraction to me?

"Everything okay?" he asked me. He frowned at his sister. "What are you saying about me? Kayla might take you seriously and not realize you have a warped sense of humor."

I rallied for his benefit. His relationship with his sister was sweet, and I liked the normalcy of seeing siblings who genuinely cared for each other beneath the bickering. Lila and I loved each other, but we didn't tease each other in the same way. Our mother humiliated us too often to even jokingly make fun of one another.

Handing me a glass of water, Cameron sank down on the couch next to me. His arm wound behind my shoulders and he held me close.

"She was telling me how you can't shut up about me," I said lightly and squeezed the top of his thigh.

"I should've known my sister would try and embarrass me. But I have no problem admitting how much I brag about you. You're awesome," he said and planted a kiss on the side of my head.

"Ugh, you two are disgusting. I'm getting a freaking toothache from all this sweetness." Scarlett's features twisted in mock distaste.

His father announced dinner, and Cameron ushered me into the dining room and gestured to a pair of chairs at the table. I sat down to his right, and before long, the Bennetts were all talking at once and sharing stories about their day. I loved hearing the family's laughter; it filled something inside of me that had been empty for a long time.

As the table quieted down, Cameron's father turned to face me. "Cameron told us you're a student at Trenton College. What are you studying?"

"I'm a journalism major. I became interested in writing since I started working for my high school newspaper."

"Do your parents work in that field?"

I shifted uncomfortably in my seat. Sometimes I wished I had a sign affixed to the front of me with a warning not to bring up my parents. "My mother is a housewife …" I stuttered over my words. With my father's death, would that label still apply? There was no such thing as a housewidow, was there? "My father was a vet, but he died two summers ago."

Maggie made a sympathetic clucking noise while Jack's eyes softened. Cameron swooped in. "You should look up some of Kayla's articles online. She's really talented."

My gloom lifted and my tone was disbelieving as I asked, "You read the articles I wrote?"

"Yes." He smirked at me. "I guessed you wouldn't brag about how crazy good you are at writing, so I did an online search and found them myself. I think my favorite was the one on safety tips for online dating. You probably saved a lot of girls from becoming the target of freaks online."

He took another piece of my heart prisoner at that moment. He sounded sincere and was telling me what I wrote *mattered*, the articles were more than merely fluff. He had also steered the conversation away from my family, and his parents began to question me about my work.

Cameron's mother had cooked beef stew with cornbread. I swirled the pieces of meat and cutup vegetables around on my plate. Out of the corner of my eye, I caught Maggie watching me play with my food. Her seeming displeasure had me inwardly cringing. I was offending her. She had cooked a wonderful meal and I was being rude by not eating it. Earnestly, I dug into the stew. After a few enthusiastic bites, I turned to his mom. "This is delicious. You'll have to give me the recipe."

Maggie beamed. "Of course."

I could play the part. I could pretend to be the normal person who polishes off her dinner and requests the recipe in order to go home and make it for her boyfriend. I wouldn't let his parents see the real me, the girl who would be using their bathroom shortly to throw up the dinner his mother worked hard to prepare.

Later, Scarlett accosted me in the hallway as I was leaving the bathroom. Cameron was helping clear the dishes with his parents. My heart momentarily stopped and I prayed she wasn't confronting me over purging in the bathroom.

Her hands were placed on her hips and the tightness around her eyes told me she was considering what to say. She sighed heavily before speaking. "I get that I'm the little sister and I shouldn't worry about my brother, but I do." As she turned, I followed her line of vision and saw Cameron chuckling with his dad, both leaning against the kitchen counter. "A lot of people think just because Cam is outgoing and funny he can't be hurt. Like he doesn't have feelings and won't experience pain like the rest of us. But that's not true and I want to make sure you're not going to stomp on my brother's heart."

My expression grew alarmed. "Why would you think I'd hurt him?"

"Don't take it personally," she said. "I can tell you really like him. I'm protective of Cam, and although he doesn't show it, he's been hurt before."

"By a girlfriend?"

I hadn't expected the surge of jealousy toward a faceless and nameless girl who broke Cameron's heart. Cameron's past relationships hadn't sounded intense enough to warrant the kind of heartbreak Scarlett was hinting at.

Instead of answering, Scarlett stepped away, unblocking my path to the kitchen. "It's not what you think. If Cam hasn't talked about his past, I shouldn't be the one to say anything."

Without replying, I continued past her. I appreciated how she was trying to look out for her brother and couldn't be angry with her for it. I'd do the same for Lila. I also couldn't fault Cameron for keeping secrets—because I had secrets of my own.

CHAPTER SEVENTEEN

"Britt! Wake up!" I pounded on her door furiously.

I stood in the foyer on our floor and tapped my foot anxiously. I'd been knocking for at least five minutes and refused to give up until she answered. Pressing my ear to the door, I heard the faint sound of the TV. Brittany needed background noise to fall asleep, but once she was out, she was practically comatose.

Finally, she swung open the door. She scowled at me as she ran her fingers through her messy hair. "What the hell, Kayla?"

"I'm late," I hissed. I was too frantic to ease her into the revelation. I didn't want to be the clichéd girl in crisis, but I had stumbled into the role regardless. As soon as I noticed the date on my wall calendar, my first instinct was to confide in my best friend. My only thought was she'd help me—wake me up from this nightmare.

"Late for what? Isn't it Sunday?" Brittany rubbed at her eyes.

"No, I'm *late*."

Her expression darkened. "Oh crap, you mean that kind of late. Damn, Kayla, haven't you seen that line fail a million times in the movies?" She chewed on a thumbnail, inheriting a portion of the anxiety I was feeling. "When were you supposed to get your period?"

"I don't know exactly." I squirmed under her scrutiny. "Like ten days ago."

"Shit, Kayla," she said and mumbled a few more expletives. "Has Cam been using a condom?"

"Yes, but I'm not exactly paying attention when we're in the middle of things. What if it broke and I didn't notice?"

"Have you said anything to him?"

I shook my head. "No. He was having his friends over last night. I didn't feel good, so I stayed here."

"I thought I heard you throwing up the other day. Have you been sick a lot? When my older sister was pregnant, she was puking every morning. She said it lasted until she was like three months along."

I blanched at Brittany's words. I ran the faucet on full blast when I threw up, hoping to cover the sound. Jessica had also given me a few strange looks when I'd emerged from the bathroom. Suspicions had been planted in their minds, and they were going to figure out how I was getting rid of the late night beer and pizza they brought home for the floor.

I couldn't be pregnant. I could barely feed myself; much less have the responsibility of feeding a baby. I closed my eyes and exhaled noisily. "I haven't been feeling well, but I never guessed I could be pregnant."

It had been more than a month since Cameron and I had visited our respective families. I never mentioned the uncomfortable conversation I had with his overprotective sister, and he never talked about the disastrous dinner with my mom. I didn't want our secrets to ruin what we had together. Instead, I continued playing make-believe, becoming addicted to the way he made me feel when we were together.

Cameron's observations about my diet forced me to change the way I ate in front of him. If I had plans to see him at night, I'd skip breakfast and lunch to eat a full meal for his benefit. Back at the dorm, I'd binge late at night on the stash of snacks I had accumulated from frequent convenience store runs. I smuggled the food past my roommates, storing it in my closet and dresser drawers instead of the kitchen. I became reliant on purging and laxatives to flush the food out of my body.

I was slowly disappearing, vanishing more and more each day in the quest to be a size zero. I couldn't stop dieting; I'd forgotten how to eat like a normal person. I should've been happy; Cameron was a great guy and he treated me wonderfully. But I couldn't stop the nagging fear that if I weren't skinny enough, he'd no longer want me.

"Kayla, you have to buy a test," Brittany was insisting.

I knew she was right. But I was terrified. What if I was pregnant? I'd been abusing my body for months—what would that have done to an unborn child? What kind of abomination would be produced from my self-loathing?

"I'll go to the drugstore now," I murmured, already lost in my own thoughts.

"Do you want me to come with you? I'll stay here with you while you take it."

Over her shoulder, I gazed forlornly out the window. The April rain was coming down in sheets. The weather felt like a reflection of what I was experiencing inside. And as much as I relied on Brittany, I suddenly craved the strength of Cameron to help me through the storm. "It's fine, no reason for us both to get soaked. Maybe I should go over to Cameron's apartment and talk to him."

"I know you're freaking out, but Cam is a good guy. He'll be there for you. And I will be, too. The college has a Planned Parenthood office on campus. We can go there if the test is positive and find out what your options are. If you're not pregnant, we'll get you on the pill." After her reassurances, Brittany launched her compact body at me and wrapped her arms around my back. "I love you. Call me if you need anything."

I had good people in my life, people who loved me. Why wasn't it enough? Why couldn't I snap out of it? Had the wiring gone wrong inside me and I'd forgotten how to be at peace with myself?

Numbly, I drove to the drugstore. My hands were trembling as I placed the pregnancy test on the counter and handed over my credit card. I was trying hard to not begin bawling in the middle of the store. I was barely hanging on, unsure if I'd ever feel good about myself again. When I lost all the weight I wanted, hit my size zero goal, I had a sinking feeling it still wouldn't be good enough.

I pulled the hood of my jacket over my head as I took the steps up to Cameron's apartment two at a time. He lived on the second floor of a house that had been converted into two separate apartments. His downstairs neighbor was his landlord, an elderly woman who kept mostly to herself.

I shoved the pregnancy test into my purse and knocked on the door. A small puddle gathered at my feet while I waited for him to answer. I knocked again, more persistent. It was only after nine and I guessed he had slept in after hanging out with his friends the night before.

"Don't you realize we're trying to sleep," a female voice said irritably as the door opened.

I stopped breathing. Involuntarily, I took a step back as I tried to register what I was seeing. Taylor was answering Cameron's doorway, dressed in one of his Rutgers t-shirts. She yawned and stretched lazily as she looked me up and down.

Taylor smirked. "Cameron didn't tell me you were coming by this morning."

I found my voice. "What are you doing here?"

"Isn't it obvious? I spent the night," she said with a shrug. Her shapely legs were bare, the t-shirt barely covering her thighs. After another yawn, she said dryly, "Sorry, we didn't get to sleep until after three."

I dug my fingernails into my palm. I should've seen this coming, I thought. I should've known better than to believe Cameron was as perfect as he appeared to be.

I had to leave. My heart was shriveling up, the pain snatching my breath away. I hadn't let anyone get that close to me in a long time, shutting myself off since my father died. Cameron had seen glimpses of the real me and I had hoped to one day let him completely. Instead, I was destined to be alone. My only possible consolation was his baby—a baby I wasn't sure I'd be able to take care of.

"Kayla ..." His voice, the drowsy voice I usually loved, broke into my thoughts.

My eyes were watery as I peeked past Kayla and saw him coming out of his bedroom. His hair stuck up in tufts and he wore a tank top and boxers. Rubbing his eyes, he stared at me, seemingly unsure if I was real or not.

There was a scream somewhere inside of me, urging to be freed. Instead, I fled as if my life depended on it. I was always running, but never reaching where I needed to be.

"Kayla! Stop!"

Blindly, I stormed down the stairs. The only thing I saw was the memory of Taylor's smug smile when she answered the door. She'd been triumphant. I had suspected for a while she wanted me out of the way, and her wish had come true. I was destroyed, lamenting how everything good in my life was always taken away prematurely.

"Kayla, please! Will you listen to me for one second?" Cameron's demanding voice was close, too close. I had to get away from him. I couldn't hear the words pass from his lips. I couldn't survive the admission of his unfaithfulness. To think of him in bed with another while I had his baby inside me brought on a powerful wave of nausea.

"Kayla," he said, breathless, grabbing me by my shoulders.

As he tried to turn me around, I pleaded, "Please, Cameron, let me go. I can't even look at you."

"I have no idea what Taylor said to you, but nothing happened. She's only here because she was too wasted last night to drive home."

I dared a glance back at him. The rain was plastering his hair to his forehead. His eyes were begging me to believe him, trying to convey he would never hurt me in that way.

"Why was she wearing nothing more than your t-shirt?"

"She asked me to borrow one to sleep in. I gave it to her before I went to bed and she crashed on the couch." I turned my head away from him, but he continued to speak. "Nothing happened."

"Cameron, it's obvious how she feels about you. I'm not sure I believe it was an innocent sleepover."

"After everyone left, she tried to kiss me," he acknowledged. "I turned her down and she apologized, saying she had too much to drink. She lives forty-five minutes away and I knew neither of us could drive. I can only imagine how it must've looked for her to answer the door."

I wiped at the moisture on my cheeks. "I should go …"

"Kayla, no." He sounded tortured. Seizing both of my hands in his, he continued, "I'm crazy about you. I don't want Taylor; I don't want anyone but you."

It was evident that he was willing me to acknowledge the truth in his words. It was jarring to be confronted with the idea that Cameron wasn't out to slaughter my fragile heart. Instead, he seemed to genuinely want only me.

Our mouths came together and we were kissing desperately. I wanted to kiss him into oblivion, revel in the taste of him intermingled with the spring rain.

His breathing was labored as he pressed his forehead to mine. "Come inside. You're soaking wet. We can talk to Taylor and she'll reassure you nothing happened."

I grimaced. "I don't want to see her. She pretty much insinuated you had slept with her."

Anger flashed in his eyes. "I'll get rid of her. I'm sorry if she made you think anything happened. I swear I'd never do that to you." Squeezing my hand, he led me toward the building. Taylor was walking into the foyer as we were heading up the stairs. She was dressed in the skirt and blouse she must have worn the night before.

Cameron scowled at her. "I don't know what kind of game you thought you were playing, but I don't want any part of it. Don't call me again."

"Cam, I'm sorry, I didn't mean to—"

"Taylor, I'm done. I tried to be your friend, but I'm over your jealous bullshit," he snarled at her.

Taylor pressed her lips together in a hard line. "Fine," she huffed out. "If you're willing to throw away years of friendship on some girl you barely know, then it's your loss." Stomping around Cameron, she grumbled in my direction, "You hurt him and you'll have to deal with me."

"Get away from me," I said softly. Her heels clicked against the wood flooring in the hallway at her retreat.

Leading me inside, Cameron shut the door with a groan. "Not the way I wanted us to start our Sunday." At my silence, Cameron peered at me curiously. "Don't let Taylor get to you. Don't give her the satisfaction of coming between us."

"That's not it." A fresh onslaught of tears threatened to spill down my cheeks as he moved closer. It was too much for me, getting off one emotional rollercoaster, only to get right back on another.

I tried to take comfort in being near him. The fabric of his tank top was clinging to his chest, soaked from kissing me in the rain. I could relive the kiss to distract me from the hurt.

"Kayla, you're shaking. Let's get you into something dry and I'll make us some coffee."

Before he could move away, I gripped his forearm. "Cameron, I came here because my period is late. I think I may be pregnant." I couldn't hold in my sobs any longer. "I brought a test over. I thought you could stay with me while I took it."

Within seconds, his arms encircled my waist and I had my head pressed against his chest. "Baby, it's going to be okay."

Tilting my head back, I stared up at him. His eyes had softened and he grazed his thumb against my cheek. "We've been careful, but I could see why you're scared. You'll take the test and whatever the result is, we'll figure it out together."

I coveted his calm and level-headedness. I was splintering into a thousand pieces, questioning how I'd ever be able to pull it together enough to raise a baby. I clutched at his damp shirt, frantic, wondering if Cameron could anchor me enough to get control of my emotions.

Releasing his shirt, I reached into my purse to retrieve the pregnancy test. "I guess I should get it over with."

There was something indiscernible in his expression, and I could tell he had more to say. I was frightened by his integrity, his readiness to do the right thing if the test came out positive. I retreated to the bathroom, fearful his words would break me even more. I was too vulnerable, weakened physically and mentally by hunger and depression.

CHAPTER EIGHTEEN

"It was negative," I said in a breathless rush, hurrying over to his bed.

At my approach, Cameron raised himself up on his elbows. Before he had a chance to reply, I jumped into his arms and buried my face in the crook of his neck. "I'm sorry for freaking out over a false alarm," I muttered into his collar.

Alone in the bathroom, staring at the lines of the pregnancy test, I willed it to be only one line. Please, don't make me have to eat, please don't force me to put on weight for a baby, I prayed silently. I knew I was sick, I could feel myself barely hanging on to my sanity.

Brittany had texted and called me a dozen times since I left the dorm. Before I relayed the news to Cameron, I sent out a quick text to let her know the test was negative. She replied she had a sense it was a false alarm and guessed my period had stopped because of all of the weight I lost. I deleted her message, vanquishing her words, hoping to deny the truth behind them.

Cameron was silent, his lips in my hair. I pulled back from him. When I met his eyes, I found I couldn't decipher his feelings. Cameron was usually an open book and I was apprehensive over what he was thinking. My gut told me I was too needy for him. He was handsome, sexy, and smart, and he didn't have to waste his time on a girl that woke up some mornings questioning whether she could make it through the day.

"Cameron?"

"Yes?" He answered me, but his thoughts seemed far away.

"What are you thinking?"

A long minute passed. "I was just thinking how I wasn't scared over the possibility of you being pregnant. I was more upset when I thought you were going to leave me because of Taylor."

I gaped at him. "I don't understand. I mean, do you want a baby?"

"I thought about it before and I definitely want kids. I'd love to be a father one day. Maybe it wouldn't be the best time for us to become parents, but we could've made things work." My Cameron, I thought affectionately, but I knew his optimism would be his undoing.

I laughed mirthlessly. "I'd be an awful mother."

"How could you say that?" he asked. "I see the way you are with your sister. You're always trying to look out for her."

"You'd be an amazing dad," I asserted. "But a child deserves a caring and loving mother."

"Just stop it, Kayla." Cameron sat up in the bed and his eyes darkened. "I can't sit here and listen to you beat yourself up." At my shocked expression, he puffed out a long sigh. "I've tried to be understanding. I can't imagine what you must have gone through when you lost your father. You're still grieving and your mother is too selfish to help you through it."

"Cameron—" I started uncertainly.

He held up his hand to silence me. "Let me finish. There are a lot of things I've wanted to say to you for a long time, but I see this vulnerable side and I didn't want

123

to hurt your feelings. But I feel like you may need to talk to someone to help you through your grief."

"What? Like a therapist?"

"Would that be so bad? Maybe it'd be easier to talk to a stranger. When I try to talk to you about certain things, I can feel you checking out. I care about you and it's killing me to see you in pain."

"You've never told me that's how you felt. I thought you were happy." I slid across the bed until my back was turned to him.

"Kayla, I'm not telling you this because I'm unhappy. I catch you in these moments where you're incredibly sweet and funny and I fall for you all over again." I squirmed out of his grasp when his arms surrounded me from behind.

"There's a but," I whispered harshly.

"*But*, there are other times when I see how sad you are. The way you barely eat, the way your clothes have started to fall off you. Kayla, when we're in bed together, you hide from me under the covers …"

"I don't have to listen to this." I stood up and took a step toward the bedroom door.

Cameron stepped around me and blocked the exit. "Why can't you see I'm only telling you this because I want to help? Your father sounds like an amazing guy and it must be hell for you to think about the day you found him. And instead of having a mom who tries to help you deal with the pain, she tries to poison you by making you feel like you're not good enough to be her daughter. I can tell you that you're beautiful and incredible until the day I die. But your mom has damaged you to the point where you'll only see yourself as worthless."

What a fool I'd been to think Cameron was oblivious to my dark side. He had only feigned ignorance, protecting me, holding on to the hope I'd find a way to pull myself out of the bottomless well I'd fallen into.

My instincts urged me to break things off with him, tell him he was off base, his theories about my life were erroneous, and I couldn't be with someone who thought I was a pathetic thing needing a savior.

But in two and a half months, my life had intersected with Cameron's in a way I couldn't brush off. I stayed at his apartment more nights than I slept at the dorm. I would drift off in his arms, safe from the nightmares, his presence chasing away the horrors inside the hidden corners of my mind.

"I'm not sure what to say," I mumbled. "I can't look you in the face and claim the things you're saying aren't true. But I want you to know no matter how messed up I am, you're important to me and I honestly have never felt this way about anyone."

His shoulders sagged with relief. "I feel the same way about you. I can't stand the thought of you hurting. Will you at least think about seeing a doctor?"

Reluctantly, I nodded. I was ashamed I needed help, but if I didn't do something, I would continue the endless spiral, falling deeper and deeper into my pit of self-loathing.

CHAPTER NINETEEN

"What's the plan for Little Kayla? Are we bringing her to the Alpha Psi Chi party?" Brittany darkened my doorway and shot Lila a sly smile. Lila dropped the magazine she was thumbing through and perked up at the mention of a party.

"You're not corrupting my sister this weekend."

Brittany pouted. "Your sister is no fun," she said to Lila before addressing me, "What's the plan then? You're not going to drag the poor girl to Cam's and force her to sit there while the two of you hook up?"

"No," I replied hotly. "I told Cameron we were having a night of sisterly bonding."

Brittany winked at Lila. "No worries, Little Kayla. Your sister sleeps like the dead. I'll spring you once she passes out."

"Would you like to eat dinner with us? I could see if Jess and Danielle want to come along, too?" I asked.

"The twins went home for the weekend, but I'll come to dinner. Are you actually going to eat this time?" Brittany's light tone sounded forced as she spoke to Lila. "Can you please tell your sister she has lost enough weight?"

As Brittany and Lila locked eyes, I could see something silent pass between them. Lila nervously bit her lip and tried to mimic Brittany's levity. "I know, right? What are you, like a hundred pounds now?"

"Hardly," I said dryly. My head bounced back and forth between the two of them. "What is this?"

"Nothing," Brittany said hurriedly. "It's just hard not to notice you're super skinny and barely eat."

"It's not like I'm underweight." I held up my arm and pointed to the skin under my arm. "Look at this, I still have batwings."

"There's not an ounce of fat on you," Brittany insisted incredulously.

Her eyes were unreadable and I had the paranoid thought she was only saying these things because she wanted to keep me in my place as her fat sidekick. I'd always been her buffer when we went out, the chunky friend forced to entertain the friend of the guy she was interested in. Brittany never voiced the truth of our arrangement, but I had silently accepted the terms long ago.

"She's right, Kayla. I only see skin and bones." Lila's small voice interrupted my thoughts.

How could they not see the fat there? Was the flesh I saw in my mind much thicker than it actually was? I shook my head to clear my thoughts. I had come so far, suffered the consequences to try and have the body I always wanted. I wouldn't let anyone's jealousy derail my plans to have the perfect shape.

"What is this, gang up on Kayla night?" I asked before sending a challenging stare toward Brittany. "I thought you wanted to do something fun with my sister."

"I'm sorry, Kayla. You're right; we should have fun tonight. Since we both have hot boyfriends that never want us out of their beds, we hardly see each other anymore."

My eyebrows pulled together. "Filter in front of my teenage sister, please."

"Sorry, Little Kayla." She nodded sagely. "Hold on to your v-card as long as possible. Once boys hear you're no longer a virgin, they expect you to spread your legs all the time."

"If my mother calls me and accuses me of corrupting my sister during her visit, I'm throwing you under the bus and letting her know exactly what wise advice you gave her."

Brittany shuddered exaggeratedly. "Your mother scares me. I've seen pit bulls with nicer dispositions."

"No kidding," I muttered

I couldn't shake the sense that Brittany and Lila had joined forces and decided I was their project for the night. When we arrived at the restaurant, they put in an order for an appetizer sampler platter. The platter was a dieter's nightmare, piled high with fried mozzarella sticks, stuffed potato skins, and Buffalo wings. Their conversation stalled when it was my turn to order, and I understood my food choices were being evaluated. With nothing on the menu with less than five hundred calories, besides an undressed salad, I settled on a chicken sandwich. I could feel the collective sigh as I handed the menu back to the waiter.

"So, how are things at home?"

My sister's eyes grew distant at my question. The familiar remorse plagued me, and I hated myself all over again for leaving home. I wanted her to know she wasn't alone in her pain. A hundred miles hadn't allowed me to escape the anguish of my father's death and my mother's harsh criticisms. "It's Hell on Earth living with Mom," Lila said quietly.

I took a small sip of my water before speaking. "I'll be home for the summer soon. I'm still writing online articles so I'll be able to work at night and we'll have all day to hang out."

Disbelief sneaked into Lila's expression. "You have a boyfriend now. And after that crap Mom pulled the last time you brought him around, it's not like you're going to have him come over again."

"I haven't talked to Cameron about the summer. I'm not sure how serious he is about us and whether he'd want to stay together once I'm back home."

"Enough with this feeling sorry for yourself, Kayla. The man can't see straight when it comes to you. He would've totally stood by you if you were really pregnant," Brittany said resolutely. I glared at her.

Lila paled. "You thought you were pregnant?"

"Brittany is overreacting. It wasn't that big of a deal." My nonchalance was failing miserably. Lila looked more upset by my casual indifference. I felt the need to clarify things for her. "My period was late because I've lost weight. It's very common to have irregular periods when you're dieting." As with most of my assertions about what is normal, I made it up as I went along. I had no idea if it was common, but I still hadn't gotten my period.

"But you told Cameron you thought you were pregnant? How did he react?" Lila leaned forward in anticipation. Her color had returned to normal and I could see she was eager to hear what happened. Maybe hearing about my endless drama would distract her from how tough things must be at home.

"He was great," I admitted. "He *is* great and everything I always wanted in a guy." I paused and tapped mindlessly on the table for a minute before continuing, "But I feel like it's too good to be real. Either his true nature is going to be revealed over time or he's going to wake up one morning and realize I'm not the girl he wants."

"I hate to be blunt." I smiled at Brittany's obvious lie. "But your mother has mind-fucked both of you for way too long. She's obviously jealous because her daughters outshine her and she wants to make you both as miserable as she is. Don't let her win. Be happy with Cameron and stop trying to make yourself 'prettier'"—Brittany used air quotes—"for her sake." Brittany sat back in her chair.

It sounded simple: Just turn off the voice inside of me insisting I was fat, ugly, and unlovable. Yet the feelings were too ingrained inside my head. My only possibility of salvation was to stop eating until the skinny girl emerged from within.

Once the food arrived, I didn't pause between bites. It was hard to put into words my mindset when I binged and purged. It was addictive—the satisfying fullness of the food resting in my stomach, followed by the sense of release when I forced it back up. Although the vomiting part was disgusting, in some ways, binging and purging was easier than not eating at all. At the basest level, I was comforted by the idea that at least I'd be able to taste some of my favorite foods.

I mumbled an excuse and bolted to the bathroom as soon as I polished off my sandwich and fries. Getting sick in public was one of the least pleasant things. It was a challenge to stay quiet as my finger jabbed into the back of my raw throat, causing me to gag loudly. In high-traffic bathrooms like the one at the restaurant, it was almost impossible to wait until the place emptied out. I could only imagine what my fellow bathroom guests thought when they heard gagging followed by the distinctive splashing when my dinner went into the toilet.

"Kayla," Lila called. Spinning around, I saw her familiar Converse sneakers behind the stall door.

"Yes?" My voice was strangled from bile and fear. My throat stung as acid sloshed against the back of my throat. I wiped at the toilet furiously with a piece of toilet paper, removing evidence of my sickness.

"What are you doing?"

"What do you think?" I snapped. "What do most people normally do in the bathroom?"

A piece of regurgitated food had splashed on my jeans. After swiping it away with my hand, I hoped the stain was small enough Lila wouldn't notice. Opening the door, I elbowed by her and headed straight to the sink. She stood silently behind me as I feverishly scrubbed at my hands with the hottest water I could stand. Finally, I met her eyes in the mirror.

The bathroom was mostly empty by then, only a single person left in one of the stalls. Lila was swimming behind me, my eyesight watery. "Please," I mouthed to her.

Comprehension dawned on her face, as she understood my request: I couldn't get into it then and there. Let me be for now. She shook her head and flew from the bathroom.

My shame overtook me. This was the example I was setting for my teenage sister. Her opinion of me would be forever altered. I would no longer be the big sister she looked up to; instead, I would be the girl who did whatever it took to get thin.

By Brittany's neutral expression when I returned to the table, I guessed Lila hadn't filled her in on the bathroom episode. I was grateful for the concession. I couldn't stand the thought of Brittany fully realizing the extremity of my dieting.

Lila cleared her throat uncomfortably. Our matching dark eyes locked across the table. We had such physical similarities that many times it did seem as if I was looking at a younger version of myself. The irony was I could see the loveliness in my sister, but not in myself. The longer I stared at her, the more I discovered the same desolation reflected in her eyes, a sadness reaching to the bottomless depths of our cores.

Later, we lay silently in bed next to each other. Brittany had begged off about an hour earlier to meet up with Kurt at a party off-campus. I had disappeared into the shower at her departure, terrified of being alone with my little sister. The hot water did nothing to ease my stress or erase the feelings of filth I had over forcing myself to throw up.

Once I was beside Lila, she rested on her left hip and stared at me wide-eyed. Lila was the one person I found it the most difficult to lie to. Although we'd been close before, our bond changed after my father's death. We relied on each other and expected the other to always be honest about what we were feeling. If I was in pain, Lila would want to share it.

"You've been puking to get skinny?"

I cowered at her directness. Lila was contradictory. My mother knew her only as a mousy girl who was an average student. But Lila was a million things more than that.

I averted my eyes. "What makes you say that?"

"I don't know," she answered sarcastically, "maybe the way you run to the bathroom after you eat and the stash of snacks I found in your closet. I've never heard of a diet where Twinkies and cupcakes help you lose weight."

"Lila, it's not that big of a deal ..."

"Of course it's a big deal! I've taken health classes, Kayla, you have an eating disorder." She sat up and her eyes grew distant. "You can't do this to yourself. If you drop dead on me like Dad ..."

I bolted up straight in the bed. "You're jumping to conclusions. It's not as bad as you think. You'd be surprised how many other college girls try to get their weight down by occasionally getting sick."

"Do you hear yourself? You sound like one of the anorexic girls from the videos they show in health class to scare us to death." Kayla bit down on her lip, apparently thinking over what to say next. "I know Mom always makes us feel like we're freakishly obese, but I thought you always understood she's wrong. We never let her force us into a diet before. We'd eat her ridiculous salads and water, but then go for McDonald's runs later. What changed?"

Her words stung. How could a sixteen-year-old girl gain this much insight while I was floundering to understand my actions? How could I sit in front of her and admit something inside of me had snapped months before? I was in so much pain, and the only way I could figure out how to get rid of it was to remove as much flesh from myself as possible.

"I'm fine, Lila. I was just tired of feeling fat all the time. I probably shouldn't be throwing up, but honestly, I don't do it that often. For the most part, I only try to watch what I eat." I shrugged.

Her expression was unimpressed. "You were home for spring break and I saw what you ate. I think most days you had a piece of bread and fruit for dinner. How can you survive on that?" Her voice broke and tears rolled down her pale cheeks. She reached for me and wrapped her arms tightly around my midsection. "Each time I see you, you're shrinking more and more into yourself. I'm scared one day I'll wake up and you'll be gone for good."

"I'm sorry, Lila. I don't know what to say. I can only say I have everything under control. Although I've lost weight, I'm perfectly healthy." My voice caught on the last phrase. Although I was skinnier, I didn't feel particularly healthy. I was tired almost constantly and my stomach hurt more often than not. The acid from throwing up was also affecting my teeth and I had to be vigilant with the use of whitening strips and baking soda rinses to avoid any further damage. I wouldn't go to the dentist for fear of my bulimia being evident as soon as I opened my mouth for the exam.

"Please try to eat more. I want my sister back. Not a skeleton that resembles her." Lila was obviously trying to dispel the heaviness of the conversation, so I didn't take offense. I only hugged her tighter and leaned my chin on top of her head.

We sat there wordlessly for a long time. I couldn't make her any promises. I was too far gone. I couldn't simply begin eating normally and allow pound after pound of fat to accumulate beneath my skin. The thought sickened me. I was sorry for the pain I was causing Lila, but gaining weight was one of my deepest and darkest fears.

CHAPTER TWENTY

The images on the TV passed before my eyes in a blur. Beautiful faces all staring back at me, secret smiles playing on their lips, bliss shining through their eyes. I envied everything about them—their effortless beauty, their thin and toned bodies. But most of all, I coveted their happiness.

I was sprawled across Cameron's couch. Minutes earlier, he had come up next to me and tried to coax me to dinner. I waved him off, but he was persistent. He had spent the past hour cooking spaghetti and meatballs while I was a motionless blob on his couch. The least I could do was eat, but at that second I'd rather have traveled to the depths of Hell than put food in my body.

My funk had worsened since Lila left to return home the previous weekend. I missed her fiercely. She had left on a sour note, her disapproval over my diet still clear in the tightness of her expression. "Think about what Dad would say," she told me. It was a manipulative thing to say and her words haunted me. I didn't want to think about my father. He was dead; thinking about him only reminded me of the years that stretched ahead of me, where I'd have to endure without him.

I tuned back into Cameron's words. "Kayla, I've been looking forward to having a romantic dinner with you all week. Can you try a little?"

My body felt heavy as I got up from the sofa. If everyone claimed I was so thin, why did I feel so weighted down? I shuffled along behind him as he led me to the table.

It was beautifully set. He had lit a single white candle and positioned it between our place settings. A filled wine glass sat beside a plate covered with steaming hot pasta smothered in marinara sauce with meatballs. Any girl would be thrilled to find her boyfriend had gone to the trouble to be romantic—but I was far from any girl.

I felt myself growing irate as I collapsed into the chair. I wasn't sure why he couldn't understand I was trying to avoid fatty foods. Instead of supporting my efforts, my friends and family seemed to be determined to undermine everything I'd done to better myself.

Cameron ate silently for several minutes. My dinner lay untouched, and I felt time slow down as I waited for him to finish. I wasn't going to be bullied into eating when food was the last thing I wanted in my body.

His eyes turned cold as he stared at me. "What are you doing? Why haven't you started eating?"

I was a petulant child, refusing to eat, despite the promises the food in front of me would make me healthy again. I pressed my lips together in a tighter line and crossed my arms over my chest.

Cameron's temper was building. I could feel the tension in the air. He was showing restraint when all he probably wanted to do was to scream at me for my irrational behavior. His voice was strained. "Kayla, you've been here all day and you haven't eaten a thing …"

My expression was deadly as we locked gazes. "When the hell did it become everyone's business whether or not I eat? Last time I checked, it was my body."

I could tell what he was thinking by the way his features twisted. This wasn't me. This wasn't the quiet and meek girl he'd been dating. This girl was bitter and wanted to unleash her rage on those around her.

"Lila called me, Kayla," Cameron said in a resigned tone. I hadn't successfully incited his anger. He refused to be pushed away. I could play chicken with him endlessly—he'd still never be the first one to yield.

"Why would my sister call you?"

"She told me she heard you throwing up in the bathroom. She found a stockpile of snacks and thinks you've been forcing yourself to get sick for a while now to lose weight…"

"Lila is sixteen years old. She's a child and has no right to make accusations and go behind my back and call my boyfriend."

"Kayla, she's scared. And so am I," he admitted. "You never want to do anything because you're tired all the time. You're constantly canceling our plans because you claim you're not feeling well …"

"I don't want to hear this. You and Lila had no right to talk about me behind my back." I jumped up from the table, knocking over my chair in the process.

"Kayla, you have to start eating better. These habits aren't healthy," he insisted. Getting out of his chair, he took careful, measured steps across the room.

"You said Scarlett does crazy diets all the time. It's not that big of a deal to try different things to lose weight," I countered.

"That's not what you're doing. Your diet has turned into something else entirely," he said softly.

"Fine! You want me to eat, then I'll eat." I shoved past him roughly and headed to his cupboards. Opening one of the cabinets, I blindly grabbed at packages of food. After ripping into a box of cookies, I shoved a handful in my mouth. Crumbs tumbled out of my mouth as I demanded, "Is this what you want? Does it make you *happy*? Because

I'm sure I won't be hearing from you once I become fat again."

"Cut it out."

I removed a box of cereal from his cabinet. I shoveled fistful after fistful of the sugary flakes into my mouth. Rummaging through his other cabinets, I found a half-empty box of doughnuts. I devoured them in quick bites, powder caking over my lips.

"This is fucking crazy, Kayla." Cameron was planted in the center of the kitchen. I saw the suffering on his face after I polished off a third donut. He appeared unsure if he should stop me since I was actually eating or if he should protest my binging in his presence.

"What, Cameron?" I taunted. "You don't like to see the fat girl inside of me eat? Or you don't like the realization that this disgusts you and deep down you're actually a hypocrite?"

"That's not it and you know me better than that." I could hear a quiet rage in his voice. "You need help and you refuse to do anything about it. You're better than this, Kayla. Your dad would hate to know his death was doing this to you."

I stopped guzzling down a can of soda at his words. "Don't you dare bring my father into this." I darted away from him, heading toward the bathroom. Three feet from the door, Cameron's strong arms encircled me from behind. "What are you doing?" I cried.

"You're not going into the bathroom and throwing that food up," he said fiercely to my back.

I tried to squirm out of his hold, but he only tightened his grip. "You're the one with the problem," I said. "Does it make you feel like a big strong man to be able to hold down your one-hundred-and-five-pound girlfriend?"

"I know you probably hate me right now, but I can't watch you hurt yourself anymore. We're going to get you help," he said, clearly agonized.

"Cameron, let me go!" I screamed.

My thoughts were irrational. I couldn't think of anything else except getting the food out of me. The more seconds that passed, the more time the food would have to digest and be stuck inside me forever.

I swung around and pelted his chests with my fists. "Why are you doing this to me? Can't you see what kind of pain I'm in? Just let me go to the bathroom. Please!"

"Kayla, please, we can get through this together. Why can't you see that you're so fucking beautiful? It wouldn't matter to me if you were three hundred pounds ..." he choked out. His eyes flooded, and I turned my face away in horror. I bucked wildly against him and his hold slipped enough to permit me to free myself from his arms and sprint into the bathroom.

Slamming the door shut and locking it, I desired nothing more than to collapse onto the floor and disappear into oblivion. Instead, I shoved my finger down my throat and vomited. By the time I was finished, my cheeks were soaked with tears. With a sob, I clutched at the edge of the porcelain sink.

How could I leave the sanctity of the bathroom? Once my body had been purged of every last morsel of food, lucidity returned. I'd just screamed at and assaulted the kindest, most honest person in my life. What kind of sane person could deal with my baggage? It was over. I suspected I'd finally pushed Cameron to the point where he'd no longer want anything to do with me.

Cameron's eyes were red-rimmed when I slunk out of the bathroom ten minutes later. My plan was to leave; to grab my things and disappear wordlessly, an attempt to give him an easy out.

"I'll just leave ..." Docile Kayla was back. My enraged other half fled the scene of the crime, leaving behind tears and recriminations in her wake.

After a couple of hesitant steps, I felt Cameron's hands wrap around my elbows. "We need to talk."

"This is too much for you. I don't need you to say the words—I get it. I'm messed up, and you don't want a head case for a girlfriend."

"That's not what I was going to say." He shook his head. "I was going to tell you we'll find someone for you to talk to. Would you just meet with a doctor? See what they have to say?"

His tone was full of hope. I don't know what I'd done to deserve him. He had the perfect opportunity to escape from my poisonous personality and he was refusing to leave.

"I'm not sure if I can," I told him. "I have a hard time picturing going to therapy and confessing all my issues to some stranger." I stared at the floor. Angus had come up next to me and rubbed against my leg. It felt like he could sense my pain and wanted to extinguish it.

"Kayla, I'm not going to sit by and do nothing. I know you refuse to believe it, but you've ruined me for any other girl. You'll always be the only girl I want. I've made so many plans for us in my head. The semester is ending and I don't want you to go back home to Red Bank. I was going to ask if you wanted to stay here for the summer until you move back to campus." He stopped his rambling speech and pressed his fingers under my chin, lifting my head to face him directly. "Kayla, I love you."

His words felt like a physical blow. I staggered backwards and set my palm over my heart. "Cameron, no …"

"I do, Kayla, I love you. I've been terrified to say it to you. I had a feeling it would freak you out, but I don't care. You need to hear that I love you so much it kills me inside to realize how much pain you're in." His eyes were full of emotion, forcing me to withstand the intensity of his feelings.

How could he love me? We'd only been together three months, three months of being plagued by my own self-hatred. Moments ago, I had gone on a rampage and attacked him, unprovoked. What had he seen inside me that made him believe he loved me?

How could I love someone? I hated myself so much at times I wished I never existed. I didn't feel like I deserved love, so how would I be able to return the sentiment?

"Cameron, I can't …" I gasped out. I couldn't bear it—I had to run away as swiftly as possible. *Run fat girl, run as fast as you can*, an inner voice taunted.

Out of the corner of my eye, I saw my purse on the floor. I made a grab for it.

"I love you Kayla and I'm not going to stop fighting for you," he said.

Who was this man before me? Cameron was the most easygoing person I'd ever met. This was Cameron showing me how deep his feelings ran, and he was primed to annihilate the walls I'd put in place.

"Stop it," I hissed. "You don't want me. I'm radioactive—I poison everything around me."

Cameron opened his mouth to protest, but I was gone before he could utter a word. His words would have fallen on deaf ears. A cacophony of voices inside my head was rising up together, blocking out everything else. Screaming, *Fat, fat, fat!* over and over again.

CHAPTER TWENTY-ONE

I was more alone than ever. Instantly, I had pushed away everyone I cared about. Lila was cold and distant; she was at a loss about how to deal with a sister no longer fitting her ideal. My roommates walked on eggshells around me, afraid to say the wrong thing and send me over the edge. And Cameron ...

I couldn't process the fallout with Cameron. It had been two sleepless nights since I last saw him. I had sent him a text, asking for my space and an empty promise I'd call him after I figured some things out. He had called me, but I let my voicemail pick up. He begged me to call him, to not run away from him, but I had nothing to say that would fix things.

The dorm was quiet as I sat alone in my room. Since it was a Saturday, my floor mates had gone out for the night. I hadn't told them about my problems with Cameron, so they assumed I was spending the night with him. I wanted so badly to talk to them at that moment, to explain my feelings without fear they'd pass judgment.

Logging onto my computer, I opened my browser and typed in: anorexia. My eyes skimmed over the medical information. There were endless websites dedicated to the dangers and complications associated with anorexia and bulimia. My mind blocked out words like "get help" and "accept your body." After scrolling through the search results, I found a site called Pro-Ana.

As I read through the forum posts, something clicked inside me. The girls on the site sounded just like me. They also only wanted to be thin and beautiful. They'd gone through similar setbacks and struggled with people saying the way they ate was "sick" and "wrong." There was even a list of tips on how to stop eating and if you were going to purge after meals, what were the best foods to eat.

I typed a quick message using the screen name DisappearingGirl21. **I could really use some advice. I've lost 40 pounds since January and everyone was saying how fab I looked once I started dropping the pounds. Now, they're accusing me of having an eating disorder and want me to start gaining weight. Right now I try to eat around 500 calories and on binge days, I'll purge out my big meal. I don't want to lose everyone in my life, there's also a guy I really care about, but I can't just pig out again and get fat. What should I do?**

Five minutes later I received a reply back from Anonymous413. **Your friends are just jealous and you should ignore what they say. Surround yourself with people who aren't haters and who won't try to put doubts in your head. Look at old pictures of yourself to recall how awful you used to look and as a reminder of how far you've come.**

My eyes cut to the family photo on my desk. I was certainly rounder in the photo, but I didn't experience disgust looking at myself forty pounds heavier. I coveted the smile of old Kayla. It lit up her entire face, crinkling the edges of her eyes.

ClaudiaNoShame piped in with a reply to my forum post. **Your best bet is to hide your ED from them. There's a ton of excuses you can give them over why** you're not eating. Like I tell people I have food allergies or I'm on meds that mess with my appetite. Or a lot of times, I carry around a piece of food, like a cookie or a bagel, and throw away little pieces when they're not looking.

I stayed online until another reply appeared from another user called ThinNatalie17. When you binge you have to be sneaky about it too. The best place to do it is in the shower. The noise of the water will drown out the sound and it'll also make clean up a cinch. If you can't do it in the shower, you can always crank up your iPod or use a bathroom with super loud hand dryers.

Hours later, after exchanging back and forth messages with the girls on Pro-Ana, I felt lighter, less anxious. Maybe I wasn't as messed up in the head as I thought. The girls insisted there was nothing wrong with wanting to be skinny. We lived in a society where thin meant beautiful.

The advice that hit home the most was I needed to stop talking about dieting and losing weight. These topics would be red flags to the people around me. I had to be a play actor, imitating a girl who ate like a normal person, hiding her dirty shame behind closed doors.

"Hi, I'd like to make an appointment to see one of the counselors."

I swallowed hard as I waited on the line for the secretary to return with open appointment times. The college offered psychiatric services for free to students. I could call and set up an evaluation session and from there the counselor would recommend services provided through the campus.

"How does Wednesday at nine sound?" The secretary chirped in my ear. I didn't have classes at the time and agreed readily. She told me to arrive ten minutes early to fill out some paperwork. I would have to decide on the spot about how to answer intrusive questions about my mental state.

After disconnecting with the health center, I debated whether to call Cameron. If I was perfectly honest with myself, I'd made the appointment solely because of him. The fact was being separated from him was killing me a little bit more each day. Each time I closed my eyes, I would see the hurt on his face as I tore out of his apartment. I would replay his words again and again. *"Kayla, I love you."*

I tried to reach inside myself and find the ability to tell him I felt the same way. But each time, I found the intense feelings I had for him locked away. It was as if I had an internal security system in place not allowing me to get too close to him. If I showed my vulnerability and permitted myself to love him, I'd never recover from the damage if he ended up hurting me.

After I'd left his apartment, I convinced myself it would be best to walk away. Nothing good could come of our relationship. I was unraveling, and I couldn't expect him to put me back together.

The problem lay with the ache I felt being apart from him. Being with him for such a short time had been a tease, and I wanted so much more. I wanted a thousand nights locked in his arms, his deep voice whispering secrets into my ear, lulling me into a dreamless sleep. With him gone, I couldn't get lost in his presence, and I found myself returning often to the day I found my father's corpse; his body already decomposing under the sweltering summer sun.

I resolved to call Cameron after I went through my first counseling session. His insistence I needed therapy hadn't resounded in me, but I could continue my playacting for his benefit. He was worth it—he was worth everything.

Time slowed down as I waited for my appointment. I hoped talking to a counselor would be enough for Cameron. If he saw how much I was willing to make an effort, maybe it would appease him for the time being. He couldn't expect me to fix everything overnight. With the encouragement of my Pro-Ana friends, I was finding myself closing in on the elusive one hundred pounds I'd decided was my new weight loss goal. It was funny how once I surpassed my previous goal weights, I had never felt satisfied. I would focus on more stubborn fat on my body I couldn't seem to get rid of.

On the night before my counseling appointment, Brittany called me from her cell phone around midnight. I could barely make out what she was saying because of the loud music blaring in the background. Brittany and the twins had headed out hours earlier to bar hop, since they didn't have classes the next day and I had begged off, figuring I'd go to bed early to make sure I got enough sleep before my therapy evaluation.

"Hello," I mumbled. I answered the phone in a half-dream state. I'd been in the midst of a nightmare where I was trapped on the ground of our backyard. I couldn't move or scream, my body glued to the freshly cut lawn.

"Kayla!" Brittany called out over the noise. Without preamble, she demanded, "Why didn't you tell me you broke up with Cam?"

"Huh?"

"We're at Hunter's," Brittany said, naming a bar in town, "and Cam is here, completely wasted. I went over to say hi and I could tell right away something was wrong. He barely mumbled a hello. When I asked him what was going on, he said you ended things with him last week. Kayla, I felt like a moron for not knowing my best friend broke up with her boyfriend!"

I had to strain to hear her over the noise of the bar. "Is he okay?"

"No, he's not okay! He looks like his dog just died! What happened?"

I groaned. "I can't get into it over the phone. I'm going to throw on some clothes and come there to talk to him. See you in a few."

Before she could reply, I hung up. I reached into my closet and put on the first thing my hand connected with, a black, knee-length dress with cap sleeves. After putting on a pair of heels, I grabbed my makeup bag, figuring I'd attempt to fix my hair and makeup while driving, and ran out of the dorm.

I had to make things right with Cameron. If I didn't work things out with him straightaway, I ran the risk of losing him forever. I was constantly putting restrictions on our relationship—how close he was allowed to get to me, how much of my body I permitted him to see—and it hadn't stopped him from relentlessly trying to break down the protective walls I had built since my father died.

For the past few weeks, I'd believed our relationship couldn't work. That it was impossible to have a boyfriend while I was obsessed with getting my body the way I wanted it. Yet, according to the new friends I made through Pro-Ana, it was possible to have a boyfriend. The key was to hide my habits from him and put on a normal façade. Shockingly, girls on the site had come forward claiming their boyfriends not only knew about their anorexia, but were also fine with it.

Hunter's was crowded when I arrived. I earned a couple of appreciative double takes as I pushed my way through, searching for Brittany or Cameron. It stung to remember how invisible I had been before I lost weight. I was finally becoming beautiful enough to be noticed.

Danielle spotted me quickly. Brittany was standing next to her and they both moved toward me after Danielle tapped my best friend on the shoulder and gestured in my direction. Brittany's eyebrows were pulled together and I could see the annoyance shining in her eyes. Gradually, I'd been pulling back from our friendship, and this was going to sting more than any of my other past mistakes. I should've turned to Brittany as soon as I fought with Cameron, but I was confused about how to explain the fallout without admitting to my eating disorder.

"You said you were seeing Cam later and that's why you weren't coming out with us tonight," Brittany said. "What else have you been lying to me about?"

Danielle seemed to notice a few bar patrons gaze at us with interest. In a harsh whisper, she commanded, "Keep it down, Britt. People are starting to stare."

"What's wrong with you? I've been there for you! I held your hand at your father's funeral! I've defended you to your crazy mom!" Brittany's skin was flushed and her fists clenched. "Now, you decide to push me away!"

"I'm sorry. I've been going through some stuff ..."

"We're all going through stuff, but it doesn't mean you ignore me for months! Do you have any clue what's going on with anyone else? Or have you become as self-absorbed as your mom?"

I took a shaky step back. Saying I was like my mom was the worst type of character assassination, and Brittany was well aware of that fact. Brittany's eyes flashed, and I realized she wasn't giving up. "Cam thinks I need mental help," I admitted softly, "so I decided I needed some time apart to figure things out."

Brittany's dangerous expression faded. "Kayla, you could've just told me."

My eyes swept between Brittany and Danielle. "I was embarrassed. It's not exactly flattering to confess your boyfriend thinks you're crazy."

"Oh, Kayla," Brittany said with an emphatic shake of her head. "Cam doesn't think you're crazy. He sees what we all do: You're grieving and need to talk to someone to work through it."

"I should've told you, but I didn't want to say it out loud, like if I talked about it, then it would be true and things were really over between us." As we talked, I was scanning the bar, trying to find him. Even if we were falling apart, I was eager to see him again. My body craved him like a drug.

"Cam is heartbroken, Kayla. If you don't want things to be over, they won't be. Cam is a fantastic guy and he's only trying to help you," Danielle said. Once she stepped aside, I was able to narrow in on Cameron. My friends had been blocking my view while they reamed me out.

His body was angled away from me and I doubted he'd caught sight of me yet. Several empty tumblers and shot glasses were littered in front of him, and I cringed. Obviously, he'd been drinking for a while, and I wasn't sure how it would affect his willingness to talk to me. He was with two friends from work, and although they seemed to like me, I wasn't sure I'd be a welcome sight after hurting their friend.

While I remained unseen, I studied him. Intoxication didn't diminish his handsomeness. His white, button-down shirt enhanced his tanned skin and the sleeves were tight around the swell of his biceps. He had done his usual haphazard hairstyle with his hair spiked in the front. He achieved sexiness effortlessly. Liquid heat churned in my belly merely from being close to him.

"Go and make nice with him. You know you want to," Brittany whispered in my ear. After a sidelong look at her, I was relieved to see her anger at me had dissipated and she had a teasing grin. Brittany was right; we'd been through a lot together, and I understood how important it was to keep our friendship intact.

Pete and Chad's eyes widened at my approach. It took a second too long for Cameron to detect my presence. Our conversation could be pointless, since the amount he'd clearly had to drink would likely make him forget anything I said. Instead of a greeting, Cameron's mouth turned down. His eyes tore away from my face and he instead faced his friends. "I'm leaving. I'll call you guys later."

Without preamble, he shot to his feet and elbowed past me. I swallowed hard and followed on his heels. Once he made it outside, I caught up to him and dug my nails into his arm to stop him. His feet stayed planted, but he refused to look at me.

"You have every right to be pissed at me," I said. "The way I acted at your house … The way I've been acting … has been unfair to you. I obviously have a problem; and instead of dealing with it, I ran away from you. I'm not the best at confrontation."

Finally, he pivoted to face me. "Why are you here? Is it to torture me some more?"

"Cameron, I never … I would never do anything to deliberately hurt you. These past few months with you have meant everything to me. You've been so good to me and I care about you so much—"

"Just stop it," he snarled as he hunched down to lean close to my face. "Stop trying to let me down easy. I told you I love you and you ran away from my house like it was on fire. Then, all I get is a text saying you need space. I should've seen this coming. I seem to have that effect on people. You're not the first person I cared about that left me." He swayed on his feet and I placed my hands on his elbows to steady him. I could hear the pain behind his words, and I understood there were mysteries about Cameron I had yet to uncover. I wanted to ask him about the person who left him, but it would have to wait for another time.

"I messed up and I'm ready to take responsibility for the way I've been acting," I said. "I made an appointment with a counselor. My first session is tomorrow."

The hard line of his jaw relaxed and I could see his eyes grow tender. He understood what a monumental step it was for me. I had closed myself off from everyone I cared about, and it was a big deal for me to agree to talk about my problems with a therapist. He blinked rapidly and I wished I could be inside his head, be privy to what he was thinking.

"That's good. I'm happy for you," he said and stepped back. My hands dropped to my sides. He bit his lip, and I wondered what he was trying to prevent himself from saying.

"I feel sick over what happened last time I saw you. It's what made me realize I need to deal with my problems." I willed him to hear the pleading in my voice. I knew I was lost, and he was one of the few things preventing me from dissolving completely.

"Kayla …" he started uncertainly.

"Can we go somewhere and talk? I can't stand how we left things."

"I don't think it's a good time right now. I drank way too much and I'll probably end up saying things I'll want to take back once I'm sober," he said, and he moved to leave.

"Cameron, you're too drunk to drive. Let me at least bring you home," I offered. "I can call Danielle to swing by and pick me up after they leave the bar. She's the designated driver for the night."

His expression was uncertain, but he couldn't argue with my logic. Cameron wasn't reckless with his body the way I was. Silently, he handed me his keys and led me to his car. My nerves made my hands unsteady as I opened the car door and climbed into the driver's seat.

The silence was oppressive inside the Mustang. Although I sensed Cameron's eyes on me as I drove, I kept my gaze fixed on the road. We were always at ease with each other, and it felt uncomfortable to sit there and not talk to or touch him. The drive to his building felt as if it took ages.

When I pulled up, I turned off the ignition and angled my body toward him. His eyes had closed, and the soft sound of his regulated breathing let me know he had fallen asleep. My fingers reached out and stroked his cheek tenderly. The movement disturbed his sleep and his hand shot out and held my fingers in place. Without a second's hesitation, I crossed the space between us and landed on his lap. I settled my knees on the outside of his thighs to be face-to-face with him.

"I've missed you," I said hoarsely.

His fingers grazed my cheek before passing over my lips. His eyes settled on my mouth and I felt a familiar burning deep inside.

"I thought you were lost to me. I put myself out there and felt like such an asshole when I realized you didn't feel the same way."

"I would never be lost to you," I whispered. I crushed my mouth against his and he parted his lips in anticipation. Each nerve ending tingled as I rocked my hips back and forth over him as we kissed. I was overcome with desire and I wanted to possess him completely in that moment.

My body hummed as he slipped his tongue down the nape of my neck. His hands cupped my breasts and I arched back to clue him in on how wild he was driving me. His palms dipped inside of the top of my dress and stroked my nipples through the cotton of my bra, "Cameron …" I moaned.

I fumbled for the buckle of his pants before pulling aside my underwear. I was ready for him and primed to explode if I didn't feel him inside me soon. After some fumbling for a condom in his wallet, he was ready for me. Once we joined, I was overcome by the feeling that I belonged with him. I gripped the back of his head and we both finished in a dizzying rush.

We didn't move right away. Instead, his hands surrounded me and I rested comfortably against his chest. It had been a departure from the past times we were intimate. My feelings of inadequacy led to quickies under the cloak of darkness or the reassurance of the blanket covering my body. For once, what I looked like never crossed my mind after our lips came together.

"I love you," he said reverently and I felt his lips brush against the top of my head. "I know you're not ready to tell me you love me, too. But it's okay. It doesn't change how I feel about you."

I snuggled closer to him and I wished I could stay in his arms forever, savor the sensations he brought on when we physically connected. I wanted to borrow his strength—he was the one steady thing in my chaotic universe. If the world outside his car windows disappeared, it wouldn't matter as long as I had him and his love.

CHAPTER TWENTY-TWO

"Are you sure you don't want me to wait for you?" Cameron asked.

After driving me back to the campus in the morning, Cameron walked me to the front of the health services building. Luckily, I'd left some clothes at his apartment and didn't have to rush back to the dorm to change first.

Sated from being with him again, I'd slept comfortably in his arms without worrying about my appointment. But since I'd been up, I'd been a ball of anxiety about what I was going to say during the session.

"No, I think I'll give you the day off from my craziness." But my joke fell flat, and I saw the worry lines crease his brow. He looked conflicted as he gazed past me at the few students that walked around the campus.

"Kayla, you're not crazy. You're not the first person to go through a rough patch in their life."

The tension in his body hinted that he wasn't speaking hypothetically. Brittany's accusations weren't without merit—I'd been self-involved. I never imagined Cameron could relate to the torment I was in. In my head, I had built him up to epic proportions. He was the perfect guy with the perfect life. The thought that he had his own demons stopped me in my tracks.

"Have you gone through a rough patch?" I asked cautiously.

He shoved his hands into the pockets of his jeans and leaned back onto his heels. "I guess. I don't know if you'd call it a rough patch, but I had a falling out with my mom and we don't talk anymore."

"What? I met your mom, she seems great. Was this recently?"

"I consider Maggie my real mother, and I've called her Mom since I was fourteen and she married my dad. My real mother has a drug problem, and she checked out of being a parent when I was nine. She was in and out of rehab until she relapsed and took off for good when I was eleven.

"We didn't hear from her for years and, honestly, I figured she was dead. Have you ever seen those composite sketches in the newspapers when they find a body? I would always study them to see if it was her—"

Horrified, I stopped him. "That's awful. I can't imagine how you must have felt not knowing what happened to her."

He nodded stiffly and I sensed his need to get through the story. He wanted to share a piece of himself with me, but talking about his mom was likely dredging up agonizing memories. "A few years ago, she started sending me letters, wanting to be involved in my life again. Nine years of no communication, and all of a sudden she wants to be welcomed with open arms. After I refused to write or call her, she started contacting my dad to see if he could convince me to get in touch with her."

"Cameron, I had no idea. Why didn't you tell me any of this before?"

"I'm fine with it, Kayla. I remember what it was like growing up with her and I can't forgive her for a lot of the crap she did. She'd leave me and my sister alone for hours to score drugs, bring junkies into the house when my dad wasn't around, steal our stuff to get money she needed for her habit—the list could go on and on. Scarlett is in touch with her, but she was a lot younger and doesn't remember things the way I do."

"I don't know what to say. I feel like such an idiot. I've been caught up in my own stuff. I didn't guess you had problems, too. At your house, Scarlett told me you were hurt before, so I assumed it was an ex-girlfriend she was talking about."

I almost wished for his sake it were an ex-girlfriend. Exes could be forgotten about, erased completely from our lives. But I was well aware of how difficult it was to obliterate a mother's poisonous influence from a psyche.

"Okay, I'm supposed to make you feel better, not lay my crap on you before you go into your appointment." He snatched a kiss before straightening up. "I'll be by later and we'll pick up your car from the bar."

I grabbed his elbow before he could slip away. "I'm sorry about your mom. If you ever want to talk about things, I'm a good listener."

"I know, but I swear I'm not torn up over it. I just thought it was important for you to hear you're not the only one with a crappy mother." His tone and expression didn't match up, and it was obvious he had a hard time talking about his mom. After another quick kiss, he walked back toward his car.

I was pensive as I watched him go. Each day I was with Cameron, he managed to surprise me. His confession hadn't lessened his appeal; instead, it made me feel drawn to him even more. He'd obviously been through a lot and still managed to survive. He gave me faith I could do the same.

The waiting room of health services was mostly empty. Only a handful of students sat slumped in the plastic chairs, and I didn't spot anyone I recognized. I checked in with the receptionist, and she handed me a stack of paperwork to fill out. I breezed through the sheets, answering the questions as vaguely as possible. The staff wouldn't refuse to see me if I didn't reveal my deepest and darkest secrets on a medical form.

After a while, a bespectacled man who looked about ten years my senior came to the door and called my name. His black hair was slicked back, he had a medium build, and he stood only a couple of inches taller than me. He introduced himself as Parker and explained he was one of the therapists working for the health services department. My stomach flipped as I followed him into a small office. There was no way I'd comfortably divulge my body image demons with a man not much older than me. How would he be able to understand my daily struggle to not be fat? How could I confess my darkest secrets, like the way I ate naked in front of my mirror some nights so the sight of my fat would stop me from overeating?

The room had a small desk and an office chair near the far wall with two additional chairs set on the opposite side of the desk. There were four cherry-wood bookshelves overflowing with large textbooks and a few miscellaneous knickknacks. I didn't see any personal photos or mementos, and I guessed it was a shared office space.

Parker's smile was noncommittal as we sat across from each other. He adjusted his black glasses and looked over the forms I'd filled out. Then he asked, "What brings you here today, Kayla?"

I fidgeted in my seat and played with the dangles on my bracelet for a few seconds before answering. "My friends and boyfriend are worried about me. I guess I've been acting a little depressed lately." He leaned back in his chair and studied me. Since I was new to therapy, I wasn't sure if this was a technique to get me to continue talking. But if it was, I obliged. "My dad died almost two years ago and it seems to have all of a sudden hit me hard."

"How have you been feeling lately?"

Like I'm drowning, I thought silently. "I'm sad a lot, probably more sad than I was right after he died."

He picked up a pen and drummed it steadily on the desk. "People grieve differently, and there's no exact time frame for how long it takes to get over a loss. You may have been in survival mode after losing your dad, and you suppressed the pain."

"I guess that makes sense. After he died, I was more worried about my sister than dealing with what it meant to live without him. My mother is ..." Explaining my mother would be like teaching a child about nuclear fusion; there was no way to put into a few words what she was like. More importantly, I couldn't detail how she made me feel. "My mother is selfish. Don't get me wrong, she was devastated over losing my dad, but instead of turning to my sister and me for comfort, she became hardened and lashed out at us every chance she got. Maybe it's because my sister and I look so much like our dad and we were a painful reminder of what she lost. We had to learn how to cope on our own."

"How are you coping now?"

The question was almost laughable. "I don't know, probably not well. I feel like part of me died with my father and maybe I'm only half existing in this world." I was surprised by the honesty of my answer. Actually, I couldn't believe how easy it was to talk to Parker. It was as if I had all this stuff bottled up inside and finally found an outlet to get it out.

"Have you found yourself retreating because of this feeling?"

"I guess I've checked out lately. Things that used to be important to me don't seem to matter as much. My grades have taken a nosedive, and I wonder if I should even bother coming back next year to finish my degree. I used to have fun going out with my friends, but now I don't have any motivation to be social.

"But what makes me mad is that everyone around me thinks I have a choice. I don't want to be this way. I fight against these depressed feelings each day, but I'm losing." I was losing so much more than fat in the past months. I was losing my identity and becoming someone unrecognizable in the mirror.

He put his pen down and leaned slightly back in his chair. "What made you decide you needed help dealing with your emotions?"

"I've been dating someone since February. Cameron makes me feel like, if I just allowed myself to get over my crap, I could be really happy with him. He has all the same qualities I admired in my dad; he's smart, thoughtful, and funny. But because of all of the doubts in my head, I can't give myself fully to him. And I want to. I want to so badly I hate myself for not being the girl he deserves." My fingers nervously twisted the hem of my shirt as I spoke. The embarrassment I had expected over confessing my inadequacies was nonexistent.

We talked for the full hour about my family and Cameron. Time flew by as I divulged information about my crumbling relationships. Parker took a few notes, but mostly he asked me questions to prompt me to talk. I was candid—to a point. I had resolved beforehand to not talk about my diet, and I kept that promise. I had an irrational fear if I confessed how far I was willing to go to stay skinny Parker would try to have me committed for my own safety. I'd taken my Pro-Ana friends' advice very seriously: Never let anyone know the truth about how I was able to stay thin.

Since the semester was drawing to a close, Parker recommended I see him once a week until summer break. It would only mean two more sessions, but he said I could continue therapy with another counselor back home. He also wanted me to learn how to cope with my grief. He gave me some information on bereavement groups I could attend, saying talking about my loss with others could help me heal. When I admitted I hadn't visited my father's gravesite since his funeral, he suggested I find a way to learn how to accept he was gone. I could go to the cemetery, or maybe write my father a letter to express how I'd been feeling.

When I left the student health services building, I felt lighter, no longer hindered by some of my depressed thoughts. Maybe the tide was finally turning for me; I had won Cameron back, and I was finally talking to someone about my problems. It didn't matter that I wasn't being totally forthcoming with Parker; a man wouldn't understand how important it was to be slender and beautiful. Instead of listening to others' voices about how I should eat, I would make my own choices.

My good mood didn't fade, not even when I saw it was my mother calling my cell phone. "Hello," I chirped as I walked back toward my room.

"Hello darling, glad to finally catch you. Have you been avoiding my calls?"

"No, of course not," I lied easily. "I've been overwhelmed with term papers."

"Well, at least I know it's not me. Lila said you haven't spoken with her since she visited."

I would have to rectify things with Lila immediately. I'd been furious after Cameron told me about Lila's part in revealing my secrets to him. After dodging her calls and emails for a whole week, I decided to let go of my grudge. I'd have to call Lila and let her know I forgave her for going to Cameron behind my back.

"Just been busy," I said.

"Good, I was worried something happened between the two of you while she was with you. She hid out in her room for days when she came back, and the only times I saw her she had a sour look on her face. I swear, Kayla, you have no idea what it's like to raise moody girls. Pray for boys when you have children," she said condescendingly.

I rolled my eyes as I sidestepped a group of students walking in the opposite direction. "Was there a reason for your call?"

"No need to get snippy, Kayla. It wouldn't kill you to call me every once in a while. I *am* a widow with only a sullen teenage girl for company."

I groaned. I should've figured she'd manipulate me with the guilt card. My mom had a way of always making me culpable for her erratic moods. "Let's not fight; I don't have the energy for it. How are you, Mom?"

"I'm okay enough, I suppose. I did get asked out on a date the other day while I was at the bank."

I wasn't sure why she was sharing this news. Men were constantly asking her out, regardless of her wedding ring. My father had almost come to blows more than once over a man trying to seduce my mother in his presence. In spite of her flaws, I believed she'd been faithful to my father. After his death, her misery was authentic enough I imagined no one would ever be able to replace him in her heart.

"Are you interested in dating?" I wasn't overly concerned about my mom entering the dating pool. I was more concerned about the poor man she managed to ensnare.

"I didn't think so, but I'm still in my forties. It's awfully young to spend the rest of my life alone. And Jake is very handsome! His family comes from money, too, so he drives a fabulous-looking Mercedes." Her voice rose to a high pitch and I could tell how excited she was. Maybe this development was a good thing. A new romance could put less pressure on Lila and me to maintain her impossible standards. To say the least, I wasn't looking forward to a summer at home and under her thumb.

"So, did you agree to go out with him?" I unlocked the outer door to the dorm with my card and pounded upstairs. My roommates' doors were all shut; it was still early enough they were likely still sleeping off the night before.

"We exchanged numbers, but I'm unsure. He's handsome and he has a job at a trading firm in New York, but he's a teensy bit younger than me."

"How much younger?" I was automatically suspicious.

After a lengthy pause, she said, "He's twenty-five."

I stopped in front of my door. "Mom, that's only four years older than me!"

"Well, it's not my fault I don't look my age. I'm not going to be ashamed younger men still find me attractive," she huffed. "I was honest about my age. If he doesn't have a problem with it, why should you?"

Slowly, I drew a breath in, feeling the air expand my lungs, taking the time to calm myself. "It's your life, Mom, but Lila is still at home with you. How do you think she's going to react if you introduce her to a guy that's practically her age?"

"I'll introduce her when I'm ready. Give me some credit, Kayla, I'm not going to simply bring strange men into my home and allow them to be around my daughter. If things get serious, then he can meet you both." Oh lord, I thought, that wouldn't be awkward *at all*.

"That's good to hear."

"How's your love life? Are you still involved with that idiotic boy?"

"Mom, you've made it perfectly clear you don't like him. Can you try not to resort to name-calling?" I had a few choice names to call her after her admission of dating someone decades younger, but my obedience was still too ingrained to say them.

"I'm your mother; shouldn't I tell you when I think you can do better? He may be marginally good looking." I tightened my grip on the phone. "But he was rude and disrespectful to your family. Not only that, how well off could he be? I can't imagine a credit card rep makes nearly enough money."

I reached for the aspirin on my dresser. I kept it on hand for my headaches, and a new one was starting. "Mom, do we have to argue the entire time we talk? Can't we have a normal conversation for once?"

My mom made an unpleasant noise, but finally sighed in defeat. "Fine. The other reason I called was to make sure you were coming home for Lila's prom next weekend. I'd like us to take some family pictures. We haven't had any since before your father died."

"Yes, of course I'll be there."

A couple of minutes later, I was finally able to hang up. I felt spent, and the good mood that followed my counseling appointment had vanished. In my head, I had a backbone, and I imagined telling my mother to stay the hell out of my life. But in reality, I still let her put doubts into my head. It was going to be a long summer at home.

CHAPTER TWENTY-THREE

"Remind me again why I'm helping you move farther away from me?" Cameron grunted as he carried another box toward the front of my house.

"Because you're the best boyfriend ever," I supplied, trailing behind him carrying more of my belongings.

He shook his head. "No, the best boyfriend would throw you over his shoulder and drag you back to his place."

I balanced the box in one hand and reached for his arm. "You know the reason isn't because I don't want to stay with you for the summer ..."

He turned to face me, and I saw the resignation on his face. "I understand you want to be here for Lila. Your sister would be more than welcome to stay with us."

"Cameron, first of all, my mother would never in a million years allow Lila to live with us an hour away from home. Secondly, my sister got a summer job at an ice cream parlor. She starts working in a couple of weeks."

He set the box down on the sidewalk and moved in closer to me. His hand slid down the side of my face, causing me to shiver involuntarily. After months of being together, Cameron could still spark the strongest physical urges in me. His eyes were always what affected me most; they were brimming with electricity. My eyes were deadened, their luster lost somewhere along the way.

His voice was pained as he spoke. "You've been doing so well these past few weeks. I'm afraid once you're home again, your mom will ruin the progress you've made."

I put my own box down and leaned into him. I looked up at him and smiled. It felt good to be cared about. Cameron would do anything for me and I understood his concern. "I'll be fine," I said. "Parker gave me the numbers of therapists in the area, and I'll make an appointment once I get settled. And it's not like we'll never see each other. I can come down to see you whenever I want or you can make the drive here."

"Judging from the way your mom looked at me the last time, I doubt I'll be welcome here. But you can stay with me as much as you want to. I'm going crazy already knowing I won't see you every day." Cameron brushed back my hair and teased me by brushing his lips across mine. I smiled and leaned into his mouth, pressing my lips roughly against his.

"I'm going to miss you, too," I said as I broke the kiss. I lifted up the box and gestured for him to follow me into the house.

When I crossed the threshold, I understood it was time for the spell to be broken. The last couple weeks of the semester had been flawless. Cameron had been by my side and supportive as I continued my final sessions with Parker. Therapy was an opportunity for me to vent about my mom and reminisce about the good times with my dad. More than once, I'd been on the verge of confessing my extreme dieting to Parker, but I couldn't bring myself to do it. I convinced myself it wasn't necessary; I had everything under control.

I spent most nights at Cameron's apartment while studying for my finals. The only time we were apart for a significant amount of time was for a final weekend of partying with my roommates before we all went home for the summer.

But the truth was that, beneath the perfect exterior I presented to everyone, the sinister side of myself had taken hold. I'd become a master of deception, so quick with my lies I could barely believe who I had become. I fooled everyone into accepting that I was no longer obsessed with my body. They'd been tricked into thinking I'd come to terms with my weight and had control of my unhealthier impulses.

Pro-Ana had made things much easier for me. The various Pro-Ana sites gave me all the tips I needed to conceal my diet from everyone else. I had stocked up on packages of bagels and muffins. They became my showpieces; I carried them around with me to put on the pretense I was actually eating them. Instead, I usually broke off pieces and shoved them into my pockets or purse. I had a close call one night when Angus attempted to rip through my purse to get to the goodies hidden inside.

At the dorm and at Cameron's apartment, I dirtied dishes and left them in the sink to leave the impression I'd finished a meal. When we ate dinner together, I'd take small bites and push around the rest of the food to make it look like I was eating a normal meal.

Discussing my diet or how much weight I wanted to lose was off-limits. If anyone brought up my weight loss, I shrugged it off and explained I wasn't actively dieting anymore.

My mother stood with her arms crossed in front of the stairs as we walked in. She gave Cameron a terse smile. "I'm sure we can take it from here, Cameron."

"Mom, he's staying for dinner," I said, wiping sweat from my brow. I was dressed in jeans, a t-shirt, and a spring jacket. Layering was the key to hiding my body from others. I used the excuse of my shyness to keep Cameron from seeing me fully undressed.

Cameron wasn't dumb, though; as we made love in the dark, I could feel his fingers pause for a second too long over my ribcage, hesitating like he was questioning whether my body was the way it was supposed to be.

My mother didn't answer. Pursing her cherry-stained lips, she spun on her high heels and stalked into the kitchen. I gave Cameron an apologetic shrug.

"Don't worry about it. I'll carry these up and meet you in your room. Do you have any other stuff in my car?"

"I think a couple of bags. I'll be up in a few."

Minutes later, after I'd retrieved my belongings and started up the staircase to my room, voices carried to me from above. I crept silently up the stairs and listened to a whispered conversation between Lila and Cameron.

"Cam, she's not looking any better. If anything, she looks worse than when I saw her before my prom," Lila was saying.

"She's been seeing a counselor and she's been eating in front of me. I don't know ... maybe it's going to take a while for her to put any weight back on," he said softly. There was an edge to his voice and I imagined the stressed look on his face.

"Could she be puking up the food you see her eat?" Lila asked.

"I don't think so. I think she suspects I'm watching her. She doesn't go to the bathroom after she eats like she used to. Her counselor wants her to see someone while she's home. Maybe if she keeps talking to someone, she'll be able to get a handle on things and gain some weight." Cameron paused for a second and the tension in the air thickened. "I'm afraid of saying anything to her. If I push her too much, I have a feeling she's just going to freak out and run as far away from me as she can."

"We have to do something! She looks like if I blow too hard in her direction, she'll fall over." I stumbled on the step where I stood, alerting them to my presence. "Kayla?" Lila called out hesitantly.

I stifled my emotions and plastered a counterfeit smile on my face. I made my way up the stairs until I reached my room. Lila was sitting on the edge of my bed and Cameron stood beside her awkwardly, his hands shoved in the pockets of his khaki shorts.

I dumped the shopping bags I had in my hands in the center of the floor. "I think that's the last of everything," I said brightly. I could see them exchange an uncertain glance, questioning how much I may have overheard. I stood beside Cameron and leaned my head against his shoulder. "What's wrong? Did you change your mind about staying for dinner?"

I was in a make-believe world, pretending to be someone I wasn't. I was wounded; pieces of myself had broken off and vanished forever. But I would never let anyone know it. I refused to be Cameron and Lila's pet project—it wasn't their responsibility to make me whole again. If I had to, I would push them all away and live by my own rules.

CHAPTER TWENTY-TWO

The walls are closing in on me here and I feel like I'm losing sight of my goals. I really need everyone's encouragement today!

I posted the Pro-Ana message and waited patiently for the supportive replies I would soon get. I was relying more and more on my virtual friends. Faceless girls were much easier to deal with than prying sisters and boyfriends.

I could no longer remember what I was trying to achieve. I understood I had aspirations when I started dieting, but it was fuzzy inside my muddled brain. I thought I'd be content when I was thin, but happiness was out of reach. Instead, I only craved invisibility. I avoided mirrors and hid under layers of clothes.

Did you make the Thinspiration book like I suggested?

Fifteen minutes later, the reply arrived from SkinnyGirl89. She was one of the regular visitors I'd come into contact with through the website. We had exchanged email addresses and cell phone numbers, too. There'd been some bonding once we found out we both lived in New Jersey, only about forty-five minutes away from each other. We vowed to be there for each other when we struggled to stick to our diet. Pro-Ana site visitors treated virtual oaths like blood bonds.

Reaching into the bottom drawer of my desk, I pulled out the scrapbook I assembled the week before. It was a collection of magazine cutouts featuring thin models with perfect bodies. They wore skimpy clothing and bikinis, outfits I'd only wear if I lost enough weight. The idea behind making a book was to look at the pictures whenever doubts threatened to make me lose my focus.

Yes, I cut out some pics from a few fashion magazines. Should I add anything else? I sent my reply and cracked my knuckles as I waited to hear back from SkinnyGirl89.

I like to add quotes to the book, too, and put them around the pictures. Here are a few favorites: "Nothing tastes as good as thin feels," "The thinner is the winner," and "Your stomach isn't growling, it's applauding."

Being home for a month had given me too much downtime, and I retreated further into myself. I no longer had the distractions of school, my college friends, or Cameron. My best friend from high school, Tami, had tried to make plans since I'd gotten back home, but I'd blown her off. Running into someone I hadn't seen in a while was unbearable; I couldn't stand the pitiful expressions. My paranoia had convinced me that after one look at me, they'd be able to see how shattered I was on the inside.

I rarely ventured out, and despite my promises to see Cameron as often as possible, we'd only seen each other twice since I moved back. I could hear the worry in his voice when I canceled plans, but I was avoiding him since his conversation with Lila. I also dodged his questions about whether I had set up an appointment with a therapist in town. I lied and said the counselor Parker recommended had a waiting list and would not be able to see me until July, a month away.

I stopped typing out my reply to SkinnyGirl89 when I heard my cell phone ring. It was Cameron's third call of the day. I had ignored the first two, lacking the motivation to make excuses about why I couldn't see him later. I knew I was just avoiding the inevitable; I couldn't keep dodging him forever.

"Hi," I answered tonelessly.

"Hey, I've been trying to get you all day. Is everything all right?"

"Yes, I'm bugging out about work. I'm trying to catch up today. I have three articles due by tonight that I've barely started."

Work was becoming my standard excuse. Since I wrote articles, I was able to fib about deadlines to avoid both Lila and Cameron. Lila was harder to evade, since we shared a wall, but I usually only ventured out of my room when she was at school. My avoidance of the two closest people to me stemmed from the idea they were exchanging notes on how I looked and how much I ate. I believed Lila kept a journal, recording each thing that passed my lips, along with a log of when I used the bathroom. I was suspicious, imagining my sister making covert calls to relay this information to Cameron.

"Kayla, why are you avoiding me? You said yesterday you'd be caught up on your articles and you'd stay at my place tonight." I could feel his frustration through the line.

"I'm not avoiding you. Of course I miss you. I'm trying to make as much money as possible so I don't have to work when school starts again."

"Kayla, you write your articles online. Why can't you bring your laptop and work here?"

I tried to sound coy. "Too many distractions?"

"Kayla, I need to see you," he said. "We're only an hour apart and I haven't been with you in two weeks. If something is going on … if there's someone else, you need to be honest with me."

The idea of there being another guy was laughable. The only man I saw on a regular basis was the guy who worked at the twenty-four-hour convenience store. I would stop there a couple of times a week to stock up on my binge foods. I'd go in there incognito, wearing a baseball cap and baggy clothes to hide my identity, and, not surprisingly, the clerk had addressed me as "sir" more than once.

As my conversation with Cameron hit a lull, I asked myself again, why couldn't I just let him go? I was hurting us both by not ending things. Still, I felt like there were two sides of my personality: There was the other Kayla, who wanted to run back to Cameron, kiss him into oblivion and forget the bullshit keeping us apart; and there was the Kayla of the here and now, who realized the minute he saw how much more weight I'd lost, he'd combine forces with my sister to stage an intervention.

"There's no one else ..." Tears strangled my words. "There will never be anyone else."

"Kayla, just get in the car and drive to my apartment. Or, I get off of work in an hour, and I can come to you. I'll do whatever it takes to see you tonight." His voice was gruff and I suddenly missed him desperately. What was wrong with me? How could my weight be more important than the feelings I had for this mind-blowing guy?

"I can't," I whispered. "I'll call you soon." I hung up and turned off my phone to prevent him from calling me back. I had to get my head together before talking to him again. Cameron deserved better and I would have to figure out if I could give him what he needed.

My mom was in the living room watching TV when I walked robotically downstairs. She'd been dating Jake for a while, which kept her distracted enough that I didn't have to deal with her overpowering personality on a regular basis. She had dropped several hints about Lila and me meeting her boyfriend, but we'd avoided it thus far.

She turned to face me, her lovely features pinched together. Although it was the middle of the afternoon on a weekday, Charlotte Marlowe was dressed to the nines. Her red silk blouse and white Capri pants were simple and stylish, and she appeared even more statuesque with her six-inch heels. My frumpy sweatpants, paired with Cameron's Rutgers sweatshirt, wouldn't go unnoticed.

"It's alive!" she quipped. "My lord, Kayla, you look like one of the extras from that zombie show your sister is so fond of." She did a quick onceover of my appearance as I collapsed onto the loveseat. Bringing my knees to my chest, I turned away from her unsettling inspection and looked toward the TV.

My mother cleared her throat. "Kayla, it's wonderful you were able to lose weight, but I think it's time to work on the rest of your appearance. How about I make an appointment for us at my salon? The staff there could do wonders with your hair and nails." My nails were brittle, splitting apart and forcing me to keep them cut to the quick. And despite the expensive conditioner my mother had purchased, my hair was thin and dull.

"I don't want to go to the salon with you," I muttered and reached for the remote.

My mother injected false cheer into her voice, her lips twisting into her version of a smile. "Kayla, we'll have loads of fun! We can go get spray tans after! It's the start of summer, and you should have some color."

I would have rather gouged my own eyes out than go with my mother for spray tans. Instead, I said dejectedly, "Maybe some other time, Mom."

"What's wrong with you? Did Cameron break up with you? Because I simply can't understand what all this moping is about."

"I don't know, Mom, maybe I miss Dad like crazy. Not all of us can move on as quickly as you can," I snapped. I covered my mouth with my hand, startled by my own outburst. Submissive Kayla was being pushed aside by angry and bitter Kayla.

My mother rose above me, her expression stern. "You have no idea what you're talking about. Your father loved me and would want to see me happy. You're disgracing his memory by wallowing in your own self-pity. When you want to act like a grown-up, come find me, and we'll talk."

I flinched at her words. Her back was rigid as she stormed from the room. If my plan was to drive everyone away, it was working perfectly. My stomach growled, begging to be fed. I drove my fingernails into my palm, hoping the pain would silence the noise in my gut, and I fell back onto the loveseat, curled into a ball. Then, I pushed my face into the cushion and screamed.

CHAPTER TWENTY-THREE

I had no idea how much time had passed while I stayed in the same position. The living room darkened, casting late-afternoon shadows across the wood flooring. I couldn't move. Nothing could rouse me, not even the insistent ringing of the doorbell. My mother strode into the room, glaring at me, before answering the door.

"I'd say what a pleasant surprise, but we'd both know that was a lie," she said. "She's in the living room. Maybe you can talk some sense into her because I'm done with her melodrama."

Heavy footsteps pounded in my direction. It took too much energy to lift my head, provoking me to stay still. A masculine growl grabbed my attention and I moved my head toward the disruption. My attention was captivated by a gorgeous set of deep blue eyes. They were filled with too many emotions for me to discern. Before I could prepare a response, a familiar pair of hands was lifting me off the loveseat. Faltering as my feet hit the ground; it took a moment for me to regain my bearings. When I came out of my stupor, I realized Cameron was standing before me.

My mother was behind him with her arms folded across her chest. They were staring at me expectantly, and it felt as if I was on trial and they were to be the ones to decide my fate. My lack of food and the sudden movement off the loveseat left me dizzy, and I grabbed the end table for balance.

I managed to croak out, "What are you doing here?"

Cameron stepped forward and cradled my face in his palms. "I was worried, Kayla. You hung up on me and then didn't answer the phone. I thought something was wrong."

"I'm sorry you wasted your time. As you can see, I'm perfectly all right," I mumbled. I tried to take a step forward, but I stumbled again. Cameron pulled me toward him. Before I could react, I felt his hands slip under the edge of my sweatshirt and wrap around my waist.

I squirmed out of his grasp, but by the look on his face I could tell I was too late. Instead of addressing me, he spun on my mother. "Do you not see her? She's been here a month. Have you bothered to *look* at her?"

My mother's mouth hung open. Cameron didn't wait for a reply. Instead, he crouched a little until his eyes were level with mine. "Babe, we're leaving here. Let's go pack your things. You can't stay in this house anymore."

He took me by the hand and led me toward the stairs. I flung his hand away. "What are you doing?"

"Kayla, you need help. I can feel the bones sticking out of your skin. I'll be the asshole here if I have to, but I'm taking you to a doctor. This has gone on long enough." He was practically snarling, and I could see a vein pulsing on his forehead.

I dug in my heels as he tried to reach for me again. "Stop it Cameron! I'm not going anywhere. I'm not someone you need to save." I narrowed my eyes before sneering, "I'm not your mom."

I had verbally punched him in the face. His jaw went slack and an angry flush colored his cheeks. "That was a really shitty thing to say. I'm going to chalk it up to you being sick and let it slide." He spoke through clenched teeth.

"It's true though, isn't it? You couldn't make her better and you can't deal with it. Now, you've decided I need mending. You're using me to make up for the things that happened to you as a kid. You couldn't be a rescuer back then and you want the chance to be my knight in shining armor."

I was a monster. His love for me was beautiful and I was twisting it into something hideous. I was trying to hurt him where I knew his deepest vulnerability lay. I wasn't merely pushing Cameron away—I was attempting to hurl him into a black hole with the promise he would never return again.

His breathing was labored and I had stunned him speechless. My mother intervened and stepped between us. The mask of disdain she typically wore in his presence faded and she spoke to him gently. "Why don't we talk outside for a minute?"

If Cameron had earned my mother's sympathy, I must've turned into something truly heinous. I forced my body to turn away as she walked him outside. I couldn't stand to see the hurt and rage directed at me. He'd let me in, revealing the ghosts from his past that haunted him, and I'd used it against him. But I was delusional enough to believe I had done it for his own good. I tried my hardest to make things work, to have a normal relationship, but I couldn't pretend any longer.

My mother was expressionless when she found me in the kitchen twenty minutes later. I was gulping down water, another pointer provided to me by Pro-Ana to stave off hunger. With a long-suffering sigh, she sank into one of the kitchen chairs and really looked at me for the first time in ages.

As seconds passed, I could no longer take the tension. "Did he leave?"

"Yes, he's gone."

The statement made me feel like I'd just been given a prognosis of a terminal disease. My breath whooshed out of me and the room started to spin. I thought I must have been having an out-of-body experience, because that couldn't possibly be what my life had come to. Being thin was supposed to be the key to unlocking the joy shut away inside of me. My intentions were never to be left alone and dejected.

My mother's gaze turned shrewd. "How much do you weigh now?"

"I'm not answering that question," I replied primly, and I returned to guzzling my water. Raw grief was a raging fire through me and I was trying to extinguish it. Once I pulled the bottle away from my mouth, I asked, "What did you say to him?"

Before she could answer, I heard the front door open and slam shut. Lila charged into the kitchen. Her backpack fell to the floor as her eyes bounced back and forth between my mother and me. "What's going on?"

"I believe your sister just broke things off with her boyfriend." My mom addressed Lila, but her eyes stayed on me.

Lila's dark eyes grew large. She demanded, "What? Is that true?"

I could hear the hurt in her tone. I wasn't surprised by her reaction; Cameron had become like a surrogate big brother to her. Besides clandestine conversations regarding my well-being, they enjoyed spending hours playing Xbox when the three of us were together. I would watch from the couch, giggling as the two of them talked trash while shooting each other with virtual machine guns.

"I don't want to talk about it," I mumbled and started to leave the kitchen. I wanted to warn them: proceed with caution. I was highly combustible, and flicking a lighter in my direction was ill advised.

Lila jumped into my path and grabbed my arms to hold me in place. This wasn't challenging for her, because she probably outweighed me by thirty pounds. Her voice was pleading. "You need help, Kayla. You're anorexic, bulimic, depressed; I could probably list your problems all day long."

"Don't do this to me, Lila," I begged quietly. "It has always been me and you against everyone else. Don't turn on me, too."

"Kayla, you promised you'd never leave me. But you are. You've stopped caring about everything. The only thing that matters to you now is what the scale says. This isn't the Kayla who came into my room at night after Dad died, wiping away my tears and telling me outrageous stories until I fell asleep."

The memory warmed me. I wasn't the greatest storyteller, but I made an effort for my fourteen-year-old bereaved sister. I would twist fairy tales, telling stories of how princesses saved princes, and I wouldn't stop talking until her eyes fluttered closed.

My mother placed her arm around Lila, a rare display of affection. "You need to get hold of yourself, Kayla. I saw your grades for the semester. I chalked it up to you getting caught up in a new relationship, but I'm starting to see there's more going on here. If you keep it up, you'll be academically dismissed from college. Also, if you insist on treating Lila and me like garbage, I'll seriously consider asking you to leave this house. You're twenty-one, old enough to take responsibility for your actions."

At Lila's silence, I understood they'd become a united front against me. My mother, a villain hiding behind her mask of exquisiteness, had poisoned my sister into believing I was the problem within our dysfunctional household. I could fill a dictionary with all the slights, all the disdainful glares, but my sister had turned amnesiac and thought I was the one who deserved to be locked away.

Wordlessly, I took flight. I had to escape. My mom was right, I was an adult and I'd make my own decisions. It was my body—*no one* was going to dictate how I treated it. I was creating new truths, a fictional tale of Kayla versus the world. Cameron, Lila, and my mother were all trying to force-feed me their ideas of how I should be. Their unwillingness to accept who I was drove me away, and I refused to relinquish control of my life.

CHAPTER TWENTY-FOUR

"Thanks for letting me stay here for a couple of days," I said awkwardly to the rail-thin girl standing in front of me. When SkinnyGirl89, aka Marti, answered the door, I was taken aback for a minute. I *couldn't* look like that. She wore a tank top and a skimpy pair of shorts. The bones of her rib cage were visible through the fabric of her shirt, and her collarbone was prominent. During our online exchanges, Marti had stated she was anorexic and proud of it for the past two years.

She was a couple of inches shorter than me, and if I had to venture a guess, she couldn't weigh more than ninety pounds. Her bleach-blond hair was assembled into a messy bun, and her overdone makeup only brought more attention to her gaunt features.

"This is going to be so fun!" Marti said happily as I followed her numbly into her apartment. "I've never had a roommate before. Not a lot of people would understand how I can't keep a lot of food in the house and why I have pictures of obese women on the fridge. I was so psyched when you called!"

I had called Marti from my car an hour after the showdown with my family. She insisted her family was just as judgmental and that I should room with her until I moved back to campus. Since she lived nearby and alone, I agreed readily and made plans to leave the next morning. Lila's pleas and my mother's cold indifference as I packed up my things haunted me as I placed my suitcase in the center of Marti's foyer.

The apartment was a two-bedroom unit in a large complex. She'd been using the second bedroom as storage for her huge collection of clothes and cosmetics, but she had cleared it out once I told her I'd come stay for the rest of the summer.

Marti explained she'd make me a key and I could come and go as I pleased. She had a bartending job a few miles away and she'd be gone most nights from five o'clock to three in the morning. She said she loved the job, trilling about how she got a kick out of wearing skimpy outfits and showing off her thin body. Her hope was to break into modeling one day, and she was saving money to build her portfolio.

We were polar opposites. Marti craved the limelight, while I wished to stay invisible, safely tucked away in the shadows. But despite our differences, I was drawn to her. She'd be my safety net, my assurance I would stay on track and not become fat again. Marti sympathized with my fears and told me to carry around a picture of myself at my plumpest as a reminder of how far I'd come.

As I turned in for the night, I could hear the bass from the radio playing next door. The walls were thin, and I was grateful for it. The music could block out the noise in my head. I'd turned off my phone hours ago, but now I powered it up as I lay in bed, sleepless. Unsurprisingly, I had several texts and voicemails from Cameron and Lila. They were unwavering in their resolve to never give up on me.

Lila's messages went from being enraged over my departure to later being apologetic and promising she'd never mention the word anorexia again as long as I came home. Cameron had called me an hour earlier and tears blurred my vision when I heard the familiar deep tenor of his voice.

"Well, I know your mom said I need to give you space and stop pressuring you to get help, but not talking to you is destroying me. I was never trying to make things harder for you and I'm sorry if that's what happened.

"Kayla, I'm not pissed about what you said about my mom and I hope it's not the reason you're refusing to talk to me. I get that you're trying to tear us apart, but I'm not letting you walk out on me. Maybe you weren't off base about some of the things you said—I do have a lot of unresolved shit I need to deal with.

"Whatever you're going through, I want to help you through it. If I came on too strong, it's only because I love you so damn much. You make everything better in my life and I only want to do the same for you. Just call me, Kayla. Please."

His words swirled around me and suffocated me with unfathomable longing. I didn't want to be in this strange bed, alone, silently reciting the rules of not eating. I wanted to be touched and loved by a man as beautiful on the inside as he was on the outside.

But I was experiencing my own personal apocalypse, and I knew I'd take him down with me. To protect him, I needed to stay away. To get past his mother's downfall, he needed to save someone. But I didn't want to be saved.

"What are you doing?" Marti asked, wandering into the kitchen the next afternoon. She grabbed a water bottle out of the fridge and sat next to me at the table wearing only a t-shirt and a thong. I had a feeling I'd have to grow accustomed to her lack of modesty.

"Adding a couple of new pages to my Thinspiration book. I want to drop these last few pounds and move on with my life. After I get below my goal weight, then maybe things can go back to normal."

Marti nodded knowingly. "I hear ya. If you drop to a couple pounds under your goal, you won't be as stressed if you gain a little bit here or there. What tips are helping you the most?"

"I think about food constantly, so I'm trying to fight my cravings. One of the things that works is I count to a hundred whenever I want something to eat. By the time I get to a hundred, I've had enough time to think of all the reasons I shouldn't eat. Another thing is I'll pinch each spot on my body where I find any fat, really hard."

Marti tapped her acrylic nails against the table while she seemed to mull over her own tips. "You know what else helps me when I want to eat? Watch people eat! It's kind of gross, especially when you see fat people doing it. Or do something else you think is revolting. Like clean the bathroom, or change kitty litter."

A buried part of me understood how sick it truly was. We were talking about how to starve ourselves in the same way people talk about the weather. It made me wonder if I should be listening to the sensible ones in my life and stop the insanity. I was on the brink of my own personal destruction, but I was too detached to care enough to stop it.

I turned the page in my Thinspiration book and froze.

I will not relent. They will not break me.

I had posted the words on a Pro-Ana forum page and printed it out afterward as a reminder of my resolve. I wrote the message during my first week back at my mom's house, at the start of my summer vacation. I was paranoid after overhearing Lila and Cameron, convinced they were concocting plans to make me fat again.

Marti may not have been the best influence, but she didn't want to undermine my goals. My object was to lose five more pounds and then return to a normal diet and a normal life. I'd stop the fasting, binging, purging, and laxative use. All the things tearing me away from the people I cared about could be in my past. I'd have it all:

my dream guy, my best friends and sister back in my life, and the perfect body.

"Try and smile, Kayla, you're scaring away my good tippers," Marti joked two weeks later as I sat on a stool at the bar she worked at. The bar was a hole-in-the-wall place named the Idle Hour with clientele who were looking to get drunk fast. About ninety percent of the patrons were single men who tended to zero in on any girl who stumbled in. Marti joked about how she brought home the leftover scraps at the end of each night.

I watched Marti working energetically, collecting bottles of alcohol to mix drinks. When I asked her before where her endless spunk came from, she told me she popped caffeine-filled diet pills throughout the day.

I took a hesitant sip of my seltzer with lemon. My life had changed drastically since I'd come to live in Toms River with Marti. My days mostly involved hanging out with Marti before she went to work. We didn't have much in common, but she passed no judgment and proved to be a distraction. There was a frantic desperation bubbling below the surface, and despite her Pro-Ana allegiances, I wondered about how content she truly was with her life.

At night, I buried myself in work, trying to take on as many article assignments as I could handle. I was sleepwalking through my life; things were crumbling around me, but nothing mattered.

Marti was a storm, and I was getting sucked into the vortex. She was outspoken, chastising me for not taking pride in my body. She relished her thinness and took pleasure in her appearance. She brought home strangers from the bar, men with blurred vision, drunken with lust for the outrageous bartender. Most nights, the sound of wall banging was what I drifted off to.

I hadn't spoken to any of my friends or family since arriving at Marti's apartment. And when I could no longer bear to listen to the pleas left on my voicemail by

Cameron, Lila, and Brittany, I changed my cell number. Messages left on Facebook and in my email inbox got deleted without being read. The only communication I had was a quick one-line email to Lila letting her know I was okay—and that was only after she threatened to report me missing if I didn't get in touch with someone immediately.

I fantasized over and over again about how things would be once I got to ninety-five pounds. I'd pack up my stuff and drive right over to Cameron's place. I'd tell him how much I'd fallen for him and that I could finally be the girl he deserved. I'd be able to take my clothes off in front of him, shamelessly, and he'd be floored at how I had the body of his wildest fantasies.

Two measly pounds stood in my way. It was all I had left to lose, and I was determined more than ever to drop them.

I wanted out of this life. I didn't want to lie awake, painfully isolated, as another faceless stranger moaned through the thin walls and Marti screamed out in ecstasy. Her lifestyle was one I couldn't understand, and resentment snaked around me. How was she able to do it? How could she let go completely with someone she barely knew when I wasn't able to do the same with the man who possessed my heart?

Marti interrupted my thoughts. "Hey, take off that sweatshirt. The guy in the corner has been eyeing you."

Daring a glance back, I saw a man with short blond hair and a lean build staring at me unabashedly. I blushed at the attention and whirled back to face Marti. "I'm not getting undressed in the middle of the bar."

When I didn't comply, she reached over and grabbed the hood of the sweatshirt. It took a few seconds for her to wrestle me out of the shirt. Although I had a tank top underneath, I felt naked and exposed. She looked me over with approval. "Much better. We work our asses off for our bodies, why wouldn't you want to show it off?" A second later, she shot me a bemused grin. "And look who decided to come this way."

My anxiety level heightened as an unfamiliar arm brushed against mine. The man took the empty bar stool next to me and didn't seem put off when I didn't acknowledge his arrival. A hand appeared in front of me. "Hi, I'm Holden."

I cast a sidelong glance in his direction. "Hi."

"Hey, can I buy you a drink?"

I tilted my head to the side and held up the seltzer. "I already have one."

"Then I guess I'll have to hang out until you need another," he said flirtatiously.

"Umm …"

Marti poked her head between the two of us, not trying to conceal the fact she'd been eavesdropping. "You have to forgive my friend. She's getting over a messy breakup. Maybe you can make her forget all about her ex."

"Marti," I hissed.

Holden took the announcement as an invitation to place his hand on my knee and lean in close. His lips brushed against my ear as he whispered, "I've been watching you all night, trying to get up the nerve to talk to you. You're so pretty, but you haven't smiled once. I'd like to have a shot at making you smile."

I felt nothing. Holden was attractive, but he stirred no emotion in me. He wasn't the one I wanted. He could never be the one to fill me with a bottomless yearning that woke me up in the middle of the night, screaming out in agony.

"I gotta go," I addressed Holden and Marti. Marti yelled out my name as I hopped off the stool, but I ignored her. I would explain things later. I didn't want an overeager stranger to fill the void inside me. She'd understand when I told her food was the only thing I wanted to relieve the emptiness.

CHAPTER TWENTY-FIVE

I was devoid of feeling by the time I finished my binge. What I had learned about purging was some foods simply refused to come back up and wound up stopping weight loss. My post-bar binge had included a box of macaroni and cheese, two cans of canned spaghetti, and a pint of ice cream—all foods that came up as easily as they went down.

I shuffled into the bathroom and turned on the shower as hot as I could stand it. I planned to allow the scalding water to wash away the filth I'd feel after throwing up in the shower. Undressing, I stepped into the water.

Piles of food poured out of me and into the pot I'd left on the ledge around the tub. I had stopped purging directly into the drain after I clogged up Marti's shower the first week I'd been living with her. Marti hadn't batted an eyelash and instead told me to keep containers in the bathroom to use for this purpose.

My throat was raw but I kept stabbing my finger against the back of my mouth. I didn't stop until I saw the last of the macaroni and cheese plop into the pot. I settled the pot outside the tub and pressed my forehead against the shower wall. I felt worthless and soiled, my tears intermingling with the shower water.

Steam billowed in front of my face and I stood in a daze for a long minute. Suddenly, I felt the world tilt. My heart was racing, and my breath was coming out in frantic, short gasps. I reached for the shower faucet, but the movement left me feeling off-balance. Black spots distorted my vision and I tried to steady myself by blindly grasping for the towel bar. My fingers slipped over the plastic and my eyes closed on their own accord. I vanished into the darkness.

The memories were there, but they weren't fully realized in my brain. I could vaguely recall shouting and cursing, a feminine and masculine voice arguing over the body they stumbled upon. There was a recollection of someone slapping my face as I tried to crawl out of my semiconscious state. Clothes were thrown on my soaking wet body, and I was dragged away by two sets of hands.

My dreams came in Technicolor, vivid and hard to distinguish from reality. In my nightmares, I was drowning, each breath sucking more water into my lungs. Hands were grasping for me from above, but I kept sinking, my weight dragging me down into nothingness.

The smell of antiseptic greeted me when I finally regained consciousness. My eyes were leaden as I attempted to open them. I blinked several times once I forced them apart and I was instantly disoriented over where I could be. Once my gaze connected with the IV inserted into my left arm, comprehension washed over me.

I realized I'd lost at least a day when I saw the sunlight streaming through the oversized windows of the hospital room. The hush in the room had led me to believe I was alone. I heard the sharp intake of my own breath when I saw my mother seated in the corner of the room.

The sound of my breathing caught her attention and she turned to me, remaining seated in the chair. She held my gaze and a thousand emotions clouded her face. She looked different; her hair was pulled back into a ponytail and her face was free of makeup. Her eyes were swollen and she appeared on the verge of crying again. She was almost unrecognizable.

"You're awake." I could hear the relief in her tone, but I couldn't quite believe it.

My mouth was dry, my lips chapped, but I managed to croak out, "I haven't seen you cry since Dad died."

"No matter what you think, you're my daughter and I love you. It's killing me to see you in this kind of pain." Her fierce declaration didn't make sense to me. The only times I had seen her that worked up was when I made a major faux pas, like wearing white after Labor Day.

I wanted to respond, but something sick and twisted inside my very being dragged my attention to the IV. I watched the liquid within the bag stream through the clear tubing, going directly to my veins. Panic took control of my mind and I demanded, "What's in the IV? What are you letting them put in me?"

"Honey, you're very sick," she said, and she stood up and moved closer to me. "You're malnourished and dehydrated. The doctors are giving you fluids and nutrients through the IV until we can talk about long-term options." Her tone was soothing, but I couldn't reconcile the woman who stood before me with my actual mother.

"Mom, you get how important it is to stay skinny. How many calories are in what they're giving me? Don't let the doctors make me fat again. Please make them stop, or I swear I'll pull this thing out!"

"Oh Kayla," she cried, "This is my fault. I'm so sorry for being a horrible mother. Your father would never forgive me if he saw you now …"

My heart fractured over the reminder of how I was disappointing my father. I dispelled his ghost and continued my begging. "Mom, I only have two pounds to lose! And then I'm done with my diet. I'll have to work to maintain it, but it'll be nothing like it is now. *Please.*"

"Kayla, what are you talking about? You were dumped at the ER by some couple that refused to give their names. The only thing they provided was your cell phone, and the nurses got my number from it. You've been in and out of consciousness for the past twelve hours. When I first came into the ER … God, the way you looked … I thought you were dead. You looked so lifeless." My mother shuddered at the memory.

I could piece together a theory about what happened. Marti and a guy she probably brought home with her had found me in the bathroom. They must've driven me to the ER and left without a second thought once I was surrounded by doctors and nurses. I wasn't surprised about the callousness of her actions; we'd both been using each other.

"But I feel fine now. I'm a little tired, but otherwise I'm as good as new. I don't need the IV any longer." My sentences came out in short breathless bursts. I found the call button on the side of my hospital bed and pressed it firmly.

"Yes?" a disembodied voice asked through the speakers.

"This is Kayla Marlowe and I need someone to come in here and take out my IV." I made an attempt to sound authoritative. I considered yanking it out of my arm, but the idea left me squeamish.

"We'll be right there," the nurse replied and clicked off.

A minute later, a petite middle-aged nurse strode into the room. "How are you feeling? Is the IV hurting you?"

My mother interjected before she had a chance. "No, she's afraid it's making her fat. Is the doctor available?"

"Mom, I can speak for myself," I said to her. "I want it out of me now! In fact, I'm not staying here another minute. I don't need anybody's help, I'm *fine.*"

"I'll page the doctor," the nurse answered coolly.

"I'm signing myself out of here, so you don't have to bother."

I heard a gasp at the doorway as the nurse scurried out of the room. My sister stood motionless, holding a vase of flowers in front of her. Her jaw dropped as she took in my appearance, and I suddenly became self-conscious about how I looked in the flimsy hospital gown.

Rushing over to me, Lila put the vase on the bedside table. "Kayla, they told me you'd wake up, but I had this awful feeling you wouldn't and they were lying to me to keep me from getting hysterical."

"I'm sorry I worried you. I had the water too hot in the shower and my blood pressure must've dropped. It was just a stupid fainting spell." Judging by the way my mother and Lila exchanged glances, I realized my family no longer accepted my lies.

"Where have you been? If you hadn't written me back, we were all a hundred percent serious about calling the police." Lila's tone was accusatory and I envisioned the hell I'd put my sister through.

"I was staying with a … friend." I was reluctant to give Marti that distinction and stumbled over the word.

"When we got the call from the hospital, I thought it had happened again. I thought you were with Dad." Lila burst into tears and my horror over the IV was forgotten. I motioned her forward and she crawled into my lap. I ran my hand up and down her back, attempting to soothe her.

My mother swallowed audibly. After she regained her composure, her voice was brisk and business-like. "Kayla, we've spoken to the doctor. You're suffering from an eating disorder and need professional help. She's making some calls to see what type of treatment options we have open to us."

"Mom, I'm in college. It's totally normal for girls to take extreme measures to stay thin …"

"That's not what this is, so save your tired excuses. I'm not saying I didn't have a part in this, but I'm ready to take responsibility. Hell, maybe I need therapy, too. But you're getting counseling, Kayla; this isn't negotiable."

"Mom, you've told me my whole life I needed to lose weight! I finally did it and now you want me to stop. Why? Are you jealous? Is it because you're no longer the skinniest in the family?"

I was trying to get a rise out of her, but my vitriol only had the effect of making despair crawl into her expression. "You're right; I have told you both you're overweight. I've belittled you and made you feel ugly and probably unloved. I can't excuse it, but your grandmother raised me to believe people valued beauty over anything else. As long as I was beautiful, the world was my oyster. She had me in beauty pageants before I was old enough to walk. She thrived on the attention as much as I did.

"I thought if I encouraged you both to look your best, maybe it would make life easier for you. But when I saw you in the ER, I realized … I knew I'd become my mother." She wiped at her eyes with a crumpled tissue she'd been holding in her lap.

I couldn't disagree with her. She'd been hell to live with. My grandmother lived in Georgia, and we only saw her twice a year for holidays. The times we were around her, she would ask us a few vague questions and then ignore us for the rest of the visit. There had always been an underlying tension between my mother and her I never understood.

"Mom, get me out of here and I'll forget it all. I'll forgive you for every single thing," I offered, my voice thick with emotion. My mother's silence confirmed my suspicion she was considering the offer.

"No!" Lila's sharp tone startled us both.

I recoiled as she glared at me.

"You're not worming your way out of dealing with your problems, Kayla. You were close to dying, and if you keep starving yourself, the next time the hospital calls us it could be to identify your body."

I couldn't breathe, much less answer my sister. A knock on my door was a welcome interruption. A tall woman with brown hair graying at the temples came into the room. She pulled her lab coat closer and stuck out her hand. "How are you feeling, Kayla? My name is Dr. Huntington, and I'm one of the residents here at the hospital."

I took her hand and then dropped it quickly. "I'm all right, I guess." My mother and Lila had left me confused. I'd been certain all I needed was to escape this place. But things were getting thrown at me I wasn't sure how to process.

"Do you want to speak with me privately, Kayla? I'm sure you have a lot of questions," the doctor said kindly.

I shook my head. The doctor pulled one of the chairs closer to the bed and watched me carefully. "I'll be honest with you, Kayla, and I hope you'll consider offering me the same courtesy. Based on your blood tests and physical exam, as well as interviewing your mother, I believe I can help you come to a decision on how you want to proceed with your treatment."

"Okay…"

"You're ninety-six pounds, which is approximately fifteen pounds less than the *minimum* of what's considered a normal weight for your height. Your electrolytes are out of balance, which is probably what caused your episode last night and the reason I ordered IV fluids. Your EKG also showed an irregular heartbeat. Based on the history provided by your family, these conditions have resulted from your struggle with anorexia and bulimia." The doctor leveled her gaze at me and paused for a beat. "Any other symptoms I should know about?"

I looked forlornly at the tree line outside my window. "I haven't had a period since April." Silence greeted me and I added tonelessly, "I also have to use laxatives to go to the bathroom."

I should've been humiliated. But I wasn't. I was disconnected from the moment. I'd hit rock bottom and if I didn't start climbing my way out of the personal Hell I was in, I would never get my life back.

"How long have you been purging and using laxatives to get rid of calories?"

Something about the woman's straightforward manner was forcing the lies back down and driving the truth out. "Since January. I've lost forty-nine pounds since then." I tried to hold back the tears threatening to spill over. "I just wanted to lose some weight. I didn't want to be fat anymore. I never thought it would turn out this way."

Lila wrapped her arms around me, and I leaned into her embrace. My mother came around to the other side of my bed and draped her arm across my shoulders. I felt stronger all of a sudden. Their support could make me face whatever was about to come my way.

"Kayla, I made a call to the River Center Clinic on your behalf. It's an inpatient clinic for eating disorders, one of the best programs in the state. They have a bed open and you can be admitted immediately after your discharge from the hospital. It's a voluntary program, which means you must decide you want to get better. Since you're still in college and on your mother's insurance, it should cover most of your stay, but your mother has volunteered to pay the difference."

"How long would I stay there?"

"Treatment is individualized, but averages between one and three months. We obviously need more information about your case, so you'd be asked to fill out several questionnaires and undergo an initial assessment by the staff at River Center. They'd work with you to create a set of individualized goals for you to reach during your stay."

My pulse quickened as I thought about the expectations placed on me. The clinic would want to control what I ate. Could I give them that power over my body? I'd been obsessed with losing weight and the thought of being fattened up against my will was excruciating.

The panic must've been clear on my face because the doctor leaned forward and I could feel the sympathy aimed at me. "Kayla, this is going to be hard, but we don't expect miracles overnight. The clinic will teach you everything you need to know about how to make smart dietary choices. Your stay will involve individual counseling, group meetings, and supervised meals. I'll get a brochure for you to look at as well as the phone number of the facility in case you have any questions."

The truth was sinking in. This was really happening. I'd been certified as being unfit to live in the real world. I was being sent away to relearn the most basic of tasks—how to eat.

CHAPTER TWENTY-SIX

As the sun set that evening, I came out of the trance I'd been in for hours. I was drowning in my own doubts. I envisioned the fat piling back onto my body. How could I stop dieting? I had suffered to get to where I was, and it was expected I give it all up. The doctor had dropped off information regarding the River Center. The nutritionists on staff eased patients into increasing their calorie intakes. Patient meal plans usually started at 1,000 to 1,500 calories per day before working up to 3,000 to 3,500 calories daily. Once weight gain was achieved, a normal diet could be resumed. When I read the numbers, I felt faint.

Lila's text alert chime brought me out of my dark thoughts. It had been going off all day and she'd been consistently sending off speedy replies. I gave her a questioning look. "You're very popular today."

She tucked a strand of hair behind her ear and said nonchalantly, "Cameron has been texting and calling me non-stop. He's been asking to see you."

"What? He knows I'm here?" I sputtered out.

"Of course he does. I've been talking to him and Brittany every day trying to figure out where you've been all this time. I had to text them both when I found out you were in the emergency room. They wanted to visit as soon as you were checked in, but Mom said it wasn't a good idea."

My mother had left an hour before to collect my things from Marti's house. I made her promise not to physically hurt the girl while she was there, but I expected Marti would receive a tongue-lashing, Charlotte Marlowe style.

I was relieved to have a reprieve from my mother. Her need to make amends was too much for me to handle on top of my decision to go to the eating disorder clinic. She desired my absolution, but I couldn't simply pretend the past hadn't shaped the broken girl I'd become.

"I can't let him see me like this," I whispered, spinning my hospital bracelet over my bony wrists.

"I know, Kayla," Lila said kindly. "He's downstairs. I'll go talk to him and tell him it's not a good time."

"He's here?"

My heart fluttered and my chest tightened. Instantly, I was floored by the sensation of missing him. He was within reach and I was going to shut him out of my life again. Cameron had a million opportunities to move on, to forget all about me, but he stubbornly refused to let me go.

"I want to see him," I said with determination. Some losses were too great to bear. My father's death was something I was still struggling with, and I didn't want to lose another man who meant the world to me. "Can you help me fix my hair in the bathroom?" I murmured to Lila.

There was so much sadness in Lila's expression each time she looked at me. Her arm steadied me as I placed my feet on the tile floor. We took baby steps into the bathroom as I dragged my IV alongside me. I had avoided the mirror since I arrived, but it was time to take an honest look at my reflection.

My fingers wrapped around the edge of the sink and a sob dragged out of my body. I couldn't bear to stare at my reflection for more than a minute. I had thought starving myself would make me beautiful, but I'd turned into a shell of what I was. My hair was dull and thin, hanging limply past my shoulders. My eyes looked hollow, with purple shadows coloring the skin underneath. The skin on my face was dry and ruddy, my lips chapped and bleeding.

I hated the mirror for showing me the truth. I was merely a husk, hollowed out completely. As I reached back to punch my fist through the glass, Lila grabbed me. I fell into her, then, and released the anguish I had bottled up for ages. I sobbed violently, blubbering against the fabric of her shirt as she held me steadfastly. We had swapped roles, and Lila had become the caretaker, the strong one.

As my moans subsided, Lila stood up straighter. "I have a brush and makeup in my purse. We'll get you ready and I'll text Cam to come up." I wanted to refuse, but my need for him was growing more insistent each second. What I felt for him outweighed my shame over my appearance. Lila continued, "Cam loves you, Kayla, and what you look like doesn't matter to him. You're still beautiful to all of us."

My sister had changed, too, in the past few months. She'd grown stronger and surer of herself. I was relieved she hadn't followed me down the thorny path I had traveled.

Fifteen minutes later, I cowered in bed, the covers pulled up to my neck when I heard a light knock at the door. My sister gave me a reassuring smile and went to answer the door. After a few seconds of indiscernible whispering, Cameron trailed Lila into the hospital room. I envisioned the warning: be prepared to behold the horror.

Shock registered in his eyes and I could see the effort he put into concealing the emotion. Instead, he managed a half-smile as he moved to the foot of the bed. My obsessions had damaged everything good in my life, and I wondered whether my relationships were beyond repair.

I tilted my head toward my sister. "Lila, can you give us a few minutes alone?"

"Sure," she offered, apparently eager to escape the awkwardness of Cameron's arrival. "I'm going to raid the cafeteria and see if I can find anything edible."

I studied him as Lila gathered up her things and headed to the door. It had been two weeks since I'd last seen him, and I felt my breath catch at the sight. He was gorgeous—there was never any doubt of that in my mind. The sun had lightened the blond streaks in his hair and a healthy-looking tan colored his skin. He must have worked at some point during the day; he wore a white, button-down shirt and black pants. My hand itched to play with the striped tie that hung loosely around his neck.

"I'm glad you're here." I was trying for honesty. Maybe if I expressed my feelings more, I'd have an easier time dealing with them.

"I had all these things to say to you, but now I'm at a loss," he said softly.

"I owe you an apology for so many things I honestly don't know where to start. But I'll start by saying sorry for the disgusting things I said to you when I saw you last. That wasn't me and I wouldn't have blamed you if you decided to never see me again after that."

"Kayla, I've been going out of my mind these past two weeks. I was freaked out over the thought something terrible had happened to you. I've never felt so helpless," he admitted.

I scooted over to the left side of the bed and motioned him over. Without a second's hesitation, he climbed in next to me. I rested my head against his shoulder and enjoyed the comfort of being next to him. "I'm starting to believe I'm truly broken. I don't know how I got to this point, but I can't continue like this."

"We're all broken in some way, Kayla. You just have to wake up each morning and find a reason to keep going," he said quietly.

"I've been selfish. The very thing I hated about my mother is the exact thing I've become. You tried to talk to me about your mom and I never tried to get you to open up more about it. One of my biggest regrets is not being there for you."

He took my hand in his and I watched as our fingers intertwined. My fingers looked frail and bony next to his large, strong hand. "My mom is in the past, Kayla. I've moved on from the things she did. There's not much to say about it."

"Cameron," I said gently. "I don't think it's completely in the past. The Vonnegut quote from your tattoo—it was your birth mom's favorite verse, not your stepmother's, right?" At his brisk nod, I continued, "Maybe you should consider meeting with her. It may help you—"

He didn't allow me to finish. "What could she possibly have to say that I'd want to hear? She left Scarlett and me for almost ten years because she couldn't stop using drugs. It's not my job to ease her guilt."

"I'm not suggesting it for her benefit. But maybe you need the closure. I'm sure you have questions you want answered." Maybe I wasn't qualified to give advice, but it was easier to sort out someone else's problems than deal with my own.

He coughed uncomfortably. "Why are we talking about this? I'm here to help you get better." A muscle twitched in his jaw. I didn't want to drop the topic, but he'd have to be the one to decide whether he wanted to see his mom and if he could forgive her. Pain flashed in his eyes. "Kayla, the time we've spent apart has been hell, but I haven't stopped loving you for one minute."

I didn't reply. Instead I hugged him tighter. He nuzzled my neck, his voice muffled as he whispered endearments, words I was too broken to hear.

Tears traveled down my cheeks. I knew the right words to say to him, but they were trapped inside. I wanted a moment to get lost in the feel of his body and the sound of his voice. Because once I said what I needed to, it was possible I might never see him again.

My mouth found the way to his on its own accord. His lips were soft and his mouth tasted sweet. The kiss was tender and alluded to the raw need we were both feeling. Our romance was addictive, a calming drug in my chaotic world.

Unshed tears clouded my vision when I opened my eyes. The tips of our noses were still touching as I held him close.

"I need to get help. The doctor here found a place for me in an eating disorders clinic," I said.

He pressed his lips to mine before replying. "Lila told me. I think it sounds great. They have visiting hours which means I can come see you."

"Cameron," I said, affectionately grazing my finger over the rough skin of his cheek. "I can't see you while I go through treatment. I believe the problem before when I went to counseling was I was going for your benefit and not for myself."

"Kayla, you have to let me in. I feel jerked around with the constant back and forth with you. Why can't you understand I want to be there for you?"

"I'm not intentionally trying to push you away this time. It's a lot to ask of you to trust me, but my reasoning is I want to go into this program with my best shot at succeeding. What I feel for you … it's intense and all-encompassing, and seeing you will only make it harder for me to focus on what I need to do to get better," I said breathlessly. I wished he could see inside me. He'd realize it was killing me to let him go. "I don't want this to be goodbye forever. But it would be selfish of me to ask you to wait for me." *Please wait for me*, I prayed silently.

His tone was gruff. "You're serious about this, aren't you? You're different already, I can tell. You really want to get better."

I squeezed my eyes shut tightly. "More than anything."

"Then, I'll stay away if that's what you want—"

I cut him off. "It's not what I want, it's what I need right now."

"Kayla, do whatever it takes to come back to me. Because, honestly, I don't think I could move on even if I wanted to. I only want you." His kiss was an oath, and I planned to hold onto it as I fought against the disease that was slowly destroying me from the inside out.

CHAPTER TWENTY-SEVEN

"This is where you'll be staying. Your roommate's name is April. She's at a group meeting, but you'll meet her this afternoon," the nurse explained as she led us to a room at the end of the hall. She unlocked it and turned to me. "Why don't I give you some time to say goodbye to your family?"

After my assent, she disappeared back down the hallway. I scanned my room. "Looks like my dorm room. It's actually an improvement over the hospital."

My room at the River Center featured a pair of twin beds, dressers, and nightstands. The floor was carpeted in dark blue, and a set of windows overlooked the front lawn. The linens were also provided, and matching floral bedspreads covered the beds.

I'd been fighting my nervousness since my mom parked the car in front of the ivy-covered brick building. The inviting exterior gave no indication of what took place inside. As we walked down the hallway toward my room, I pictured the pain of all the past patients seeping into the walls. The patient dorms, lounge areas, cafeteria, and treatment rooms were all housed in the single three-story building.

I rolled my suitcase to the middle of the floor. The clinic provided a lot of the items I needed for my stay, so I'd packed lightly. I was given a list of things not to bring before I left the hospital. On the forbidden list were fashion magazines, tank tops, short skirts and shorts, and over-the-counter medicines. The toughest thing for me to leave behind was my laptop. After I took a minute to think about it, I realized it would probably be best, since I'd be cut off from my Pro-Ana network. The clinic had desktop computers, but their use was monitored.

"At least you're used to sharing a room. I was never able to get along with other girls and couldn't imagine being forced to live with a stranger," my mom remarked, sitting on the edge of the bed. Lila rolled her eyes behind my mom's back. We'd heard time and again how girls were always jealous of my mother and that was the reason she never had girlfriends. Thankfully, my mother was going to attend family therapy sessions as part of my treatment. If her behavior didn't change as well, I'd have a struggle changing my own.

"Maybe I'll luck out and have another roommate like Brittany," I said.

I had called Brittany the night before and we'd talked for over an hour. She'd tried to reach me in the midst of my pandemonium, and I wanted her to know I was sorry for not returning her calls.

I confessed everything that had been going on with me, down to the last dirty detail. I was surprised to learn she suspected I had an eating disorder, but that she couldn't figure out a way to confront me about it without initiating the collapse of our friendship. I promised to stay in touch as often as I could while staying at the clinic. I didn't have a clue whether I'd be finished with treatment in time for the start of the fall semester in September, but I didn't doubt we'd remain close, whether I returned to school or not. I was appreciating my roommate a lot more since living with Marti for two weeks.

"So, I guess this is goodbye for now," I said uncertainly to my family.

"You get an hour for visitors each night. Lila and I can come by as often as you want us to. I'm also meeting with your therapist once a week. She thought I should start off the sessions without you attending," my mom explained, brushing an imagined piece of lint from her blouse. The clinic made her uneasy. I could see it in her darting eyes and gritted teeth. I wondered if she had mentally compared me to the girls we'd seen on our arrival, the doll-like girls with very little flesh, their heads appearing oversized compared with their compact bodies. As we walked the halls of the clinic, I imagined myself in a warped beauty pageant, with my mother and Lila as the judges, comparing my bony frame against those of the other patients, mentally deciding how sick I truly was.

I hastened the goodbye. The sooner I came to accept that as my new reality, the easier the transition would be. I would set small and achievable goals to get me through the initial difficult days. That world was unfamiliar and terrifying. But I was my father's daughter. And if there was one thing I always admired about my dad, it was his ability to make the best of the most impossible situations.

The hours that followed were a rush of unfamiliar faces, all wanting something from me. I was weighed, measured, and poked with needles until the counselors and nurses were satisfied. The clinic performed blind weigh-ins: they would know how much I weighed, but it would remain a mystery to me. The purpose was to curb the obsession over what number appeared on the scale. The blood work was required to see what type of nutrients my body had been deprived of during my months of starvation.

I met with my individual counselor, a woman named Noreen. I liked her carefree manner and imagined I'd eventually feel comfortable enough talking to her about my deepest secrets. She was also in charge of several of the group meetings held at the clinic. The groups covered topics like self-esteem building, nutrition education, and body image.

I met my roommate April before dinnertime. She was tiny; I guessed her height was just under five feet. Her curly ginger hair was cut to her chin and her blue eyes sparkled when she introduced herself. April didn't look a day over fourteen-years-old. I hid my astonishment over her revelation she was nineteen. She was a sweet girl, offering up my choice of beds despite her being in the room first. I liked the way she laughed; it was deep and came from the belly. I didn't foresee any conflict arising between us during my stay.

April seemed to sense my unease as we walked down the hall to the dining area. It would be my first supervised meal at River Center. During my stay at the hospital, I picked at the trays of food sent to my room. I guessed the doctors didn't press the issue since I was hooked up to an IV and I was being checked into a residential eating disorder program. April assured me although we'd be watched while we ate, no one was going to force the food down my throat. It felt like she could see inside my head and understood my nightmare visions of nurses shoving feeding tubes up my nostrils.

I was also told I should squash any thoughts of throwing up after eating. An escort went with patients if they decided to use the bathroom after meals.

A nutritionist had filled me on my meal plan and what to expect as my body adjusted to eating three meals and two snacks per day. However, nothing could prepare me for the overwhelming emotions I felt sitting in front of a plate of food in a room full of watchful eyes. The meal wasn't extravagant, just grilled chicken with brown rice and steamed broccoli. My brain registered the food as healthy, but I couldn't bring myself to pick up the fork. I was crippled by my illness, a prisoner to the idea that food was the enemy.

I closed my eyes and took a few long and cleansing breaths. Parker had talked about goal setting, and I suspected that this would be a part of my recovery. I told myself if I could eat that meal, I'd give myself a reward at the end. I decided if I ate dinner, I'd spend my free time downloading every cheesy love song on my iPod that reminded me of Cameron. The thought made me smile and I mechanically pierced a spear of broccoli and lifted it to my lips. I washed the food down with milk and concentrated on eating another piece of food.

I held back tears of frustration as I continued to eat. To an outsider, my behavior probably made little sense. All I had to do was eat. It was a simple enough thing to do. But I had to knock down the mental barriers first.

Making it through my first meal went unrewarded. Instead of downloading songs, I laid curled up on my bed. My arms clutched my stomach tightly as cramps stung my insides. "Are you okay?" April asked hesitantly from her side of the room.

"No, something's wrong. Please, can you find me a nurse?"

Pity flashed in her eyes, but she complied. A minute later, one of the nurses was escorted by April to our room. "What's wrong Kayla?"

"I have this horrible pain in my stomach. I'm also feeling bloated. I need something to help stop it. Can I have a diuretic or a laxative?" I moaned out my question.

"Kayla, we talked to you about this when you checked in. Your body needs to get accustomed to eating a regular diet again. We don't provide medications to get rid of the calories you take in." Her tone was gentle, but firm. I disliked her at once for her part in my misery.

"This isn't normal. This isn't going to make me better," I cried.

April sank on her knees next to my bed. "You're going to feel wretched for a while, but it stops. I've been here three weeks and my stomach is no longer swelling up like a balloon after each time I eat."

My inner demons struggled against my will to survive. I was going to get fat. This was what I had signed up for and I'd have to learn to live with it. Eating wasn't going to kill me, but the hunger could.

The first night, April stayed with me. I appreciated the gesture, because I knew she was missing out on her free time for the evening. She was on the other side, working her way toward a return to her normal life, and still she was willing to reach out and lift me out of my unsettling thoughts.

Recovery wasn't going to be painless. I was going to have to claw my bloodied and damaged body out of the hole I'd fallen into.

"It gets better, Kayla," April said as I sobbed into my pillow. "I felt the same way you did when I first came here. I thought no one would get what I'd gone through. But when I started meeting the other girls, I realized I wasn't the only one hurting. There's always a story worse than yours, more tragedy than you can imagine. But we all want to get better, that's why we came here."

I used my shirt sleeve to wipe away my tears. "Why are you here?"

"Because I wanted to be a prima ballerina," she said, and she did a brief pirouette around the room. I was able to manage a smile. She added, "Did you ever hear of the diet philosophy of ballerinas? It's simply 'do not eat.'" Breathlessly, she fell back onto her bed. "There's no such thing as a chubby ballerina. I've dreamed of being part of the New York City Ballet since I was a little girl, and it was clear early on that food would only get in the way of my dreams."

"What happened to you?"

"I stopped growing. Ballerinas are beautiful, tall and elegant, and I'm stuck in the body of a ten-year-old boy," she said wryly. "Everything seemed to fall apart for me at once. I blew a couple of auditions and was told I'd never be good enough to make it as a professional dancer. All that time I wasted on something that wasn't going to happen. Not to mention the torture I put my body through. I thought about killing myself so many times …"

"Oh, God, I'm so sorry," I murmured.

She rose up on her elbows and stared at me across the room. "My problem was I let being a ballerina define who I was. Without it, life didn't make sense. I'm here because I want to know if I can still be happy without dancing."

"Have you figured it out?"

"Not completely, but I'm learning to enjoy food again and not treat it like it'll bite me back. I definitely don't miss being so hungry that I'd put whitening strips on my teeth to keep myself from eating." She paused and said thoughtfully, "The thing about this place is it lets you escape your real life and figure out how to be happy again."

"Thanks. It's nice of you to share all that stuff," I said awkwardly.

April's laughter was abrupt. "You get used to all the over-sharing too. Within two seconds of meeting someone, they're telling you all about how crappy their lives are." When I didn't respond, she commanded, "Try and get some sleep. It'll make things easier on you. Tomorrow, I'll introduce you to the rest of the gang on the Island of Misfit Toys."

CHAPTER TWENTY-EIGHT

The schedule at River Center was regimented. Each morning, I woke up knowing exactly what to expect. Structure was intended to give us the best shot at sanity. Breakfast, lunch, dinner, and snacks were all supervised and at the same time each day. I was expected to attend two group meetings per day along with two individual counseling sessions each week. My mother was attending the family counseling sessions alone for the time being, but I was expected to join her as part of my treatment.

True to her word, April introduced me to the friends she had made during her stay. During group meetings, I'd hear their horror stories and the lengths they went to for thinness. I wasn't forced to share my past; the staff explained I'd talk during group meetings when I was ready. However, hearing the other girls' tales did make me feel an instant kinship with them.

It was our own little world inside the River Center. The rules were different there, and it was up to us to learn how to make it on the outside. Field trips involved outings to coffee shops and restaurants. We were lost children who needed to be taught again how to order and eat in public. Back at the center, there were meal preparation classes where we were instructed on how to make healthy, well-balanced meals.

Fun was allowed, but like everything else it was monitored. If I ran too hard on the treadmill, I was told it was time to stop. If I went onto a website that wasn't considered conducive to my recovery, a staff member told me to get off the site and find another activity for my free time.

Besides being anorexic and bulimic, I was diagnosed by my therapist as having depression and body dysmorphic disorder. My counselor described body dysmorphic disorder as a type of mental illness where a person becomes obsessed with an imagined flaw. I finally understood all the times I thought I saw a reflection of an obese girl in the mirror, it hadn't been real.

Multiple diagnoses made me feel like I was all sorts of crazy. On the other hand, I thought if the doctors could name what I had, I could be mended. I was prescribed antidepressants, but warned they weren't a miracle fix and it'd take weeks for the full effects to kick in. I wished for an easy way to be cured. Like whatever was wrong with me could be surgically removed and the despair would be gone instantaneously.

On my tenth day of the program, I woke up feeling different. I decided it would be the day to stop feeling sorry for myself. My symptoms, since I'd begun eating a regular diet, were easing, and I was more energized. My inner anguish over stepping on the scale each morning had diminished. I didn't see the number, but I accepted my weight was climbing.

Normally silent during cognitive group therapy, I felt the urge to share with my friends. The goal of cognitive group therapy was to transform negative thoughts and behaviors into positive ones. During the session, the counselor, Mary, was discussing how we had to give up the idea of perfectionism and break away from the all or nothing way of living our lives.

Mary took note of my enthusiastic nodding as something clicked inside of me. "Kayla, did you have something you wanted to share?"

I cleared my throat. "Looking back at the past few months, I'm starting to understand why I wanted to be skinny so badly. I needed to be skinny because to me that meant I'd be perfect in my mother's eyes. She's been so unhappy since my father died; I thought if I could just be what she wanted, we'd both find a way to move on."

"Do you think it made her happy?"

"I thought so for a while. I received so much positive attention when I first lost weight. My mom kept going on about how great I looked, and my friends told me how envious they were of my body. It was almost addictive to hear their compliments. After so much time being told how fat and plain I was, I wanted to hear I was pretty.

"But I think I gave her too much power in our relationship. Why should my weight affect whether or not she's happy? Being thin isn't going to bring my father back to life," I said. I chewed on a hangnail as I felt the stares of the other patients.

Mary sent a nod of approval my way before segueing into another part of the group discussion. I'd been skeptical about the therapy, but I couldn't deny how good it felt to self-reflect over the destructive nature of the relationship with my mother.

Hours later, April and another patient named Chelsea gathered around my bed. I could tell by their expressions they were excited about something. April wasn't a major rule-breaker at the River Center, but she did have a tendency to push the limits. One of her new life goals, she'd stated, was to get me to loosen up.

My eyebrows pulled together in confusion as they started to giggle. "Doesn't the schedule say we're supposed to be meditating and writing in our journals?"

"Ha," April barked out. "You weren't meditating. You had that pining look you get when you're thinking about Cameron."

I shut my journal and sat up straighter. "You got me. I was trying to decide if I should write him a letter or not."

April waved me off. "You could do that any time. I could write it for you if I want." She teased me in a singsong voice, "Dear Cameron, I'm making my roommate loonier than she already is by going on about how crazy sexy you are. Let me tell you all the dirty things I want you to do to me once I break out of this place—"

I shut her up by tossing a pillow at her head. "You're a pain in the ass. Anyway, what mayhem are the two of you planning?"

With a sly smile, Chelsea produced a small plate behind her back. On the plate was a brownie with a dollop of whipped cream and a cherry. Chelsea said, "I snagged it from the dinner cart. I figured we could share it."

Her suggestion sounded innocent enough, but desserts were not given freely at the River Center. Sweets could be a trigger for binge eating, and our nutritional goals included learning the ability to eat them in moderation. The staff decided on a patient-by-patient basis whether you received dessert and, if you did, it was usually only twice a week.

A reprimand was on my tongue, but I reminded myself about the group talk on perfectionism. I had to stop trying to please everyone else and think for myself.

Chelsea broke the brownie into three pieces and handed me the largest section. Taking a bite was practically effortless. The mental hurdles I had to jump over in order to eat had diminished.

"This isn't even that yummy, but you may be onto something. This is kind of fun," I mumbled while chewing on a large chunk of the brownie and watching the girls dig greedily into their pieces.

"Wow, I would've shoved a brownie down your throat sooner if I knew that was all it took to get you to smile," April joked.

"I've missed this," I sighed. "I remember sitting around with my roommates, eating pizza and cookies for dessert and just goofing off. I wasn't always thinking about exit strategies and how I could avoid invitations to dinner." As an afterthought, I added, "I'm over being the downer of the group."

"I second that," April said. "I may not ever be a prima ballerina, but to be honest, I haven't enjoyed dancing in years. When I get released, I want to do something totally reckless and spontaneous. Like go backpacking around Europe or sign up to work on a cruise ship."

"I'm going back to college when I get out of here. I dropped out because I had so much anxiety about trying to be social with other students," Chelsea said. Chelsea was a year older than me and had been at the clinic two and a half months. She had explained after we met each time she was on the verge of release, she experienced a setback that kept her from leaving.

"I'd like to finish school, too," I said. "It's going to be my senior year, but after my crappy grades last semester, I may not graduate on time. After that I'd like to get a job with a newspaper or magazine. Maybe eventually start a magazine featuring real girls and not only fashion models."

"Isn't she adorable?" April asked Chelsea jokingly. "You forgot to mention how you'll marry Cameron and bear his children."

I smiled at her prediction. "Of course I want a future with Cameron, but maybe I shouldn't get my hopes up. I haven't talked to him in weeks and I have no clue when I'll be ready to see him again. We're not together, so he could meet someone else and fall in love with her."

April said, "No way. From what you told me, it sounds like an epic romance. You went through way too many crappy times together to not end up happy at the end of it all. It gives me hope for my love life. I was always too busy and obsessed with dancing for a boyfriend. While I'm schlepping around the world, I plan to have a few flings to make up for it," she said dreamily.

"I bet you will," I said. "You'll have to send me postcards and tell me all about the guys you meet."

"You can count on it. I'll let you live vicariously through me as long as you promise to try to make things work with Cameron," she said narrowing her eyes.

"Fair enough," I replied.

"We should hold our own therapy sessions in here. We'll have brownies and talk about all the ways having an eating disorder sucks," Chelsea said while using her thumb to wipe off a smudge of chocolate left on the corner of her mouth.

"It does suck," April agreed readily. "The worst part was when my family found out about it. They kept saying things like 'snap out of it.' Like it was that easy. Did they honestly believe I want to be like this?"

"I hated how my friends and family tried to pigeonhole me. Like because I'm not a size zero, they thought I didn't have a problem," Chelsea added. Chelsea had an average build and long black hair reaching toward her waist. From group sessions, I learned Chelsea struggled with binge eating and bulimia. "We're real people, not all of us are going to fit the textbook definition of having an eating disorder."

"I couldn't stand how my eating dictated my life. I had to avoid people and places because they would get in the way of starving myself or going on one of my binges," I said.

They both nodded and the room quieted. We became lost in the past, mourning all we'd lost because of our illnesses. I thought about the dinner dates with Cameron I had turned down, the times I'd told Brittany and the twins I was too tired to go out to The Court for dinner and drinks. I could never get those missed moments back, but I could plan for a brighter future.

CHAPTER TWENTY-NINE

"I looked in the mirror today and I think it was the first time in a long time I was able to see what I really looked like," I told my therapist, Noreen, a week later.

"What was your reaction?"

"I've avoided mirrors a lot and I think it was to prevent myself from seeing the real me. Where's all the fat I thought was on my body? Because all I see is flesh sticking to my bones. Being under a hundred pounds was never my dieting goal. But once I got there, it still wasn't good enough," I explained.

"Are you learning to accept your body?"

"It's hard, but I'm getting there. I mean that's what you guys preach here, right? Getting rid of all the dangerous and destructive feelings that got me to this point." I pursed my lips and felt my shoulders tense. "My problem is I have a tendency to *feel* too much. I was able to be apathetic after my dad died, shut everything off to survive. Once all those feelings I pushed down came back to haunt me, I felt suffocated by my emotions."

"How can you change the way you handle your emotions to make better choices?" she asked.

I had become accustomed to the probing questions. Being more of an introvert, it had been a little strange for me to constantly talk about myself and hyper-analyze my every action. From sun up to sun down, every activity was about how to change the way you were on the inside as a way to survive outside of those walls.

"I guess I need to find a happy medium. Not turn everything off, but not obsess over every tiny setback, either," I answered.

Half an hour later, I finished my session and headed in the direction of my room. Each meeting with my counselor left me with a lot to think about, and I liked having time alone afterward to process all that was said. I was learning to not tune out the voice of reason inside me that wanted to heal and move on from the past.

When I entered the room, I noticed a few pieces of mail were left on my bed. My initial guess was most of the letters were from Lila. Although she visited with my mom at least twice a week, she liked to send me notes on the days she didn't see me. She'd gotten it into her head she was going to help build up my self-esteem, and the letters were homage to all the ways I was awesome. She certainly laid it on thick, but they did have the desired effect of making me smile and laugh.

My mom was making progress, but my expectations were modest. Whether or not she was able to accept Lila and me as we were was insignificant. I couldn't give her words that much influence over my life anymore. She was trying, and I gave her credit for it. Lila had confessed they went shopping together and my mom hadn't made one derogatory remark about my sister's clothing size.

I picked up one of the envelopes that were on the bed. Cameron's tight scrawl was instantly recognizable on the envelope. My heart stopped for a minute, and I had to remind myself to breathe. My fingers trembled as I tore into the envelope and drew out the lined sheet of paper.

Dear Kayla,

I swore I was going to leave you alone, but Angus insisted on writing you. He misses you like crazy and wanted me to pass along the message. To be honest, we both do.

Lila told me you're doing great there. Maybe I'm being selfish because when I heard that, the only thing I could think of was you'd be coming back to me soon.

I get the reasons we can't be together right now, but it still sucks. I don't want to be without you and I freak out when I think that things may be over for good between us. I don't want to lose you. I can't lose you.

I'm here when you're ready to talk. I'm not trying to put any pressure on you, but I didn't want you to think I forgot about you either. Angus is keeping the spot on my bed warm for you and it's ready whenever you want to come back.

Love,

Cameron

"You look like you're about to pass out, Kayla. Who's the letter from?"

Before I could respond to April, she scanned the letter behind me. I'd been immersed in Cameron's words and hadn't heard her come back to our room. She let out a low whistle. "Damn, Kayla, if you're not going to take back that spot on his bed, I'll volunteer."

I playfully shoved her. "Hands off. I'm thinking it was impulsive of me to decide not to be in touch with him while I'm here. I really want to write him back. What do you think?"

"Yes!" April shouted. "I'd kill someone to find a guy like that. You're lucky I like you or I'd totally try to steal him from you. It's so romantic he wrote you a love letter."

I bit down hard on my lower lip. "It's embarrassing to think back about how ugly I was to him when we were together. I said and did some messed up things."

Cameron's letter couldn't have come at a better time. I needed the reassurance he still had feelings for me. I'd let him go because I was trying to give him the opportunity to walk away. But the truth was most of my daydreams involved being released from River Center and hurling myself back into his arms. The only thing holding me back was the constant playback in my head of all the ways I'd screwed things up.

"This disease is ugly. Kind of ironic, I guess, since we're doing it to be pretty." April shrugged her delicate shoulders and handed me the notebook that had been resting on my nightstand. "Write him back. If you think about it too much, you'll probably change your mind."

April had a point. There was a litany of reasons to keep Cameron at bay. Yet, he was the one bright spot in the dark days from before. I was finally able to start believing he loved me. He'd said it before, but I hadn't thought I was good enough for him. As if he loved the counterfeit Kayla I chose to show him, and not the real version. I imagined if I gained weight, he would leave me.

"I think my hang-up is I met him while I was at one of my lowest points. Like the thought that something good could come out of anything about that time in my life is impossible. But I wasn't always miserable. I could forget sometimes what was going on with me and have an amazing time with him."

"Just because it wasn't the right time to meet someone doesn't mean jack. It happens that way sometimes. You're not looking for love and it finds you regardless and bowls you over."

I reached for the notebook. Pleased her harassment worked, April left me alone to figure out what I wanted to say to Cameron. Her release was imminent and I was already imagining how much I'd miss her. Friendships grew fast at the River Center.

I'd failed to tell Cameron how I felt for most of our relationship. But I wanted to be candid with him going forward.

Cameron,

I miss you too. And give Angus a kiss from me. On second thought, maybe a hug would suffice.

I hated being here at first. It was crappy to give up control and trust a bunch of strangers to help me. But I made some friends and the staff is actually not evil minions like I initially thought.

Don't be afraid of losing me. My heart will always belong to you. As much as I tried to deny it, you've had me since you gave me one of your cheesy grins and shoved a credit card application in my face. I ran away from you out of fear. I thought something that powerful and passionate couldn't be real.

I don't know if I'll ever be completely "cured" but I'm dealing with my baggage. I still need some time to work through everything, but I want to come back to you too. I'll be in touch when I can.

Love,
Kayla

CHAPTER THIRTY

"Kayla! What the hell! I didn't know you were coming back!" Brittany squealed. She charged me and pulled me in tight for a hug. I laughed at her greeting. I was just as excited to see her.

"I thought I'd surprise you. I was only released a couple of days ago. The counselors didn't want me to miss the start of the semester. I'm still going to do therapy, but just on an outpatient basis," I said in a rush.

The hurdles I'd faced at the start of treatment had been easier to get through the longer I stayed at the River Center. By the end, I wasn't the girl full of resentment and despair who sat in the back of group meetings, not truly hearing what anybody had to say. I could listen and relate to the emotions of the other patients. We were all lost in some way, trying to find our way back.

"I'm so flipping happy right now! I thought I was going to have to get a blow-up doll and pretend you lived here to keep the college from giving away your room," Brittany said, giggling.

We were back in the same townhouse as the year before. The college used a lottery system to determine housing. Since Brittany and Danielle had lucked out and received top picks, they were able to select our old dorm, as well as Jessica and me as their roommates.

I followed Brittany into her empty room as she dragged in her suitcase. I had arrived a couple of hours before and had half my belongings unpacked already. "Well you know how my summer was," I said. "What about your own?"

"Not as exciting as yours. I heard from your mom you were living with a crack head whore—can't wait to hear the stories about that. Mostly, I spent time with Kurt and helped out at my parents' restaurant."

I held no resentment toward Marti. I felt sorry for her, if anything. Her dream of becoming a model was unlikely, and I hoped she stopped hurting herself in order to make it happen. I had sent her a text before I left for the clinic to let her know I was going to get treatment. She sent me a text back saying she felt sorry for me and not to let the doctors turn me into a fat cow. Part of my recovery was cutting off contact with her and the rest of the girls I'd found through Pro-Ana. In the future, I wanted to share my story and hoped to change the unhealthy mindset of women like me.

"I'm glad you and Kurt are still together. You make a good couple," I said as she unzipped her suitcase.

"I think so, too. But I may need you to feign another fainting spell in a room of hotties in case it doesn't work out," she quipped.

"I'm at your service," I said with a laugh.

Brittany stopped unpacking and stared at me shrewdly. "You're back."

She didn't have to elaborate. What was left unsaid was I had disappeared for half a year. The Kayla she befriended in freshman year, the girl who bought her M&Ms and trashy romance novels after each boy broke her heart, was back in her life.

"How has your mom been? Did the therapists recommend shock therapy after her sessions?"

"Nothing quite that extreme, but I think counseling is helping her, too. We talked a lot during family counseling, and it seems like a lot of her screwy ideas about beauty came from how she was raised as a pageant princess. Also, she was so angry after my dad died, blaming him for not taking care of his body better and having a heart attack. That was the reason she went after my sister and me about our weight," I explained.

"I still think she's horrible, but for your sister's sake maybe she'll stop being so damn wicked all the time."

"I'm not expecting miracles overnight, but she's trying. Lila sees that and she's having an easier time living with her. Lila has come a long way too. Without having me to lean on, she's become her own person."

Lila shined now, and she'd discovered a confidence she didn't know she had. She had told my mom she was no longer forfeiting control over her life. Not only would she eat what she wanted, but she'd also choose her own friends and boyfriend. My mom wouldn't concede complete control, but at least Lila had found her voice. Their new dynamic alleviated the guilt I typically felt when I returned to college.

Brittany interrupted my thoughts. "Does anyone else know you're back?" Brittany lifted her eyebrows suggestively.

"Not yet. I thought I'd plan something nice and surprise him. I hinted in an email to him last week I was hoping to be released soon," I explained.

After I talked it over with my therapist, I started exchanging emails with Cameron about three weeks earlier. We hadn't gotten into anything too heavy. They were mostly light-hearted notes that made me smile. I wasn't afraid of our relationship anymore. I was only filled with hopeful expectation when I thought about Cameron.

"Well, I've been stalking him on Facebook all summer to make sure I didn't see any posts or pictures of girls trying to make a move on him while you were away. He's barely been online. I'm assuming he spent the summer pining for you, which makes it safe for you to be with him again," Brittany said. "Enough boy talk for now. Get your lazy ass downstairs and help me bring up the rest of the stuff."

"Glad to see you're over treating me with kid gloves."

As I followed her down the stairs, she spun on me suddenly. "I'm not sure what the rules are for talking about your appearance. But I just want you to know I think you look good. You look healthy."

More importantly, I felt healthy. Before I left the clinic, I found out my weight. I was one hundred and ten pounds. I'd gained fourteen pounds during treatment. I wasn't the same person leaving the facility. The number didn't send me into a spiral, and I was at peace knowing my weight would most likely climb as I continued to eat a normal diet. I was comfortable in my own skin, and it felt incredible.

I was a work in progress, and two months at the River Center wouldn't fix all the things in my life. I'd probably always have to remind myself to eat healthy and not plot out elaborate ways to stay skinny. I also had to deal with the conflicting emotions brought on by my parents. But I was gaining confidence in myself, and none of my problems seemed insurmountable any longer. The uncertainty of life didn't cripple me as it had before.

Another change was my newfound willingness to ask for help when I needed it. Being in therapy or on antidepressants didn't mean I was weak. They were only an acknowledgement that I was tired of struggling and needed help.

"Thanks Britt." I rolled my eyes. "Now let's get all your crap moved in so you can help me think up ways to win my guy back."

I nixed most of Brittany's plans to wow Cameron, since the majority of them were inspired by her latest obsession with BDSM books. As much as I wanted to rock

Cameron's world, I also wanted him to see the real me. I'd kept myself hidden, and a part of being the braver Kayla was showing him the pieces of me he'd been missing.

It was after six when the door to Cameron's apartment opened. Angus ran over to greet his owner, and I giggled at the startled expression on his face when he saw me in his kitchen. His voice was strangled. "Kayla …"

It was a little cruel to scare him, and I was probably lucky he hadn't chased me with the baseball bat he kept by the door in case of burglars. However, the look on his face was priceless.

"Your landlord remembered me and let me in here. You probably should think about living in a building with better security," I teased.

Then the room fell away, and I was suddenly in his arms. The past dissolved, and it was only the two of us again. There was no hesitation as his lips found mine in a sensual kiss. I took him in completely, lost in how much I'd missed the taste of him. When we broke apart, he didn't release me. His eyes held mine while his fingers slid over my jaw line.

"When did you get here?"

"About an hour ago," I said and kissed him again. I wanted to fuse our lips together and never stop feeling them against my own. They were beautiful and sexy and when he deepened the kiss, they made everything below my belly clench tighter. Breathless from his kiss, I panted as I tried to speak. "I made us dinner. We took cooking classes in the center and it turns out I'm not half bad. You were always cooking for me, so I thought I'd return the favor."

Cameron's intense stare told me he understood. It was monumental for me—and one of many firsts I hoped to conquer with him before the end of the night. My eyes drank him in. He was casually sexy in a polo shirt and khaki pants, and I ran my hands down the front of the shirt. His chest and abs felt hard against my palms and lust snuck into his expression.

His eyes became hooded, and I suspected he knew the panty-dropping effect the look would have on me. I grimaced and slipped out of his arms. "I had a whole seduction plan mapped out in my head, and you're ruining it."

"Babe, I'm already seduced. If it didn't smell so damn good, I'd say to hell with dinner and take you right here."

"Hmmm …" I was tempted, and I licked my lips as I fantasized over all the things we could do at that moment.

His jaw worked back and forth. "You're killing me here, Kayla."

I chuckled. "Okay, dinner first and everything else … soon." I pecked his cheek and took him by the hand to lead him into the kitchen. I pushed him gently down into a chair. Retrieving the plates from his counter, I presented him the food with exaggerated arm movements. "I call it chicken a la Kayla, but basically it's just grilled chicken mixed with brown rice and veggies."

I was a ball of nerves as I sat across from him. I took a deep breath and dug into the food. After a minute of silence, I peeked up to look at him. He was watching me, a small smile on his lips.

"What? Do I have food on my face?"

"No, I just didn't expect this. I normally hate surprises, but this is the best possible one," he said before taking a bite of his food. Pointing at me with his fork, he remarked, "This is really good by the way." He chewed thoughtfully for a moment. "How was the rest of your time at the center?"

"A lot of the same stuff repeated over and over. To be honest, I started to get really sick of talking about myself. I found a lot of the girls' stories interesting, though. It gave me the idea to maybe start an online magazine featuring real girls and honest stories about struggles women in my age group face." I put down my fork and looked at him in earnest. "A lot of the stuff they went through made me stop feeling sorry for myself. I've experienced loss, but I also have a lot to be grateful for."

"Your magazine sounds like a good idea. Maybe you can hire me. Instead of signing people up for credit cards, I could sign them up for magazine subscriptions," he said. "Are you going to keep in touch with any of the patients there?"

"I'd like that. I made a few good friends. April was released two weeks before me and mailed me a postcard before getting on a plane for Europe. I have a feeling she's going to be okay back out in the real world."

"What about you? Are you going to be okay?" His voice was laced with concern and I was again thankful for the day I met him. The feeling was new to me; I never understood how someone could completely change your world. Our lives were intertwined and I could share anything with him, my bliss and my despair.

"Yes," I said softly. "I'm going to be okay."

I was learning every day to let go of my need to be perfect. I had to embrace my flaws and understand they were what made me special. I had more weight to gain and I'd always have to monitor my relationship with food, but the hopelessness plaguing me for months was becoming a distant nightmare.

His penetrating stare brought heat to my face. Before things progressed, I wanted to confess all my secrets to him. I didn't want him to question my feelings and whether I only said things in the heat of the moment.

I nervously sucked on my lower lip before I spoke. Angus pressed against my leg, and I took a minute to pet him, gathering my thoughts. I'd never put myself out there before. It felt like I was about to free-fall, not sure if there was anyone to catch me at the bottom.

"I missed you insanely during the summer," I admitted shyly. "I kept looking back at our relationship and wishing I could obliterate every shitty thing I said or did to push you away. When we were together, it didn't matter how much I wanted to be in my own Hell alone—you never let me. And I didn't understand why; I *couldn't* understand why. I kept thinking you must be some type of masochist.

"After I started believing I was worth something, it became clear. You love me as much as I love you. Because I'd do the same for you. I'd face anything with you, Cameron, because you've possessed every last bit of my heart."

"Jesus, Kayla …" His eyes flashed with a burning need, and I lurched into his arms. "Babe, I love you," he said. "I love you so damn much." His mouth melted against my neck and I sighed with contentment. I loved him. I loved him completely, and I wasn't afraid to give him all of me.

CHAPTER THIRTY-ONE

Cameron cradled me against him and kissed my hair, telling me he loved me again. Sliding off his lap, I gripped both his hands in mine. My eyes were shining as I tugged him away from the table. Once we arrived in his bedroom, I released him.

"One of the things we learn about in treatment is to have confidence in our bodies. My problems with how I looked not only affected me, they also hurt our connection. Although I loved the things you did to my body when we slept together, there was always my own self-doubt holding me back. I used every excuse to keep you from seeing me completely naked." I shoved him lightly once we reached the side of his bed. He gamely sat on the edge.

Before I could lose my nerve, I slipped my white t-shirt over my head. Unbuttoning my skirt, I shimmied until it fell to the floor. I took a second to relish Cameron's expression as he took his time exploring my body with his eyes. Instead of the humiliation I expected when I stood before him in my bra and panties, I felt sexy and desirable.

As I unclasped my white lacy bra and peeled off my matching underwear, I tried to infuse some playfulness into the intense moment. I danced side to side and threw off my undergarments with exaggerated flourish.

My heart was racing, but my head was quiet. To pose naked for the man I loved was empowering, and I was ecstatic to be released from the neuroses that had prevented me from doing it earlier. I pouted and settled my hands on my hips.

"Cameron, this is the part where you take off your clothes," I said with exasperation.

He leaned back, resting on his elbows. "Hell no, I'm enjoying the view way too much. Could you do a few more of those dance moves?"

I was mesmerized by the way he ran his gaze over every inch of my skin. He took his time, but his tight grip on the edge of the bed told me how badly he wanted to touch me. My palms sank into the bed as I kneeled above him. My hair fell in front of my face as I positioned my mouth within inches of his lips. He sucked in a shaky breath.

His arms curled around me and his hands cupped my behind. I pressed my breasts against his chest and he fell back flat on his back. My hands tugged urgently at his shirt and he reached his arms up while I peeled it off of him.

As our mouths came together, I was burning up from the inside out. His mouth was warm and his tongue collided with mine. Our kisses were reckless, our lips moving in a frenzy, not able to get enough of one another.

"You … are … incredibly …beautiful," he panted out between kisses, his mouth then trailing from my ear along my jaw line.

My hand clutched his hair and his chin tilted up, allowing me better access to his neck. I ran my tongue over his skin, relishing the delicious masculine taste of him. He groaned as I dragged my mouth down the front of his bare chest. I pressed butterfly kisses over the hem of his pants, sneaking a glance at his black boxers peeking out of his waistband.

His hands reached under my armpits and yanked me away from the button of his pants. "I need to feel you right now. If I'm not inside of you within the next thirty seconds, I'm going to start believing this is just one crazy intense dream."

I nodded without taking my eyes off him. I didn't want to close my eyes and risk missing a second of the most erotic experience of my life. His hand covered mine and guided me to the buckle of his belt. After I unfastened his pants, he pulled them off, leaving him clad only in his boxers. As he pulled me tightly, I could feel how ready he was to be inside me.

He apparently wanted the same assurance from me and I moaned as his fingers entered me. I tossed my head back and moved against his fingers. His free hand roamed over my breast, his thumb sliding over my nipple.

"Kayla, look at me," he said urgently. I forced my gaze back to his as he continued to do things to my body that were inciting raw need inside of me. "I love you. I love seeing you like this and knowing I can do this to you."

I couldn't form a coherent answer. All I could manage was "I love you" before sensation took over. I held back until he removed his boxers and slipped on a condom. He felt right inside me, as if he was filling up the empty space I'd always suspected was there.

We finished together, our eyes locked the entire time. It was raw and intense and I fantasized about doing it again and again until our bodies were completely spent. That was what had been missing the entire time between us; loving one another with abandon.

Afterward, I curled into his side and he brushed the hair away from my eyes. I rested my chin on his chest and smiled at him. He craned his neck and kissed the tip of my nose.

"Not to inflate your ego or anything, but that was … wow," I murmured.

"I'm not going to lie. I'm feeling very manly right now after seeing how hot I get you." His teasing tone caressed my ears and I closed my eyes.

I could have stayed that way forever: loving him, being loved by him. I might never be perfect, but I fit perfectly with him.

CHAPTER THIRTY-TWO

"Kayla, when you said we should visit your father, I was figuring you meant we were going to the cemetery," Cameron said as I parked my Jeep. Without a reply, I jumped out and walked around to the back of the car. After opening the trunk, I handed him two fishing poles. I carried the tackle box while using my free hand to slam the trunk close again.

Cameron was close on my heels as I stomped over the graveled parking lot. "I thought the only reason I never went to the cemetery was because I refused to accept my dad's death. But the more I thought about it, the more I realized he wouldn't be there. My dad hated cemeteries as much as I did. If I wanted to be close to him, I should go somewhere he loved." I motioned to our surroundings. "This lake was my dad's favorite fishing spot. Lila and I have been coming here since we were babies."

Cameron stopped and took time to appreciate the surroundings. It was a small, secluded lake shrouded from the nearby highway by a line of towering pines. There was a small beach where Lila and I would wade while my dad casted nearby. We would bring a picnic lunch and run and swim for the day. I did a quick scan of the perimeter. "I only see a couple of anglers across the lake, so we'll stay on this end. Since it's the end of August, we're fishing for bass. Trout season doesn't start until the end of the month."

He cocked his head and grinned at me. "Did I ever tell you how sexy it is to hear you talk like a middle-aged fisherman?"

I playfully shoved him. Then I reached into my beach bag to pull out a picnic blanket. "We could set up here."

Once we'd unloaded the fishing gear, I reached out for his hand and squeezed it. "Thanks for coming with me today. I wanted to remember the fun I had with my dad and not dwell on the bad stuff."

"I wish I could've met him. I'd like to thank him for having such an incredible daughter." Without fail, Cameron would say something utterly perfect and remind me again why I fell in love with him.

"He'd be a huge fan of yours. Besides the fact you're a lover of dogs and cars, you would win him over with how you treat his daughter like a princess." My chest tightened momentarily, but I'd learned to allow myself to grieve for my dad instead of rejecting my feelings.

After a minute, Cameron broke the silence. "I got a call for an interview next week. The position is for an assistant in the HR department of a consulting firm."

I squealed. "That's amazing! I thought you only sent out your resume a few days ago. That must be a good sign if you're already getting calls."

Cameron wanted to eventually have his own business, but he acknowledged the goal was likely to be years away. In the meantime, he only wanted to find a job where he didn't feel the urge to turn to hard liquor to get through most days.

"You'll have to help me brush up on my interview skills." He shot me an overzealous grin. "Hi, I'm Cameron Bennett, and if you hire me it'll be the best decision you ever made for this company."

I bumped my hip against his leg and giggled. "You're interviewing for a job, not trying to sell a used car."

"Okay, I'll try to bring it down a notch. I don't want to reek of desperation," he said.

I sat on the blanket and Cameron squeezed next to me. I rested my head on his shoulder and watched the sun reflect off the surface of the still water. I brought my father's face to my mind and welcomed his presence. Maybe he was with me, watching out for me. Since meeting Cameron, I had started believing in fate. And maybe my father had a hand in bringing an incredible guy into my life.

"I was thinking …" Cameron started uncertainly. At my questioning look, he continued, "I was thinking of seeing my mom. You know, my real mom."

"Oh?" I prompted gently. His relationship with his mother was a landmine I had to tread carefully over. Thinking of the cavernous hole she had left in her son's heart made me resent her. But I also understood Cameron would have that pain to carry with him until he dealt with the past.

"I do have a lot of pent-up shit I want to say to her. And you were right. I'm not over everything. My dad gave me these books of hers she left behind and that's how I found the Vonnegut passage. I read those books over and over again, trying to get inside her head, trying to make sense of why she made the decisions she did." I gripped the hem of his shirt and moved the fabric away to reveal his tattoo. I stroked it as he continued to speak. "So, it's probably going to suck and be awkward, but I was hoping you'd come with me when I see her."

"Of course," I said. His head tilted toward me and he kissed me gently. "I love you." I hadn't been able to say it for ages, but the words kept slipping from my lips as if my heart was trying to make up for all the time it had been closed off.

"I love you," he said. "But I still plan to catch a bigger fish than you."

"Want to bet on it?" I challenged. "Loser has to clean and filet the day's catch."

"Fine, you're on," he agreed.

As we started preparing our lines, I peeked at him. His blue eyes were filled with mischief and he was trying to hide an ecstatic smile. His attitude was contagious, and I found myself beaming. His movements were confident and strong, and the way he held himself was sexy as hell.

He was it for me. He didn't cause a mere fluttering in my belly, he ignited explosions. I was lucky to be with a guy who not only loved me, but who also helped me appreciate my body again. Instead of despising what was on the outside, I found myself daydreaming over what Cameron would do at night to my body.

Having an eating disorder was an ugly thing, but I had survived it. I didn't become a tragedy, a warning to girls of what happens when you starve yourself for beauty. At the end, I'd chosen love.

And each time I stumbled, each time I felt the urge to deny my body what it needed to be healthy, I would remind myself of that choice.

The End

For questions or recovery assistance:

National Eating Disorders Association

1-800-931-2237

http://www.nationaleatingdisorders.org/

ACKNOWLEDGMENTS

My husband Bryan, my love and my everything, I wouldn't be who I am without you.

My children, your love is always my biggest inspiration.

Lynn, a fabulous editor who has helped me become a better writer.

My parents and sisters, thanks for your awesomeness and allowing me to put parts of you in my novels.

To the rest of my friends and family, I love you all and will be eternally grateful for how much you've helped me succeed.

To Jo, thanks for your work on the book and for always be a supporter for aspiring and indie writers.

ABOUT THE AUTHOR

Heather Topham Wood's obsession with novels began in childhood while growing up in a shore town in New Jersey. Writing since her teens, she recently returned to penning novels after a successful career as a freelance writer. She's the author of the paranormal romance *Second Sight* series and the standalone *The Disappearing Girl*.

Heather graduated from the College of New Jersey in 2005 and holds a bachelor's degree in English. Her freelance work has appeared in publications such as *USA Today*, Livestrong.com, *Outlook by the Bay* and *Step in Style* magazine. She resides in Trenton, New Jersey with her husband and two sons. Besides writing, Heather is a pop culture fanatic and has an obsession with supernatural novels and TV shows.

Follow Heather on Facebook, Twitter and her blog to keep posted on her upcoming works:

https://twitter.com/woodtop255
http://authorheather.com
https://www.facebook.com/HeatherTophamWood

Made in the USA
San Bernardino, CA
21 April 2016